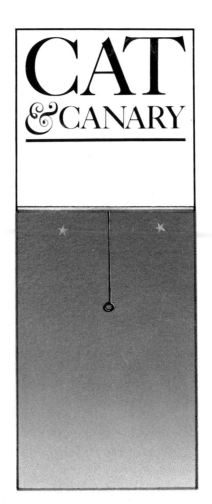

First published in the United States 1985 by
Dial Books for Young Readers
A Division of E. P. Dutton, Inc.
2 Park Avenue
New York, New York 10016
Published in Great Britain by Andersen Press Ltd.
Printed in Italy
First Edition
US
10 9 8 7 6 5 4 3 2 1

Library of Congress Cataloging in Publication Data
Foreman, Michael, 1938–
Cat and canary.
Summary: A city cat who has always wanted
to fly lives out his fantasy.
1. Children's stories, English. [1. Cats—Fiction.
2. Birds—Fiction. 3. Flight—Fiction.] I. Title.
PZ7.F7583Cat 1985   [E]   84-9568
ISBN 0-8037-0137-3

CAT
& CANARY
MICHAEL FOREMAN

Dial Books for Young Readers / New York

E. P. DUTTON, INC.

It was dawn in the city. Cat watched the winter sky change from night to day. Canary was still asleep in her cage.

Every day Cat watched his master get ready for work. Every day the man said, "You are lucky. You just lie around the house all day, lazy cat." Then he put on his hat and coat and went to work.

But every day as soon as the man had left, Cat let Canary out of her cage. Canary always flew around the room a few times. Then they had breakfast together and went up to the roof.

Cat watched Canary dive and whirl around in the sky. He wished he could fly with his friend above the streets and bridges to the land beyond the river.

Cat often watched other cats on other roofs chasing birds.

He never chased birds. After all, his best friend was a canary.

All the birds flocked to his roof.

Most days his roof was a blizzard of birds.

One windy day Cat found a kite tangled on
a television antenna. When he untied it, he
became caught in the string. Suddenly the wind
came up and Cat was whisked into the air and
over the streets. The cats on the other roofs
were amazed to see Cat flying.

Winds rushing between the high buildings blew him

higher until he was flying among the tallest skyscrapers.

Canary tried desperately to keep up with him.

Cat was thrilled to be suddenly soaring free as a bird.

The sun turned the great buildings to gold and silver,

and threw Cat's giant shadow across surprised people far below.

But soon the sun was covered by storm clouds

and Cat no longer felt free as a bird.

The huge buildings now looked dangerous and threatening.

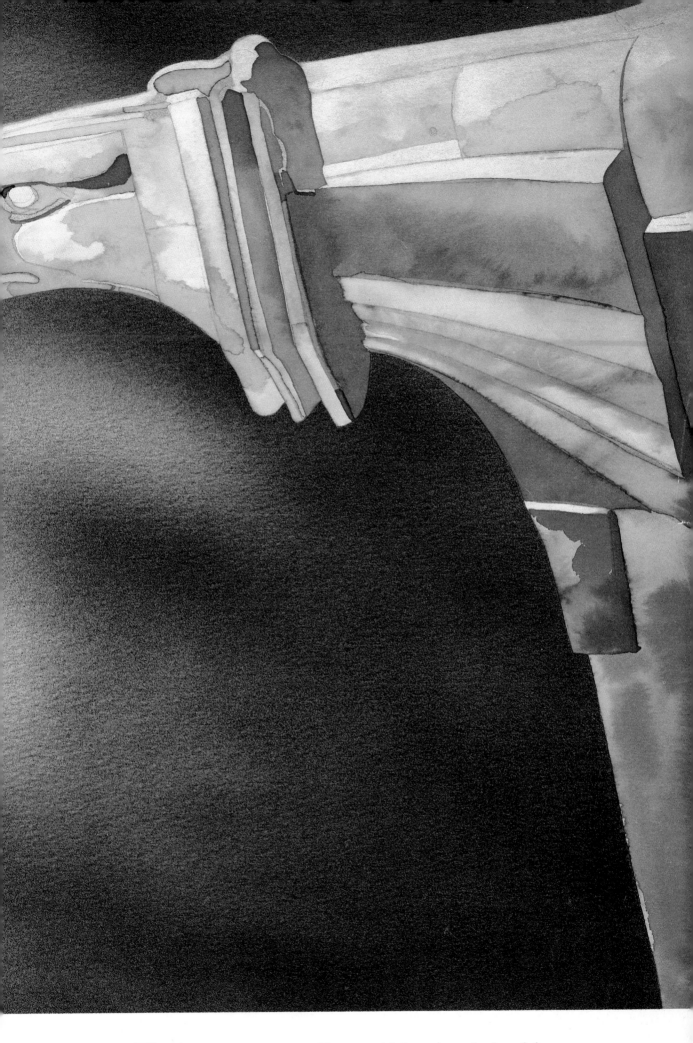

There was no way Cat could control the kite.

He was being blown farther and farther from home.

Below he could see the icy river. Snow began to fall.

Just as Cat was about to give up, Canary appeared with a
large flock of birds. They took the kite strings and turned
toward home.

Down they went, through the snow toward

the bright flashing lights of the city.

They landed on their roof just as their master turned the corner. The man did not see them. His head was bent against the wind, and snow blew into his face and down his neck. "Oh, to be a cat," he thought, "to stay home where it's cozy and do nothing."

Cat waved to the birds and tied the kite back onto the television antenna. "Tomorrow," he thought, "if we all fly together, we can go to the land beyond the river and still be back by nightfall."

Then Cat and Canary raced downstairs. When their master opened the door, Canary was swinging in the cage and Cat was curled up on the mat with his eyes closed.

"What a lazy cat!" said the man. "I bet you haven't moved all day."

and continued as he made his way up the rickety wooden staircase. The stairs creaked and gave slightly under his weight, even though he prided himself on being slim. This whole place could come down and collapse in a heap of brick dust and rotting timbers. From behind many of the doors he passed on the ground floor and first floor landings came the click-click-click of typewriters as their keys were hammered energetically. People with important things to say, revolutionary propaganda to be spread at the greatest possible speed.

He reached the second floor. The dust here wasn't as thick in the air as it had been on the ground floor, and the smell of damp had eased. He guessed the row of buildings had been put up right on the bare earth. The smell of damp was actually that of damp soil.

There was typing coming from behind the door next to the sign 'British Communist Party'. The door itself needed a coat of paint; the green paint with which it had been painted was flaking off, exposing the wood beneath.

Danvers knocked at the door, turned the handle and stepped inside. A girl of about his age with long, stringy black hair hanging down, almost obscuring her face, sat at a desk, a typewriter in front of her. A young man was standing next to her. They both looked suspiciously at Danvers. The young man, Danvers spotted, had eyes of different colours: one brown, one blue, an oddity which momentarily took him aback.

'Yes?' demanded the young woman.

Danvers guessed she'd taken one look at him and reckoned he wasn't a fellow comrade. He took his warrant card from his pocket and held it out to her. 'Detective Sergeant Danvers,' he introduced himself.

Without a word, the young man hurried to the door and darted quickly out of it. The natural reaction of a revolutionary when the police turn up, thought Danvers ironically.

The young woman scowled and glared at Danvers. 'This is private property!' she snapped. 'You can't do anything here without a warrant. If you haven't got a warrant, you can get out!'

Danvers regarded her, keeping a façade of calm. He'd expected something like this hostile reaction. 'I'm not here to search anything or anyone, or arrest anyone,' he told her. 'I just want to ask some questions.'

'I don't have to answer any questions!' barked the girl. Then her voice rose and she shouted at him, 'So you can get out!'

An inner door and an older woman looked out. 'Trouble, Naomi?' she enquired. And then she saw Danvers and her mouth opened in surprise.

'Good Lord!' she said. 'Bobby Danvers!'

Danvers felt himself colouring. Suddenly, he felt awkward and clumsy. The woman standing looking at him, in bemused surprise, was someone he hadn't seen for many years. Lady Amelia Fairfax.

'What are you doing here?' she asked.

'He's police!' scowled Naomi, and she looked as if she was going to spit on the floor at Danvers' feet.

Lady Amelia grinned. *She must be at least thirty*, thought Danvers, *but she looks so . . . young!*

'Well, well!' smiled Lady Amelia. 'I bet the colonel wasn't amused. A son of his, working for a living.'

'If you can call being a copper working!' snorted the young woman. 'They don't work; they persecute the poor and the oppressed!'

Danvers ignored the young woman and kept his concentration on Lady Amelia. He gave a shrug. 'Father and I don't talk much these days,' he said.

'No? Well, I don't keep up with society gossip,' said Lady Amelia. 'So, back to my earlier question: what are you doing here?'

'We're investigating the murder of Lord Amersham.'

She looked at him, momentarily bewildered, and then she let out a laugh.

'I thought he was shot outside his house in Regent's Park,' she said. 'At least, that's what it said in the papers. Or have they got it wrong, like so many things?'

'No, he was shot there,' admitted Danvers.

'So why have you come all the way to the East End for your enquiries?'

'He's come to fit someone up!' snapped Naomi. 'Some poor out-of-work soul who'll get thrown in jail, and who'll vanish with no questions asked. Murder solved! The Empire is safe!'

Danvers looked at her thoughtfully. When it was put that way, that *was* why he was here. Not to frame anyone, but – if Churchill had his way – to find some unfortunate with socialist leanings who carried out the murder.

'You're frightening him, Naomi,' Lady Amelia chided her mockingly. She gave Danvers a smile. 'Why don't you come into the office, Bobby . . .'

'Detective Sergeant Danvers,' Danvers corrected her.

She wasn't fazed. 'Detective Sergeant,' she repeated, rolling the words around her mouth with a mocking tone. 'For one thing, it won't make our members happy if they come in here and find a member of the constabulary.' She gestured at the door to the inner room.

'Whatever he says, don't trust him!' scowled Naomi.

'Of course I won't,' said Lady Amelia. 'I've known Bobby since he was small, when he used to steal sweets from his sister.'

'I never stole sweets!' Danvers protested. Then he groaned inwardly as he saw the girl, Naomi, grin delightedly. *They're playing with me*, he thought. *I should be like Stark, grim and silent, untouchable. But instead, they're having their fun with me.*

His ears still burning with embarrassment, he walked over to door to the inner room and followed Lady Amelia in.

Stark sat in the lounge of the small hotel in Cadogan Gardens. It was a very pleasant place: armchairs of brown leather, oak side tables and coffee tables, with heavy brass ashtrays on them, and flowers in vases as an added decoration. The walls hung with prints of hunting scenes. The atmosphere reminded Stark of a gentleman's club. Hardly the base for a group of what had been described as 'rabid revolutionaries'.

He heard footsteps coming down the nearby stairs and turned to look. Michael Collins had descended the stairs and was walking into the lounge area. He was accompanied by two men.

Even if he hadn't seen the photographs of Collins already, Stark would have recognized him from the description alone. The Big Fella, as he was known in Ireland. And he was big. Tall, broad-shouldered, a large face with a slightly punched-in nose, and with a self-confident swagger as he walked that told everyone that he, Michael Collins, was the man in charge. Most of the photos in his file had showed Collins defiantly in uniform as the Commander of the IRA, and in those he had stood head and shoulders above his comrades. In the photos of him in civilian clothes with his fellow Sinn Féin politicians, he had also loomed over most of them, with the exception of the equally tall Éamon de Valera. But in those photos, de Valera had presented a thin, lugubrious figure, while Collins had seemed so much larger than life that the photo could barely contain him. In the flesh, as he was now, he seemed even larger. The Big Fella indeed.

Collins strode towards Stark, holding out his hand. 'Detective Chief Inspector Stark, I believe,' he said, a bland smile on his big features. 'I got your message saying you wished to talk to me.'

Stark shook his hand.

'I hope you don't mind my bringing my colleagues with me, Chief Inspector?' said Collins, gesturing at the two men with him. 'We were talking together when I got your message, and I felt it would have been rude to exclude them.'

Stark looked at the other two, recognizing them immediately from the files he had studied the previous night. Robert Erskine Childers and Ned Broy. Childers the intellectual, Broy the hard man. 'Not at all,' said Stark politely.

'Witnesses,' hissed the smaller man, Broy.

'I beg your pardon?' asked Stark.

'None of us says anything without a witness,' growled Broy. 'Especially to the police.' And he glared darkly at Stark.

'Now, now, Ned,' smiled Collins. 'I'm sure we have nothing to worry about from Mr Stark. After all, his grandmother was an Irish lass from Cork.'

Clever, thought Stark. *He's letting me know he knows all about me. More to the point, he's telling me that his most likely source is from inside our own: the Metropolitan Police, or possibly even Special Branch.*

'She was indeed,' nodded Stark. 'And, like many from Cork, she came to England to earn herself a living.'

'As I did myself,' said Collins.

Collins watched Stark, waiting for him to respond. *He's giving me the cue to say something about working at the Post Office, to let him know that I know about him, too*, thought Stark. Instead, he turned to Childers and said, 'Mr Childers, it is a great pleasure to meet you. I enjoyed your novel *Riddle of the Sands* very much indeed.'

A small smile of pleasure appeared on Childers's face. 'Thank you,' he said. 'With recent events, many have forgotten that I am actually a writer rather than a politician.'

'We'll never forget that in Ireland, Bob,' said Broy fiercely. 'Ireland is a land of poets and writers. And warriors.'

'As you can see by his attitude, Mr Stark, Ned here is not a lover of things British,' said Collins, that same cocky grin on his face.

'No true Irishman would be after hundreds of years of servitude and cruelty,' snapped Broy.

'True,' said Collins calmly, 'but let's keep that for the talks. The chief inspector is here to talk about other things, I'm sure.'

'I am indeed,' said Stark. 'I'm investigating the shooting of Lord Amersham.'

Stark noticed that Childers and Broy exchanged puzzled looks, but Collins remained impassive, that same half-smile on his face. *He knows*, thought Stark. *He knew I was coming before I got here, and he knew already why.*

'What's that got to do with us?' demanded Childers.

'We're exploring many avenues of enquiry,' said Stark blandly. 'One is that Lord Amersham was opposed to the talks you're currently undertaking with the British government.'

'So?' demanded Childers, his tone hostile. Any friendliness he'd previously shown towards Stark had vanished.

'Jaysus, they're trying to pin this on us, Mick!' said Broy angrily, turning to Collins.

Calm as ever, Collins shook his head. 'I don't think so, Ned. After all, we're the most public of men. Everywhere we go, we're watched by the gentlemen of the press.' His smile broadened and he added, 'And Special Branch. If any of us had shot the old wretch, they'd know already.'

By God, he's a cool customer, thought Stark. He wondered just how much Collins knew about the files on him and his colleagues at Special Branch. 'You're absolutely right, Mr Collins,' he said. 'But it has been suggested that there may be some among your supporters here in England who might see Lord Amersham as an obstacle worth removing.'

'And you expect us to turn them in?' spat Broy, his face contorted with fury.

'I expect you to help us with our enquiries,' replied Stark smoothly and calmly.

'I hope you're not suggesting you'll be using heavy-handed police actions with us,' said Childers coldly. 'We are an official political delegation, with all the immunity and protection that goes with it.'

'Peace, fellas!' protested Collins, for the first time a note of irritation entering his voice. 'Can't you see the man's only doing his job?' The big Irishman turned to Stark. 'You know that Lord Amersham was no friend to Ireland. I'm not going to play the hypocrite and shed crocodile tears for him. He and his kind killed enough good Irish people over the years.'

'The Black and Tans!' snarled Broy.

Collins waved a hand at Broy to calm him down, then continued, 'You've been told to question us. Why? Not because anyone thinks we had anything to do with the murder. So . . . to rattle us?'

'We won't be rattled,' put in Childers. 'We've waited too long for this moment.'

Collins chuckled. 'Jaysus, Bob, you've waited hardly any time at all. You're English.'

Stark saw Childers bridle. 'My mother was as Irish as yours, Mick,' he said.

Stark noticed that Collins leaned forward to utter a retort, but then thought better of it. Instead, he smiled and patted Childers affectionately on the shoulder. 'Just joking, Bob,' he grinned.

Although Childers nodded in acceptance of the apology, Stark saw that he wasn't mollified. *There's tension between them*, he thought. *Mainly from Childers. He's an Anglo-Irish Protestant from the upper classes. The rest of the delegation are dyed-in-the-peat Irish Republicans, with centuries of oppression by the British to their names. Childers feels different, an outsider, and wishes he wasn't.*

Suddenly, Collins got to his feet. 'I'd love to carry on talking with you, Mr Stark,' he said. 'As you know, we Irish love a good conversation. But we have things to prepare for very important meetings.'

Stark nodded and rose to his feet, as did Childers and Broy. 'Of course,' he said. He held out his hand and Collins took it in a firm grip. 'I thank you, gentlemen, for your time. And, if you should hear of anything that may help us in this case, I'd be grateful if you'd send a message to me at Scotland Yard.'

'You'll get no help from us!' spat Broy.

Collins smiled. 'We certainly will, Chief Inspector,' he said, still wearing that same smile. He released Stark's hand and turned to the other two. 'Come, lads, we have work to do.'

With that, the three left the lounge and headed towards the stairs.

I've been played for a fool, thought Stark. *Someone has sent me along either to stir things up, or to send a message to Collins. The trouble is, I don't know what the message was. But I get the impression Collins does.*

As he left the hotel, he was feeling angry. Someone was using him. It was nothing to do with discovering who murdered Lord Amersham, but everything to do with the treaty negotiations. Who? Special Branch? Or someone behind them? And why?

SIX

D anvers sat in the small, cramped, shabby office, his notebook open on his lap, but he felt overwhelmed. So far there had been nothing to write, nothing that would help the investigation, anyway.

To his surprise, Lady Amelia Fairfax seemed very much at home here. She'd always been a bit of a maverick, Danvers knew that, but he'd never pictured her in this cramped office overflowing with leaflets and books and newspapers, all promoting the communist cause. She'd found herself space among all the papers that were everywhere, even on the chairs, by simply moving a pile of books on to a pile of leaflets that looked as if they were going to cascade to the floor at any moment.

'The last time I saw you,' she said, 'you were about ten.'

'I was eight,' Danvers corrected her. 'Summer, 1908. You were having a row with your mother.'

Lady Amelia looked at him and frowned. 'Was I?'

'She didn't want you to marry to Lord Fairfax.'

Lady Amelia studied him thoughtfully. 'Either you have a very good memory or you're making it up from hindsight.'

'It was a very memorable row,' said Danvers. 'It was in the lounge of the Russell Hotel. I was there with my mother.'

Lady Amelia held up a hand to silence him. 'Yes, I remember it very well, also,' she said ruefully. 'One hates to admit that one's parents may be right, but . . .' She shrugged. 'How about you and your father?'

'We disagree,' replied Danvers flatly. 'As a result, we don't talk.'

'Your mother?'

'She believes he's right. Or she has to pretend to believe he's right, and so stand by his views.'

'So you don't see her, either?'

'No,' confirmed Danvers. Then, in a less abrasive tone, he added, 'I do see my little sister sometimes.'

'Lettie,' nodded Lady Amelia.

'She keeps me up to date, although she doesn't tell my father she's seen me.' Then Danvers seemed to remember why he was here and abruptly adopted an official tone. 'Lord Amersham,' he said.

'A pig,' said Lady Amelia calmly. 'Whoever killed him has done womankind a favour. And many other sections of the population, I should guess.'

Danvers regarded her, still puzzled. He gestured at the shabby office around them. 'I still don't understand . . .' he began.

She finished the sentence for him. 'Why an aristocrat like me should be working for the Communist Party?'

He nodded.

'For a start, I'm just filling in for Sylvia Pankhurst for a couple of days while she's away raising much-needed funds. I said I'd go through the correspondence for her. If you don't keep on top of it, it can be overwhelming. But I do believe in the cause. Do you know how much of the wealth of this country is owned by just a few?'

'No, but I'm sure you're going to tell me.'

Lady Amelia stopped herself, then she smiled. 'The statistics,' she said. 'The Party's very good at them. But every statistic is also a person.' Suddenly, she changed tack. 'What makes you think the murder of that pig, Amersham, is connected to the Communist Party?'

'It's just one line of enquiry,' said Danvers blandly.

'No, it isn't,' said Lady Amelia. 'The murder only happened yesterday, yet you're here today. Are you also talking to his various mistresses so swiftly? Or their husbands? Or knocking on doors in the Irish areas? Or talking to the Jews? Lord Amersham was a well-known anti-Semite.'

'Other officers are carrying out different aspects of the investigation,' said Danvers. 'It's a wide-ranging enquiry.'

Lady Amelia laughed. 'I bet it is,' she said. 'I can think of plenty of people who'd be queuing up to see him dead.'

'But not all of them own a gun,' said Danvers.

She looked at him, her face thoughtful. 'I don't have a gun,' she said. 'Nor does Naomi.'

'Do any of your people have a gun?' he asked.

Even as he finished the question, and saw the tight look on her face, he knew he'd made a mistake. She stood up, her manner now stiff and formal.

'I think our interview is at an end, Sergeant,' she said. 'Unless you have a warrant for my arrest?'

Danvers hesitated, then he gave a silent sigh and stood up. 'No,' he said. 'As I said to the girl outside—'

'She's not just a "girl",' said Lady Amelia. 'She has a name. Naomi.'

'As I told her, I don't have any warrants. I'm just looking for information that may lead me to a murderer.'

'Then look closer to home,' said Lady Amelia. 'In your own social circle.'

As she led him towards the door, he said, 'I'm not part of that social circle any more.'

She opened the door. 'Yes, you are,' she said. 'More than you think.' Then she called to the girl at the typewriter. 'Naomi, the sergeant is leaving.'

SEVEN

'Excuse me, sir.'

Stark looked up from the notes he was making to the uniformed sergeant who'd just knocked at his door and looked in.

'Lady Amersham has returned from Scotland, sir. Chief Superintendent Benson thought you ought to know.'

'Did he?' said Stark. 'Did the chief superintendent say anything else?'

'He said she was expecting you.'

Yes, thought Stark with a sinking feeling. *That's all I need.* A grieving widow, and one with close contacts at the highest levels of society and politics. They ought to have special inspectors for this sort of thing, the type who know how to talk to these people, the right kind of social etiquette, an understanding of the nods and winks and certain handshakes. Of course, he had such a one in Danvers. The right kind of background, the right connections, the right school. Danvers would know the right way to talk to Lady Amersham. They possibly even had acquaintances in common. But Danvers was busy talking to communists.

He sighed, got up and made for the door.

Danvers stood on the pavement outside the building that housed the British Communist Party offices, filled with impotent rage. He'd been made a fool of by Lady Amelia and that girl, Naomi. The only saving grace was that no one else had been there to see his humiliation. He'd allowed them to kick him out! How? He was a police officer. Not just a police officer, a detective sergeant, and he'd been sent off with a flea in his ear like some irritating child.

When had the tone of the meeting changed? When he'd asked if 'any of her people' had a gun. The effect had been so immediate that the harshness with which Lady Amelia had ordered him out of the office could only have been a defence mechanism. He'd struck home. Someone there had a gun, and Lady Amelia knew it.

He saw a uniformed constable appear from around the corner of the street and amble towards him, going nowhere, just walking his beat.

'Constable!' he called.

The constable stopped and looked quizzically as Danvers hurried towards him. Danvers showed his warrant card, and immediately there was a change in the constable's manner. He was suddenly alert, but at the same time wary. A detective from Scotland Yard. It could only mean trouble.

'Is this your beat?' asked Danvers.

'Yes, sir.'

Danvers jerked a thumb towards the building that harboured the Communist Party. 'Do you know the people in that building?'

The constable looked towards the building and hesitated a moment before replying cagily, 'I know some of them, sir.'

'The British Communist Party. They have offices there.'

'I know *of* them, sir. But I don't know them particularly, nor their offices. They're not very welcoming to the police, and unless I have a specific complaint—'

'Yes, yes,' said Danvers impatiently. 'Have you heard any rumours about them? Particularly, if any of them have been heard of as owning a gun.'

'A gun, sir?'

'A pistol.'

The constable shook his head. 'Not as I've heard, sir. If I had, I'd have had to investigate.' He saw that this answer didn't please Danvers, so he added, 'Though it wouldn't surprise me if one of them might, sir. They're generally harmless, just spouting slogans and things, but there are a few rough types who hang about with them.' He gestured towards the end of the street. 'You might get more information from the Dragon Arms. It's a pub round the corner in Eccles Lane, and I believe some of them hang around in there.' He winked and said, 'The landlord's name is Charlie Wilson. He's a great one for hearing things that have turned out to be useful. But don't give him more than five bob. It'll make him greedy.'

'Thank you, constable,' said Danvers. 'If there's a result because of this, I'll see that you get mentioned. What's your name and station?'

'PC 236 Charles, sir. John Charles. Stepney station.'

Danvers nodded. 'Thank you again, Constable.'

Danvers headed in the direction PC Charles had indicated, took a right, and found himself in a narrow warren of lanes and back alleys. Here, in these enclosed and tight streets, the smells of the poor were kept captured, unable to be blown away by draughts and winds. The smell of boiled cabbage. Urine from the gutters mixed with the smell of washing. The acrid, sooty taint from thousands of coal fires hung heavy in the air, mingling with the decay of damp, catching Danvers in the nostrils and throat.

It's no wonder so many of them die, thought Danvers. *The wonder is that so many survive. Fertile ground for the communists.*

Danvers walked along until he came to a pub on the corner of Eccles Lane. The Dragon Arms. An unusual name, he reflected. Usually pubs were called things like the King's Head or the Queen's Arms. Who'd ever heard of a dragon with arms? Maybe it had once been called something similar, like the Dragoon Arms, and a less than literate sign-painter had accidentally changed its name.

He pushed open the door and stepped in, and was immediately assailed by the heady suffocating odour of beer and cheap gin. The interior of the pub was dark, light filtering in through the coloured glass of the windows, the gloom eased by the glow of a fire burning in the grate. At this time of day there weren't too many customers. Three men dressed in working clothes sat at one table, half-drunk pints of beer in front of them, and they turned and looked at Danvers as the door shut behind him. A few other men sat on their own at other tables, reading news-papers. There were two women as well, drinks in front of them on the tables. Many of them had pieces of paper on which they were making marks with stubby pencils. Choosing their bets for the day, realized Danvers. Selecting the horses of their choice before going off to make contact with their street bookie and passing over their slip and cash. An illegal act, liable to a fine.

The double standard, thought Danvers. *My father can place bets on today's races with his bookmaker because he is Colonel Danvers, and he has an account with an on-course bookmaker, even though that bookmaker may never actually go to a race-course. These men and their bookmaker can be arrested and charged. It's a wonder there hasn't been a revolution here already.*

The barman watched warily as Danvers approached, and when Danvers reached the bar and took out his warrant card, the barman shook his head. 'No need for that,' he grunted. 'I knew who you were the moment you walked in.'

'I'm looking for Charlie Wilson,' said Danvers, keeping his voice low.

'In that case, you've found him,' said the barman. 'What can I do for you?'

'I'm after some information.' Danvers lowered his voice even more, to almost a whisper. No sense in alerting the whole bar and warning off someone who might be involved.

Wilson turned and called to a man sitting at one of the tables, 'I'm just going down to the cellar to check a barrel. If anyone wants me, tell 'em I'll only be a minute.'

'Right you are, Charlie,' nodded the man. He went back to his newspaper, although Danvers could feel the man's eyes on him as he followed Wilson to the hatch in the floor behind the bar and then down the creaky wooden steps to the cellar, where the barrels were stored.

'Who gave you my name?'

'The local constable. John Charles. He thought you might be able to help me.'

'That depends,' said Wilson. Danvers took two half-crowns from his pocket and passed them to Wilson. The barman nodded and slipped them into his pocket. 'What do you want to know?'

'I understand that some Communist Party people come in here.'

Wilson gave a derisory laugh. 'That lot!' he snorted. 'Revolution! They couldn't organize a bunk-up in a brothel. Spend all their time talking and arguing among themselves.'

'Have you ever seen any of them with a gun?'

Immediately, Wilson was wary, suspicious. 'Gun?'

'A pistol.'

'Why?'

'It's just some information we've received. I'm double-checking it.'

'What have you heard?' asked Wilson warily.

'Just what I've said,' replied Danvers. 'A man who's got a

pistol, who comes in here, who's associated with that crowd. Has he waved that pistol around in here?'

Wilson was silent, weighing the implications of his answer, then he said, 'I'm guessing this information is worth more than five bob.'

'Maybe,' shrugged Danvers. 'That depends how good it is.'

Wilson fell silent again, studying Danvers. Then he said, 'Let's see that warrant card.'

Danvers took out his warrant card and handed it to Wilson, who studied it carefully before returning it.

'What's he done?' Wilson asked.

'We don't know,' said Danvers. 'Reports of a man with a gun who comes in here, who we think might be able to help us with our enquiries.'

Wilson thought it over some more, then said, 'Another half-crown.'

'How do I know it'll be worth it?' asked Danvers. 'Of course, we could always make this official. You come to the Yard with me.'

Wilson laughed sarcastically. 'And do what? You think you'll get any more out of me playing the heavy? I've done nothing wrong, copper, and you doing that could mess up a whole lot of arrangements I've got with your blokes.'

'Good point,' nodded Danvers. He took another half-crown from his pocket and handed it to Wilson. 'Name?'

'I don't know his whole name. He's called Dan. He doesn't come in here all the time, just sometimes with that crowd from the commie office. When he does, he gets drunk and mouthy, talking about what we ought to do with the toffs. Shoot 'em, he says, like they done in Russia. I always put it down to just talk – that's all that lot do is talk. But one day he pulls out this pistol. Says he bought it back from the war and he's gonna make 'em pay. Says him and all the other ex-soldiers is owed big time by them in power. Says they're scum and vermin, and he's the man to deal with 'em.'

'What happened? When he pulled out the pistol.'

'The others got alarmed and told him to put it away. He was raging drunk and told 'em there'd be no proper revolution until a few of the toffs was shot dead.'

'When was this?'

'He's been coming in here with 'em, on and off, for about four months. This was about two weeks ago when he did the business with the gun.'

'And since then?'

Wilson shook his head. 'He's been in, but no sign of the gun.'

'Where does he live?'

Wilson shook his head. 'No idea. Not round here, that's for sure, or I'd know. He only came in with that commie crowd.'

'His name?'

'Like I said, I only picked up his first name. Dan.' He shook his head. 'More than that, I don't know.'

'What's he look like? How old is he?'

'Mid-twenties, about five feet eight tall. Dark hair, thinning on top. Cheap, worn clothes. A drinker.' He shrugged. 'They'll know who he is at the commie offices, though. He was in very thick with them. As far as I could tell, he was actually a member of their party, not just a hanger-on, from things he said. You could always ask them.'

EIGHT

Stark hadn't really taken much notice of the house the last time he'd been inside it; then his attention had been on the dead body of Lord Amersham lying on the dining table. Now he was in the drawing room, sitting uncomfortably on a settee, facing Lady Amersham who sat bolt upright on a hard-backed chair, clad in stark, unadorned black, her widow's weeds. If she was suffering heartfelt grief at her loss, Stark saw no sign of it.

The room itself was oppressive: dark browns and dark green on the walls, heavy brocade curtains. Most of the pictures on the wall were military portraits.

'I'm sorry to trouble you at this difficult time, Lady Amersham,' began Stark.

Lady Amersham made no reply, just sat as still as a statue on her chair and fixed the chief inspector with a gimlet stare that did not hide her disapproval of this situation.

'Can you think of anyone who might have borne a grudge against your husband?' he asked.

Lady Amersham continued to fix him with her unflinching glare. 'My husband was one of the most respected men in England,' she said.

'True,' nodded Stark. *I have to play this one cagily*, he thought. *This woman is no tear-stained, grieving widow. She is the fierce guardian of her husband's reputation, and woe betide anyone who dares to try to sully that reputation.* 'But a man such as Lord Amersham does not achieve high office without arousing feelings of resentment or jealousy in others.'

She sat there, stiff-backed, unmoving, her look the same as she replied coldly, 'My husband was the exception. Everyone who knew him had the greatest admiration for him. Especially for his charitable work.'

'His charitable work?' queried Stark.

Lady Amersham visibly bridled at this. 'I am surprised you are not aware of the great amount of work he has done for charity, especially for those who fought in the Great War.'

'We are still at the early stage of the investigation—' began Stark apologetically.

Lady Amersham interrupted him. 'He was the President of the Passchendaele Memorial Fund Charitable Commission.'

I was at Passchendaele, thought Stark bitterly. *There was precious little sight of your husband or his cronies in the trenches there when the fighting was at its cruellest.*

Lady Amersham continued listing the different worthy organizations her husband had presided over or sat on the boards of. No mention of housemaids or other servants taken advantage of, or aristocratic wives adulterously bedded, nor his opinions of people whose politics differed from his own – communists, socialists, suffragettes – nor of the Irish or Jews. Stark wondered if Lord Amersham's charitable work on behalf of fallen soldiers stretched to those troops from far-flung parts of the Empire who had fought and died to protect it – especially those from India and Africa. Somehow he doubted it.

'The nature of the way he died suggests this was not a random killing,' said Stark carefully. *How else do I put it without crossing the bounds of propriety?* he considered. Three bullets fired expertly. A skilled assassin, either a professional for hire or a marksman bearing a personal grudge. 'What we are trying to establish—'

He was interrupted by a knock at the door and the butler appearing.

'Excuse me, my lady . . .' the butler began apologetically, before he was interrupted by the figure of Winston Churchill brushing him aside as he strode into the room.

'Beatrice! My sincere apologies! I was held up or I would have been here sooner!'

Like a human whirlwind, Churchill handed the butler his hat and then proceeded to pace around on the carpet, addressing Lady Amersham as if she was a world leader to be won over. 'A tragedy, not just for you but for the country!'

Lady Amersham said nothing, but watched the pacing Churchill warily.

She does not trust him either, Stark realized. She worries what he will say, what he will reveal.

'I came once I heard that you were coming here, Chief Inspector,' said Churchill, turning his attention to Stark. 'At a time like this, Lady Amersham needs the support of her true friends.' He shook his head, a scowl on his face. 'Alastair will be avenged – you have my word on that, Beatrice. Chief Inspector Stark is one of our finest men. Tenacious. And a war hero. He volunteered – not one of your conscripts! Promoted through the ranks, in the field, to become captain. Wounded. Decorated. DSM – that's right, isn't it Stark? Distinguished Service Medal.'

He's been checking up on me since we last met, thought Stark. 'Yes, sir,' he said quietly.

'See, Beatrice! He's one of ours. That's why I know we'll get the swine who did this!'

'I thank you for your solicitations, Winston,' said Lady Amersham, still tight-lipped. She did not rise to greet him, or take his hands in gratitude as some would have done on such an occasion. But then, she was Lady Amersham. Widow of Lord Amersham, pillar of the establishment, a former officer with the Hussars who'd fought with distinction in the Boer War and other wars in far-flung places, a politician, a member of the government.

She's as hard as nails, thought Stark.

'Is there anything else, Stark?' asked Churchill. 'We don't want to upset Lady Amersham any more than is necessary at a time like this.'

So, that's why he's really here. To stop me talking to her. 'No, I think I have everything I need from Lady Amersham, thank you.'

She did not rise to say goodbye to them, just nodded brusquely in response to Churchill's slight bow of farewell and Stark's similar nod of his head to her as he got up.

The butler followed them to the front door, handing Churchill his hat as they left. The front door had barely closed when Churchill spun round on Stark, once more his aggressive self. 'What the hell do you mean by questioning the Irish delegation?' he demanded angrily.

So that's why he came, Stark realized. *Not to stop her talking, but to rage against me.*

'I told you where your line of enquiry should be! The Bolsheviks! They hated him.'

'Lady Amersham seems to disagree with you, sir,' said Stark calmly. 'She says that Lord Amersham had no enemies.'

'Of course she does! She's distraught with grief, man!'

Hardly, thought Stark. *Unless she has an odd way of showing grief.*

'I ask you again, why did you go to question Collins and the others?'

'I was acting on information received, sir.'

'From whom?'

Stark hesitated, then reached a decision: *I'm not getting caught up as the scapegoat in whatever political battles are going on here.* 'Special Branch, sir,' he said.

Churchill swore. 'I knew it!' he burst angrily. 'This is politics, Stark! There are people – powerful people – in Whitehall who want these Irish talks to fail. They will do anything to stop the talks succeeding.' He wagged a warning finger in Stark's face. 'Don't let them use you! You're a good man, Stark. You can see what's happening in this country. Subversion. Treason. All under the cover of democracy.' He snorted. 'They want to do the same here as happened in Russia. Murder the Royal family. Stamp out the aristocracy. Turn Britain into a Bolshevik state. Well, we're not going to let that happen!' He shook his head. 'These are difficult times. Turbulent times. What happens in the next few years will determine the future of this country – and the Empire. The assassination of Alastair Amersham is a part of that. That's why we have to stamp on it now!' He patted Stark affectionately on the shoulder. 'Keep up the good work, Chief Inspector. Fight the good fight.' Then he looked Stark firmly in the face as he added, 'And stay away from the Irish delegation. Is that clear?'

'Very clear, sir,' nodded Stark.

He watched Churchill stomp across the pavement to his waiting car.

Well, that's me warned off, he thought. Stay away from the Irish delegation. *Stay away from any leads that might point in that direction. Stay away from Lady Amersham. Do not ask her any questions.*

He was intrigued that Churchill had seen fit to check on him, on his war experiences. His promotion to captain. The DSM. Being wounded. Was it that information that had led to Churchill's change of attitude towards him: from the belligerence of their first meeting to the almost affectionate way Churchill had treated him today – like trusted confidantes, two comrades fighting on the same side? Of course, that was Churchill's way. He was a clever politician. He would bully and bluster people into doing what he wanted, and – if that didn't work – he would do his best to make people like him, warm to him. Feel they were on the same side.

But not me, thought Stark. *I don't trust you, Winston.*

But then, he didn't trust any politicians.

NINE

When Stark got back to Scotland Yard, he found Danvers waiting for him in their shared office. The sergeant leapt to his feet as Stark as came in. 'I think I've got a lead, sir!' he said urgently.

'The Communist Party?'

'Yes, sir.'

'Go on.'

'I called at the offices as you said, and met someone there I know – Lady Amelia Fairfax. She's an old friend of the family.'

Yes, she would be, thought Stark wryly.

'At first it was all very friendly, even when I said I was there asking questions about the murder of Lord Amersham, whom she hated. Her attitude changed abruptly when I asked if any of her people had a gun.'

'Protecting someone?' murmured Stark.

'Yes, that's what I thought. So I started asking questions locally about anyone who might have been seen in the BCP offices, who was known to carry a gun. The beat constable directed me to a local pub, the Dragon Arms.'

'Get to the point, Sergeant,' urged Stark impatiently. 'Did you get a name?'

'Partly, sir. Someone called Dan. He's an ex-soldier with a grievance against the ruling classes. The landlord of the pub told me he'd seen him waving a pistol around once when he was drunk, mouthing off about killing aristocrats.'

'Did you get a description?'

'He's in his mid-twenties, about five feet eight inches tall. Dark hair, thinning on top. Cheap, worn clothes.'

It can't be that simple, thought Stark. But sometimes things *were* that simple.

'It could be just drunk talk, sir.'

'Yes, it could, but it's the best lead we've had so far. In fact, it's the only lead we've got. What's his connection with the communists?'

'It seems he's a member of the Party.'

'That's excellent work, Sergeant. Well done. So now we can get his name and address from them. From your old family friend, Lady Amelia Fairfax.'

Danvers looked awkward. 'I doubt if she'd give it to me, sir. She was very curt with me once I asked that question about someone with a gun.'

Stark had to force himself not to laugh at the sergeant's discomfort. 'She kicked you out?'

'Yes, sir,' admitted Danvers unhappily.

Stark could picture the encounter. He knew of Lady Amelia Fairfax's reputation from reports in the press. A strident radical, a disgrace to her class, according to the outraged press editorials.

A woman of very forceful opinions. She would have chewed Danvers up and spat him out. It would be no use sending him back to insist she gave him the man's name and address, nor would it be any use sending uniform to do that. She would simply tie them up in knots, even if they went with a search warrant, and precious time would be slipping away. If this Dan character was their culprit, they needed to catch him before he murdered someone else on his quest to kill off the aristocracy. If he wasn't, they needed to eliminate him from this case and save wasting precious time on him.

'Right, Sergeant,' he announced. 'It's time to upset some people.'

Stark strode up the stairs of the old building that housed the Communist Party offices, two uniformed constables following him. He felt the stairs shudder under their weight, and wondered if they might collapse, sending them crashing down. It always amazed him that these old decrepit, tumble-down buildings seemed to remain standing. He guessed it was only the presence of the buildings on either side that kept places like this from falling over.

Stark had left Danvers down in the street, along with two more uniformed officers, ostensibly to keep an eye on anyone entering or leaving the building, but mainly to spare Danvers the embarrassment of another encounter with Lady Amelia Fairfax. Lady Amelia had seen Danvers off with a flea in his ear because he was a nice young man with good manners. It was time for her to meet a rougher type of policeman.

He reached the landing and the sign on the wall that said 'British Communist Party', pushed the door open and was inside the reception area before the girl at the desk could begin to open her mouth in protest.

'You two guard the door,' he commanded the constables.

The girl at the desk found her voice. 'What the hell do you think you're doing?!' she demanded angrily.

'Police,' said Stark curtly. 'I'm Detective Chief Inspector Stark from Scotland Yard. Is Lady Amelia Fairfax here?'

The girl, Naomi, stared at Stark, partly bewildered by this whirlwind entrance. Then she recovered herself. 'Have you got a warrant?' she demanded aggressively.

'Yes,' said Stark.

Naomi looked at him, momentarily taken aback. Then she demanded, 'Let me see it.'

'I'll show it to Lady Amelia,' said Stark curtly.

'She isn't in,' said Naomi.

'In that case I'll wait for her in her office,' said Stark, and he strode towards the inner door as Naomi leapt to her feet and shouted, 'No! You can't!'

The inner door opened and a tall woman Stark recognized immediately from the pictures he'd seen in the papers as Lady Amelia Fairfax stood in the doorway, looking out at him and the two uniformed officers.

'What's going on?' she demanded.

'I am Detective Chief Inspector Stark from Scotland Yard,' Stark repeated.

'He says he's got a warrant!' shouted Naomi.

'I have some questions to ask you,' said Stark.

'And I have no intention of answering them,' snapped back Lady Amelia.

'Very well,' nodded Stark quietly. He turned to the two uniformed officers and pointed at Naomi. 'Evans, arrest that young woman. Handcuff her and take her to the car waiting downstairs. Smith, gather all the documents you can find here, bag them up and take them to my office.'

'Yes, sir,' said Evans, and he produced a pair of handcuffs and headed for the shocked Naomi, while the other uniformed policeman made for a filing cabinet.

'Wait!' shouted Lady Amelia.

'Wait,' echoed Stark, and the two uniformed officers stopped.

'Very well,' she said. 'Let us go to the office.'

'Wait here,' Stark ordered the two policemen. 'See that no one comes in, or leaves.'

He followed Lady Amelia into the inner office. She shut the door.

'So, Bobby Danvers has sent his bully-boy boss,' she said tartly.

'I am investigating a murder. I believe there could be another. My intention is to stop that happening.'

'By terrifying women.'

Stark couldn't stop a small smile appearing on his face. 'With respect, Lady Amelia, you do not seem to be a person who is easily terrified.'

'I do not use that title,' she said curtly.

Except when it suits you, reflected Stark. *When you want to pull rank.* 'Mrs Fairfax,' he amended.

She bridled at that, too.

'Or, if that doesn't suit you, perhaps you'd tell me how you'd like me to address you,' he added.

She hesitated, unsure of him, then reluctantly said in pinched tones, 'If this is going to be a formal interview, then perhaps we'd better stick to Lady Amelia.'

As I thought, Stark smiled inwardly. *When in a tight spot, wave the aristocratic flag.* 'It is,' said Stark. 'I'm making enquiries about a man who we have been led to believe is a member of this organization. His name's Dan. He's an ex-soldier.'

'I would imagine there are plenty of ex-soldiers called Dan around.'

'Yes, but not all of them spend a lot of time here at these offices. A member of your organization, so we understand. He's very vocal in expressing his opinion about the ruling classes.'

'As are many of our members, Chief Inspector. But I doubt if that comes as a surprise to you.'

'He's in his mid-twenties. About five feet eight inches tall. Slim build. Dark hair, thinning on top. Carries a revolver.'

Lady Amelia fixed him with a challenging glare. 'And you want me to identify him to you?'

'Yes,' nodded Stark.

She shook her head. 'In that case you are very misguided about the idea of comradeship.'

Stark nodded, then said calmly, 'And you are very misguided about the role of the police. A murder has been committed. As I said, we feel there is a possibility that the culprit could strike again. We need to talk to this man, at least to eliminate him from our enquiries. I believe that you – and very likely that young lady in the outer office – know this man and will be able to give us his name and where we can find him.'

Lady Amelia gave a short and derisive laugh. 'Just like that?'

'Yes,' said Stark. 'If you do not, I will arrest you both for obstructing the police in their duties while carrying out a murder investigation. We will then be forced to go through all your files and records and list every name and address we can find.'

'Those files are confidential!' she snapped, outraged.

'Not if I deem them to be vital evidence,' said Stark.

'Do you really have a warrant?' challenged Lady Amelia.

'Yes,' said Stark, and he produced the warrant he'd obtained earlier. 'I would have preferred not to use it, but I will do so if you insist on being obstructive.' He looked at her keenly as he added, 'I'm sure you will be pleased to be able to say you have been arrested and spent time in jail. It will help your image with your supporters. I also hope that, because of your social position, *Lady* Amelia, *you* will be treated well. But not everyone enjoys their spell in prison.'

'You are threatening Naomi!' she burst out angrily.

'Not at all,' said Stark. 'I'm just letting you know the reality of the situation. As far as the young lady is concerned, whether she decides to help us, or go to jail, is up to her. It is a choice she makes.'

'But you are not asking her your questions,' Lady Amelia pointed out.

'I will ask her as soon as I have finished talking to you. But my guess is she is so loyal to you, once she knows you have refused to give the information, she will also refuse. And both of you will be arrested, and my men will go through your files and I will get the information I'm looking for, anyway. Plus, I expect, much more information besides.'

Lady Amelia's eyes burned as she glared at Stark. 'Are we now living in a dictatorship?' she demanded, tight-lipped.

'Not yet,' he responded. 'Not until the communists take over.'

Lady Amelia fell silent, and Stark could see she was weighing up her options.

'You bastard!' she hissed.

Stark nodded. 'Yes,' he said. 'I've often been called that. But usually by criminals once they've been caught.'

'You are asking me to give up an innocent man.'

'No,' Stark corrected her. 'Contrary to the opinion some have about the police, I have never framed a person yet, or falsified evidence against them. If he is innocent, he will be released, I promise you.'

'And you expect me to believe you?'

'That is up to you,' said Stark.

Lady Amelia fell silent and turned away from Stark, further weighing up her options. Finally, she headed for the outer office. Stark followed her, standing in the open doorway between the two offices and watching as she went to a filing cabinet, opened it and began to rummage through a tray of index cards.

Naomi had stopped work and watched Lady Amelia with a wary expression on her face, now and then shooting a hostile glance at the two uniformed constables who stood impassively, waiting.

Lady Amelia took a card from the index, closed the filing cabinet, then strode back to her office. Stark stood aside to let her enter the room, then closed the door. She handed him the small card. On it was written: Dan Harker, Flat 2, 33 Emery Street, Bethnal Green.

He wrote the name and address down, then returned the card to Lady Amelia.

'Thank you,' said Stark.

TEN

S tark came out of the inner office and addressed one of the constables waiting for him.

'You, stay here,' he instructed. 'No one is to leave here, or enter, until I send you a message.'

Lady Amelia Fairfax stood in the doorway of her office and glared at Stark. 'Keeping us prisoners, Chief Inspector?' she asked sarcastically. 'You must think we are very dangerous.'

'No, but I think you're capable of getting a message to Mr Harker to warn him,' replied Stark.

He gestured at the other constable to follow him out of the office and down the stairs. Danvers was waiting for him in the street.

'Our man is Dan Harker, Flat Two, Thirty-three, Emery Street,' said Stark.

Danvers stared at him, surprised. 'Lady Amelia volunteered that information?' he asked, stunned.

'In a manner of speaking,' said Stark. He turned to the constables. 'Are you locals?' he asked.

One of the men nodded.

'Do you know where Emery Street is?'

'It's over in Bethnal Green, sir,' the constable replied. 'It's not on our beat, but I know whose it is. Willie Roberts. A constable who works out of Bethnal Green.'

'Good,' nodded Stark. 'Let's go and find this Willie Roberts.'

It took less than half an hour. They found PC Roberts at Bethnal Green police station and followed him to Emery Street. On the way, Stark questioned the constable about Harker, but Roberts admitted that he didn't know too much about the man.

'I've had to talk to him a couple of times, that's all.'

'About what?'

'Being drunk and disorderly on the street.'

'What's he like when he's drunk?'

'Aggressive.'

'And when he's sober?'

The constable shrugged. 'I don't think I've seen much of him when he's sober, sir.'

'Do you know if he owns a gun?'

The constable shook his head. 'Sorry, sir. If he does, he didn't tell me about it. But then, he wouldn't.' He hesitated, then added, 'Mind, he did threaten to shoot me once.'

'What?'

'I just put it down to the drink talking. Drunks do that. Talk about what they're going to do, but half the time they never do once they've sobered up.'

Roberts stopped at the end of a short street. 'Here we are, sir,' he said. 'Emery Street.' He pointed at a house. 'That's number thirty-three. Flat two is that window on the left of the front door.'

Stark studied the house. The window the police constable had indicated was dirty with grime, but Stark could see that a make-shift curtain was pulled across it.

'Stay here,' he ordered.

He walked across the road to stand beside the window of Flat two, listening. There were no sounds from inside. Either Harker was out or he was keeping quiet. Perhaps he was asleep. Many serious drinkers slept during the day. Stark listened for a few more minutes, then returned to Danvers and the uniformed constables.

'Is he in there, sir?' asked Danvers.

'Difficult to say,' said Stark. 'I couldn't hear any noises from inside. But we're going to play this as if he is.' He turned to Roberts. 'Tell me about the layout of the house.'

'Four rooms on the ground floor, two on each side of the passage,' responded the constable. 'Three rooms upstairs. All let out. Like I say, Harker lives in the room at the front of the house, on the left.'

'Anyone live with him?'

The constable shook his head. 'Not as far as I know, sir.'

'Is the street door locked?'

'No, sir. It's a lodging house. Street door's always open.'

'Where are the stairs?'

'At the far end of the passage, by the back door.'

'What's out the back?'

'A small yard, with a privy and a shed.'

'Is there a way out through the yard?'

Again, Roberts shook his head. 'No, sir. There's a brick wall at the back, and behind that there's a lane.'

Stark turned to two of the officers. 'Higgins and Prescott, get into the back lane, just in case he does a bolt for it over the wall.'

'Yes, sir,' nodded the two policemen, and they headed for the back lane.

'This could be dangerous, sir,' said Danvers, concerned. 'If he is armed, he's likely to start shooting as soon as he knows it's the police.'

'My opinion exactly, Sergeant. Which is why I'm going to be using subterfuge and then, if we're lucky with that, a bit of brute force. I want you outside in the street with a couple of men, guarding the front door.' He looked at Roberts. 'You're with me, Constable.' He pointed at another officer. 'You, stand at the bottom of the stairs.'

Stark headed back across the road, followed by Roberts and the other constable, and entered the house. He gestured the constable to the bottom of the stairs, then indicated for Roberts to stand on the other side of the door, out of the way of any bullets if Harker started shooting through the door. When the two officers were in place, Stark tapped gently on the door and called out in a low voice, 'Dan Harker?'

There was no reply, but Stark was sure he heard movement inside the room. He banged on the door again, harder this time, and raised his voice a little as he repeated, 'Dan Harker?'

This time a gruff voice growled back, 'Who wants him?'

'Ernie,' said Stark. 'Naomi from the office sent me.'

'What office?' asked Harker, his tone suspicious.

'The Party office,' said Stark.

There was another pause, then Harker asked, 'What's she want?'

'She asked me to give you a message.'

'What's the message?'

'She wrote it down and put it in an envelope and told me to make sure I give it you personal.'

'All right. Hang on,' growled Harker.

There was the sound of a key turning in the lock and then Stark saw the handle turn. Immediately, Stark hurled himself at the door. There was a cry of pain from inside as the door hit Harker, and then Stark and the constable were in the room. Stark threw himself at Harker, bringing him crashing to the floor, the constable throwing himself on the man as he kicked and writhed.

'Sergeant!' bellowed Stark.

Danvers hurtled into the room, the other constables behind him, and they joined in grabbing hold of the struggling man. It only took a few moments and then Harker was standing, held by two officers, his hands handcuffed behind him.

'Daniel Harker,' said Stark. 'I am arresting you on suspicion of being involved in a murder. Anything you say may be noted and may be used in evidence.'

Harker stared at Stark, shock clear on his face. 'No!' he shouted. 'I'm protected!'

Protected? Stark studied Harker's face, his eyes. Protected by whom?

'The rest of this interview will take place at Scotland Yard,' said Stark. He turned to Danvers. 'Sergeant, search his room while I take Mr Harker in. And don't forget the privy and the shed in the yard.'

ELEVEN

The interrogation room in the basement of Scotland Yard was small and cramped. The lack of any natural light added to the oppressive atmosphere, just the harsh light from the one unshaded bulb dangling from the ceiling. The room stank of sweat and damp. Stark hated this room. In this kind of intimidating atmosphere, suspects would often say what they thought their interrogator wanted to hear, rather than tell the truth. When he could, Stark preferred to talk to suspects in his office, put them at their ease, lull them into making a mistake, contradict themselves. But *this* case was the investigation into the murder of Lord Amersham, peer of the realm and member of the Cabinet. It was being followed by those in government and the press, and that meant doing everything by the book. Which was why Stark was now sitting on a hard wooden chair, facing Dan Harker across a bare table. Two uniformed constables stood just behind Harker, ready to subdue him if he became aggressive.

Harker sat, sullen, watchful, his eyes on Stark's face the whole time.

'You said you were protected,' said Stark. 'Who by?'

Harker didn't respond. Instead, he continued to watch Stark cautiously. He's weighing things up, realized Stark. He's weighing *me* up, trying to work out what I know.

'Do you know Lord Amersham?' asked Stark.

At these words, Harker's attitude changed from fear and wariness to one of puzzlement. 'Who?' he asked.

'Lord Amersham,' repeated Stark.

'No,' said Harker. 'Why?'

'Lord Amersham was shot and killed yesterday. Where were you yesterday morning?'

It was as if a switch had been thrown; suddenly, all the anxiety disappeared from Harker's manner and he visibly relaxed.

It isn't him, Stark realized. *He's killed someone, but not Lord Amersham.*

'It wasn't me,' said Harker, shaking his head. He leaned forward and added firmly, 'And you can't fit me up for it, either.'

'You said you were protected,' said Stark. 'Who by?'

'You asked me that before.'

'I'm asking you again.'

Harker shook his head. 'You must have misheard me.'

'No,' said Stark. 'Who do you claim is protecting you? And why?'

Harker stared back at Stark, but with a new confidence. 'I'm saying nothing,' he said. He twisted his head round and looked at the two uniformed officers, before turning his attention back to Stark and saying in a challenging, almost smug, voice, 'And it won't do you any good to try to beat anything out of me.'

Stark bridled at this. 'I don't beat prisoners,' he said curtly.

'No?' said Harker. 'There's plenty who do.'

There was a tap at the door and Danvers peered in. 'I'm sorry to interrupt, sir,' he said. 'But I have some information.'

Stark got up and headed for the door. 'Keep an eye on him,' he told the constables.

Outside in the corridor, Danvers opened the bag he was holding. 'We found the gun, sir. But it's a Webley. An 11.2 millimetre.'

'Thank you, Sergeant. I don't need the full spec. I get the picture.'

'Yes, sir. We double-checked every nook and cranny in case he had another gun, but there was no sign of anything.'

'There won't be,' said Stark angrily. 'He didn't do it.'

Danvers frowned. 'But the information . . .'

'I'm sure the information was good, and I'm also sure that Harker is a dangerous man who quite likely killed someone. But I'm pretty sure he didn't shoot Lord Amersham.'

'Chief Inspector Stark!'

Stark and Danvers both turned at the voice, and saw the figure of Chief Inspector Burns approaching them along the corridor.

'Chief Inspector Burns,' nodded Stark in wary greeting. He gestured at Danvers. 'I don't believe you've met Sergeant Danvers.'

Burns smiled and shook Danvers' hand. 'A pleasure to meet you, Sergeant,' he said. He turned back to Stark. 'We need to talk.'

'I'm in the middle of an interview,' said Stark.

'I know,' nodded Burns. 'That is why we need to talk.'

Stark hesitated. He wanted to tell Burns to get lost, that this was *his* case, not Special Branch's. But he already knew that the interview was a waste of time, Harker wasn't the murderer.

Stark turned to Danvers. 'Sergeant, continue the interview with Mr Harker,' he said.

'Yes, sir,' nodded Danvers, and Stark saw the pride in his eyes at being given this task.

As Stark and Burns head towards Stark's office, Burns murmured approvingly, 'Good move. Flatter your sergeant. You ought to go into politics, Chief Inspector.'

Stark didn't reply, just led the way in a sour silence. He waited until they were in his office and had closed the door, before turning to Burns and saying accusingly, 'He's one of yours, isn't he?'

'Yes,' nodded Burns. Curious, he asked, 'Did he say as much to you?'

'No,' replied Stark. 'He just said he was protected, but he didn't say who by. Once you arrived, you provided the answer.'

'It's always useful to have someone inside these revolutionary organizations to keep an eye on them,' said Burns. 'Let us know what's what, what they're planning. We created the perfect cover for him: the angry radical, bitter about the war, harbouring resentment against the upper classes. But I can assure you, he didn't shoot Lord Amersham.'

'I know,' said Stark. 'For one thing, his weapon's a different calibre. But I'd already worked out he hadn't done it.'

'Actually, you've done us a favour by arresting him. Given him even greater credibility in the eyes of his communist comrades.' Burns smiled. 'Perhaps you could get your chaps to rough him up a bit. That would give him even greater clout with the revolutionary masses.'

'You didn't think to inform me about him? You knew we'd be investigating the communists.'

'If you remember, we had suggested a more fruitful line of enquiry.'

'The Irish delegation,' nodded Stark. 'I went to see them.'

'We know,' said Burns. 'And?'

'They knew I was coming,' said Stark.

'Of course,' said Burns. 'You made an appointment to see them.'

'I meant they knew I was coming to see them before I made the appointment.'

Burns frowned. 'What makes you say that?'

'A feeling.'

Burns smiled. 'The policeman's famous hunch,' he said. 'Possibly a bit exaggerated in this instance.'

'The point is, you knew that Winston Churchill had ordered me to investigate the Bolsheviks, and you knew I would be going to the British Communist Party, but you didn't give me any advance notice about Dan Harker,' snapped Stark.

'If we had, you wouldn't have made such a fuss with Lady Amelia about finding him,' replied Burns. 'As I said, the fact that you did has turned out very well for us. His credibility inside the organization is assured. Thank you, Chief Inspector.' He smiled, and then added in a cautious tone, 'You will be releasing him now, of course.'

'What about the other murder?' asked Stark.

Immediately, Burns was alert, wary. 'What other murder?' he asked suspiciously.

'The one you used as leverage to get Harker to work for you,' said Stark.

Burns shook his head. His smug confidence had been momentarily rattled. 'I don't know what you're talking about,' he said.

'Harker murdered someone. You offered him immunity from prosecution if he worked for you. That's the "protection" he was referring to.'

Burns was no longer smiling. 'There was no such murder,' he said flatly. 'There is no such protection. Dan Harker is an operative of ours, working undercover for the good of this country. We are grateful for your cooperation, but we must insist you release him immediately.' When Stark didn't respond, he added, 'We are on the same side.'

Stark gave a curt nod, and Burns left.

Stark returned to the interrogation room and gestured for Danvers to join him in the corridor. Just before he closed the door behind them, he shot a look at Harker, who appeared just as smugly confident as he had when Stark had been questioning him.

Danvers shook his head. 'I can't shake him, sir,' he said. 'I think you're right. Not only is he not our man, but I don't think he has any information that can help us.'

'Except one thing,' scowled Stark. 'He's a plant inside the Communist Party from Special Branch.'

Danvers stared at Stark. 'So he's one of us?' he said.

Stark shook his head. 'He's never one of us, Sergeant,' he said grimly. 'But he's got nothing to do with the murder of Lord Amersham. Kick him out.'

'And then what, sir?'

'And then go home. That's what I'm going to do. We'll reappraise everything in the morning.'

TWELVE

H is parents and Stephen were sitting at the table in the kitchen having their supper when Stark arrived home.

'I didn't know what time you'd be home,' said his mother defensively. 'You've been coming home at all hours of late.'

She got up to go to the range, where the saucepans were keeping hot, but Stark stopped her. 'Don't worry, Mum,' said Stark. 'Sit down and finish. I'll have mine afterwards.'

He went back out to the hallway, where he took off his jacket and overcoat and hung them up. He was about to head back to the kitchen when he became aware that Henry had followed him and was standing in the narrow passage, blocking his way. His father had the newspaper in his hand and an angry expression on his face.

'Is this how little you think of us?' Henry burst out, and he brandished the newspaper at his son.

Stark stared at his father, bewildered. 'I'm sorry, I don't know what you mean.'

'How do you think me and your mum feel having to find out what you're up to by reading about it in the papers?' His father opened the newspaper and read out, '*The net is closing in on the killers of Lord Amersham. Detective Chief Inspector Stark of Scotland Yard informs us that they hope to have the murderous Bolsheviks behind the assassination in custody soon.*'

Stark shook his head. 'None of that is true.'

'But it's in the papers!'

'That doesn't make it true. I never said that to them. We don't know if it's Bolsheviks who are behind the murder—'

'Well, someone thinks they are! And that's another thing. You didn't even tell us you were on this case!'

'I'm not allowed to discuss cases outside of Scotland Yard.'

'Not even something like this? The murder of someone as important as Lord Amersham?'

'It doesn't matter if it's the murder of Lord Amersham or someone who stole a watch, we're not supposed to talk about it outside of our colleagues in the police force.'

'Well, someone's talked about it to the newspapers!'

And I know who, thought Stark grimly. Churchill, eager to push his anti-Bolshevik agenda.

'It's not right!' his father continued. 'The neighbours read this and ask us about it, and we don't know anything. It's not fair!'

'I've told you, Dad, I haven't talked to the newspapers. I haven't talked to anybody about this except the people at the Yard.'

'It's still not right!' Henry insisted. 'You ought to tell us things.'

With that, he headed back along the passage to the kitchen and returned to his place at the table. As he picked up his knife and fork and resumed his meal, Stark came into the kitchen.

'You're right,' he said quietly, addressing his remarks not just to his father, but to his mother and to Stephen. 'I'm sorry I haven't let you know what's happening.' He pointed at the news-paper which his father had deposited on an armchair. 'I am investigating the murder of Lord Amersham. As chief inspector, I'm the senior officer on the case. Because of Lord Amersham being who he was, there's a lot of interest in this case, so I think we can expect more reports in the papers. I promise that if I say anything to the press, I shall let you all know in advance. So far I haven't said anything to them, but if they don't know something, a lot of the time they make it up.'

'What are Bolsheviks?' asked Stephen.

Stark smiled. He was glad the boy's reading was coming along. 'Bolsheviks is another word for communists,' he said. 'They're people who believe in getting rid of the upper classes.'

'They're savages,' Henry snorted. 'They killed the Russian

tsar and all his family. They want to get rid of the King and Queen, and the government.'

'Why does the paper say you're going to arrest them?' asked Stephen, puzzled.

'Because someone in government has told them that's who did the murder,' said Stark. 'The truth is, Stephen, we don't know who did it. That's what my job is: to try to find out.'

'If the government say the Bolshies did it, they did,' stated Henry flatly.

'Possibly,' said Stark.

Sarah had finished her meal. She got up, took her plate out to the scullery, then went to the range and began to serve Stark's meal on to a plate. 'Wash your hands,' she ordered him.

Stark headed out to the scullery and the cold tap over the sink. *I'm thirty-four and they still treat me like an errant child*, he reflected. *But that's the price I pay for having them look after Stephen.*

Later, when the meal was finished and the plates cleared away, Stark sat down at the table and watched as his father and Stephen laid sheets of newspaper on the table to protect it, then took the pieces of the model plane they were making from a drawer. A sharp knife was produced, and a pot of glue with a brush.

The shape of the Sopwith Camel was already clear: the relatively short body, the round propeller casing at the nose, the upper wing of the biplane ready to fix to the struts coming up from the lower wing and the fuselage. Stark had seen plenty of them in action over the trenches of Flanders during the last year of the war, twisting and turning in the sky with an agility that had been lacking in the earlier planes.

As Stark watched Stephen cut and shape the pieces of wood under Henry's painstaking directions, once again he felt the surge of admiration at the careful, precise work that he'd had as a child when watching his father at work as a carpenter.

'Do you want to do some cutting, Dad?' asked Stephen.

Stark shook his head. 'No, I'll leave that to you and Grandad,' he said. 'You're better at it than I am. I'll do some gluing.'

'You'd better not mess it up,' growled Henry. 'You always made a mess when you were a kid.'

'Yes, but I'm older now. I've learned to be more careful,' said Stark. And he winked at Stephen, who grinned back.

*   *   *

The tap-tap-tap at the door of his flat interrupted Danvers as he pored over the copies he'd made of the reports from the uniformed officers: witness statements, speculations, theories. He knew he should have let it drop, relax, get his mind off it for this evening, but he also knew that *this* was his big chance. The murder of Lord Amersham. One of the most high-profile cases the Yard had ever had. There was the promise of promotion here. He would show them all that *he* was the man who would take the police force forward. Superintendent Barnes, Stark, Special Branch, his father, Lady Amelia Fairfax, that girl Naomi. There had been enough sneers and doubters when he said he was going into the police force. He was sure the answer to the murder lay somewhere in these documents he had laid out on his small sideboard and his other chair. And now he was being interrupted.

He opened the door and was surprised to see his sister standing there. 'Lettie!' It was always a pleasure to see Lettie, even if she did bring with her unpleasant memories of his father and home. 'Come in! I'll just clear these papers up and find you a chair!'

Two chairs. That was all he had in this room. *A bijou apartment*; that was how the agent had described it. In real terms, it meant a tiny living room, with a gas fire and one gas ring on which to boil a kettle; and a small box room which housed a very narrow single bed. There was also a toilet and basin in the small bathroom, a luxury considering that most of the population of London still had to use outside privies.

'You should have told me you were coming. We could have arranged to meet somewhere nicer. The Connaught.'

For once, Lettie didn't comment. Usually, when she called, she made well-intentioned but disparaging remarks about the small flat, wondering why he didn't provide himself with a better standard of accommodation.

'Because I'm only on a policeman's pay, Let,' he told her every time. 'Even as a detective. Yes, I might find somewhere larger further out, but this is Russell Square, and Bloomsbury isn't cheap, you know.'

Danvers cleared the papers into a pile and dumped them on the sideboard.

'If you give me a minute, I'll get myself cleaned up and we can pop out somewhere.'

'No.'

There was something in Lettie's voice, a note of despair, and Danvers stopped what he was doing and turned to her, suddenly anxious. 'What is it?' he asked. 'Is Mama all right?'

'Yes,' she said, but her voice was still strange. Anxious.

Danvers gestured to her to sit, and she lowered herself into the chair. 'Come on, Lettie, what is it? What's wrong?'

He looked at his sister as she sat awkwardly on the chair. He'd always felt protective towards Lettie. Eighteen now, but still a child in so many ways. Danvers put that down to the dominant stance of his father, determined to rule the roost at home, crushing his wife and children into moulds of his wanting. He had never allowed Lettie to gain her independence, take risks, show a bit of wildness. No, the *family name* was far too important for that.

'I saw Bunty Wickham yesterday,' said Lettie. She hesitated, and Danvers saw she was doing her best to stop herself bursting into tears. Lettie forced a not very convincing smile. 'You know what a terrible gossip she is.'

Yes, Danvers did. One evening, at a dance, he'd had a mild flirtation with her, and the next morning an exaggerated report of his antics had blazed around their circle like wildfire. 'Like an octopus,' she had said. 'Really, my dear, his hands were all over me!'

'Anything that Bunty Wickham says needs to be taken with a very large pinch of salt,' said Danvers.

'Yes, I know. Anyway, she said that the police are looking into Lord Amersham's private life. You know . . . his . . . relationships.' She looked at Danvers. 'Is that true?'

'Among other things,' said Danvers cautiously. 'To be honest, there are lots of different avenues to explore. Politics, for one.'

She dropped her head, nodding. 'Who'll be looking into it?'

'All of us?'

'You?'

'Well, of course. My boss, Chief Inspector Stark, is in charge of the case, and I'm already closely involved. Although it's early days yet.'

'The questions about Lord Amersham's private life. How . . . discreet will people be?'

'As discreet as we can be, but everyone knows what sort of man he was.' A sudden realization hit him, and he stared at his sister in shock.

'Lettie. You're not saying that you . . .'

'No, no, no!' Her face as she looked at him was a mixture of shock and revulsion.

'But then why . . .'

'It's Mama and Papa.'

Danvers stared at her, bewildered. 'What is?'

'I'm sure it's nothing!' burst out Lettie, and she jerked to her feet and began to pace about the room, agitated. 'It really is nothing, but the police may not see it that way. I mean, *you* will, obviously, but your superior . . .'

'For God's sake, Lettie, just tell me!'

'It was about a month ago. Papa was away on business, and Lord Amersham called at the house. He said he was there to talk about this charity of his, the Passchendaele Memorial Fund. Because Papa was away, he talked to Mama about it.'

'Just the two of them?'

'Yes.'

'And you were there?'

'I was there when he arrived, but I had to go out. I was meeting Felicity Lamb. Anyway, a few days later Papa returned home in a fearful rage. He'd been told that Lord Amersham had been with Mama alone in the library, and he began to shout at her. You know what a temper he has.'

'Only too well,' said Danvers ruefully.

'Papa said that Lord Amersham had the worst of reputations, and no decent woman would entertain him, certainly not privately. He . . . he . . .' She stopped. 'He demanded to know what had taken place between them, and even when Mama promised him it had only been a conversation about Lord Amersham's Memorial Fund, he wasn't placated. He said that if *that* man came to the house again, he would . . . he would shoot him like a dog.'

'Who heard this exchange?' asked Danvers.

'Everyone in the house. You know how loud Papa's voice is when he gets angry.'

'And who, exactly, was in the house?'

'Me. Bridges. Mrs Henderson. Millie.'

His father's valet, the housekeeper, the maid. Which meant, with Millie's gossipy tongue, the threat would be common knowledge.

'And then . . .' Lettie was continuing, her manner even more awkward. 'And then, about a week later, Lord Amersham returned. Once again, Papa was away . . .'

'It seems Lord Amersham timed his visits carefully,' commented Danvers wryly.

'I was in the drawing room when he arrived. Mrs Henderson answered the door and Lord Amersham asked if he could see Papa. Mrs Henderson told him that Papa was away from the house, and Lord Amersham asked if he could see Mama. Mrs Henderson told him that Mama was also away. I got the impression that Lord Amersham didn't believe her.'

'Was Mama at home?'

'Yes. But she had given orders that if Lord Amersham called again, he was to be told that she was not available.'

'And then what happened?'

Lettie gave a shudder at the memory. 'Lord Amersham said he would like to leave a note for Mama, and asked for a pen and paper. As Mrs Henderson went to get them, Papa returned. His business had obviously finished early.'

'Or he had been watching the house,' observed Danvers quietly.

'Nonsense!' said Lettie. 'Why would he do such a thing?'

Because jealousy makes us all act like fools, thought Danvers sadly. 'What happened then between Papa and Lord Amersham?' he asked.

'Papa exploded! He demanded to know what Lord Amersham was doing in his house. Lord Amersham said that he had come to continue a conversation he'd had about the Passchendaele Memorial Fund, about raising funds for it. Papa . . . Papa virtually accused him of lying. He raged. He jabbed his finger at Lord Amersham, and at one moment I thought he was going to attack him.'

'What did Lord Amersham do?'

'Nothing. He just sort of looked at Papa with a sort of cold sneer on his face, which only made things worse. Finally he said, "You are a fool, Danvers, and beneath my contempt." And with that he left.'

'What happened then? With Mama?'

'Yes,' nodded Lettie. 'Papa went and found Mama and started raging at her, accusing her of encouraging Lord Amersham. He said there'd be no more of this. He said . . . He said if he shot Lord Amersham, no court would find him guilty because of the man's appalling reputation. In fact, he said there were many who would applaud his actions.'

She fell silent.

'And when was all this?' asked Danvers.

'Lord Amersham's last visit was just over a fortnight ago.' She looked at her brother, agonized. 'What can we do, Bobby?'

Danvers stood up and took his sister by the hand. 'Lettie, it's highly unlikely that Papa would have carried out his threat.'

'I know, but the police won't know that!'

'I am the police,' Danvers reminded her.

'I mean the people at the top. This chief inspector they talk about in the newspapers.'

'Chief Inspector Stark,' said Danvers. 'He's a good man, Lettie. Intelligent.'

'But say Papa is arrested? If it all comes out . . .' She shook her head miserably. 'Think of what people will say about Mama.'

'You don't mean you think that Mama and Lord Amersham . . .?'

'No! No! But you know what people are like; they'll say there's no smoke without fire.' She squeezed his hand and looked at him appealingly. 'Will you have a word with this Inspector Stark? Explain to him. Stop anything happening before loose gossip turns into . . . I don't know . . . accusations.'

Danvers hesitated. Yes, he knew he'd have to pass this on to Stark, but he also knew that the chief inspector was not the kind to hide things under the carpet. That was one of the reasons he was so unpopular with the senior ranks at Scotland Yard. 'Leave it to me, Lettie. I'll see what I can do,' he promised. But he already knew that even by mentioning it to Stark, he would be putting his father in the frame as a suspect.

THIRTEEN

Stark was in the kitchen, polishing his boots, when the sound of the door knocker echoed down the passage from the street door.

'I wonder who that is?' asked Henry. 'You expecting anyone?'

Stark looked at the clock on the mantelpiece. Quarter past eight. His car wasn't due this morning until half past eight. Maybe the driver was early, for some reason.

His mother was in the scullery with Stephen, getting him washed and ready for school. His father was sitting by the range, reading yesterday's newspaper.

'I'll go,' said Stark.

He went along the passage, taking his jacket from the coat stand and pulling it on before he opened the door. Sergeant Danvers was standing there, and the worried expression on his face made Stark immediately alert. 'I'm sorry to call on you at home, sir, but something has happened that I need to tell you about before you start work.'

'Who is it?' Henry called.

'It's someone from work,' Stark called back.

Sarah appeared from the scullery and smiled when she saw Danvers. 'Sergeant Danvers, isn't it? You came with the note from Paul the other day.'

'Yes, indeed, Mrs Stark, and I'm very sorry to call at this hour.'

'That's all right.'

'He's called on work business,' said Stark.

'Then you'd better come in. It's not the weather for standing on the doorstep. Paul, take Sergeant Danvers into the front parlour.'

Stark gestured for Danvers to enter the house.

'First door on your right,' he muttered.

'Thank you, sir,' said Danvers, and he walked down the narrow passage to the door.

The front parlour, thought Stark. *Reserved for funerals, weddings, and very special guests.* It was Danvers' upper-class

accent that had made Sarah direct him to this special room, where
everything was kept polished and untouched. If he'd been an
ordinary working-class constable, he'd have been invited to the
kitchen, a much warmer and friendlier place.

'What's happened?' asked Stark. He gestured to one of the
chairs. 'You'd better sit down.'

Danvers sank down on to one of the heavily cushioned chairs.
'I've never really talked to you about my family, sir,' he began.

'I read your application form,' said Stark. 'I can guess some
of it. Public school. Very respectable family.' He gave Danvers
a thoughtful look. 'Not the traditional background for someone
in the police force.'

'No, sir. But I am serious about making it my career.'

'I know you are, Sergeant. So, this concerns your family.'

'My father, actually.'

Danvers sat in silence, looking miserable.

'I think some words would be a good idea,' prompted Stark.
'Telepathy isn't my strongest point.'

'Sorry, sir,' said Danvers awkwardly. 'It's wondering where to
begin.'

'The start is usually a good place,' said Stark gently.

Danvers nodded. 'My sister, Lettie, called to see me yesterday
evening.' And then, slowly at first, Danvers told Stark the story
his sister had told him the night before.

Stark waited until he was sure Danvers had finished, then
asked, 'And how likely do you think it is that your father may
have carried out his threat?'

'Highly unlikely, to be frank. And certainly not in a public
place. That would bring too much disgrace on the family name.'

'But you felt it important enough to come to me here?'

'Because it would be bound to come out! And you need to
know before word reaches the Yard. I trust the servants absolutely,
but who's to say who Lord Amersham may have told?'

Stark nodded. 'Yes, a good point.' He regarded his sergeant
quizzically. 'I get the impression from things you've said that
you and your father don't get on.'

'Yes, that's true,' replied Danvers.

'Does he have a temper?'

Danvers nodded unhappily. 'Yes,' he admitted.

'So he *could* have carried out his threat? That's obviously what your sister thinks; otherwise she wouldn't have come to tell you about it.'

'Yes,' said Danvers. 'Lettie thinks . . . She thinks he's capable of it. He's very protective of our family's reputation.'

'Your father will have to be interviewed,' said Stark.

'I know, sir.'

'You can't do it. That would be in breach of all the rules.'

'Yes, sir.'

'Which means, as the chief officer in this case, I'll do it.'

Danvers looked at him gratefully. 'Thank you, sir. I hoped you'd say that. But . . . but I must warn you, he can be . . . aggressive.'

'Even to the police?'

'Yes, sir.' Danvers gave a rueful smile. 'He's quite democratic about expressing his opinions, regardless of rank or status.'

'To Lord Amersham, for example.'

'Exactly, sir.'

'Thank you, Sergeant. I have been warned and will be prepared.'

'I didn't mean . . .' began Danvers apologetically.

'Don't worry, Sergeant.' Stark waved a hand to calm the sergeant down. 'In my position, I have often been on the end of adverse attitudes. But it will help me if you tell me about the household – who I can expect to find when I call.'

'Yes, sir. My father is generally at home.'

'Colonel Danvers.'

'Yes, sir.'

'Colonel of what?'

'The cavalry.'

'Served?'

'Sudan. The Boer War.'

'Your mother?'

'She's usually at home, but my guess is she'll stay out of it, in her room, once she realizes the reason for your visit. My father will certainly order her to her room.'

'Your sister?'

'Letitia. I call her Lettie. She's eighteen. I doubt if she'll be at home. She prefers to go out, seeing friends, or trips to museums and things. Anything, rather than stay home with father. As I said, he can be quite abrasive.'

'Servants?'

'Just the three. Bridges, father's valet, Mrs Henderson the housekeeper, and Millie the maid.'

Just three servants, thought Stark. He liked Danvers, but he couldn't help feeling a touch of resentment at the sergeant's casual attitude that having servants was the norm. Yes, in his class, they were. He wondered how Danvers viewed him, his boss, living in this cramped terraced house in one of London's poorer districts.

He dismissed the thought. *We are not to blame for our backgrounds or where we come from*, he told himself. 'Right. I'll go and see your father this morning, first thing, as soon as my driver arrives. You go to the Yard and assess any new information that may have come in overnight. I'll join you there.'

'Right, sir. Is there any particular line of enquiry you want to look at?'

'Yes. Line up some contacts among the Jewish community. Lord Amersham was virulently anti-Semitic. His public comments about Jews won't have endeared him to some, especially his negative comments about those Jewish immigrants who've recently arrived from Russia. There may be something there – some angry immigrant who's lost everything and feels Lord Amersham's words are too much to bear.'

Danvers nodded. 'There was a chap at school with me who was Jewish. We were quite friendly. Would it be all right if I approached him to see if he can put me in the right direction, the right people to talk to, that sort of thing?'

The old school tie network, thought Stark. 'Good idea, Sergeant. At the moment we're still clutching at straws. Who knows which part of the enquiry will turn up the right straw.'

FOURTEEN

Stark's car pulled up outside the Danvers family's house in Hampstead, a large, old red-brick house set in its own grounds, with a stone wall around it.

'Wait here,' he instructed his driver.

He pushed open the ornate wrought-iron gate and walked up the path to the house and rang the bell. After the briefest of delays the door was opened by a short, thin, elderly man in a valet's suit who looked enquiringly out at Stark.

'You must be Mr Bridges,' said Stark. 'I am Chief Inspector Stark from Scotland Yard, and I wish to see Colonel Danvers. Is he available?'

Bridges opened the door wider. 'If you'd care to step inside, sir, I'll see if the colonel is free.'

So, at least he's at home, thought Stark as he stepped into the hallway. Would he see him? The upper classes could be very dismissive of what they considered the *lower orders*, and that included rank-and-file police officers. But he was sure that the colonel would know that Stark was his son's immediate boss, and that fact might arouse the colonel's curiosity about this unexpected visit.

Stark stood in the lobby and looked around him, and into the house itself, taking in the outer hallway with its pattern of black-and-white floor tiles, gold-coloured embossed wallpaper, with paintings and prints of rural scenes adorning the walls. *My God, the hallway on its own is bigger than our living room, bigger than most of the rooms in my own home.* His *rented* home. Very few people in Camden Town or the surrounding areas owned their own homes; all were rented. And this was where Robert Danvers had grown up. In this comfortable, spacious financial security. And he'd given it up to move into a small flat in Russell Square and work as a police detective. Why? As a child, even as a man, Stark would have given his back teeth to live somewhere like this.

Bridges returned. 'The colonel will see you. He is in the library. If you'll follow me, Chief Inspector.'

They set off, out of the hallway and through a large, thickly carpeted room furnished with heavy, dark oak chairs, a table large enough to seat eight people, a grand piano in one corner, before arriving at a set of double doors. Bridges knocked, opened them, then announced, 'Detective Chief Inspector Stark of Scotland Yard, Colonel Danvers.'

He stood aside and Stark entered.

Colonel Danvers was standing with his back to the large, ornate fireplace; there was no fire in it, just paper spills and kindling ready to light.

Stark shot a glance around the library. Rows and rows of books, as one would have expected, but somehow they looked as if they were ornaments, not for actually being taken off the shelves and read. As with the hallway, the pictures on the walls here were of rural scenes, mostly hunting. The tables and chairs shone with polish, and it suddenly struck Stark that this room was the Danvers family's equivalent of his own front parlour: for show only, for guests, not for actual use.

Colonel Danvers was about sixty, the same age as Stark's own father. He was a man of medium height, carrying a lot of weight around his stomach. The result of too much good food and too many bottles of wine. He also had that same disapproving scowl on his face that Stark's father had. *Was this the same with all fathers?* Stark wondered. Disapproval and disappointment at their sons?

'Thank you for seeing me, Colonel Danvers,' said Stark.

Danvers did not reply, nor did he invite Stark to sit down. He just remained standing stiffly in front of the unlit fire, watching the chief inspector suspiciously.

'I'm investigating the murder of Lord Amersham, and we have received information that you and Lord Amersham had an altercation recently,' said Stark, coming straight to the point.

He looks just like an older version of my sergeant, he thought. The eyes, the nose, the mouth, the forehead, the chin, all the same. A copy, but aged by years and too much comfortable living. Was this how Robert Danvers would look in forty years' time? Is that the same for all of us? We all become our fathers?

'What information? Who from?' growled Colonel Danvers.

'I'm afraid that must be confidential for the moment,' said Stark. 'Is there any truth in the story?'

Danvers remained silent, his mouth pursed tight and his eyes fixed on the chief inspector's face.

This is a man with a very short temper, Stark reminded himself. 'I must ask you again, sir, is there any truth—'

'I don't wish to discuss it!' snapped Danvers.

'I respect that, sir, but I have been empowered by the government to find the murderer, and in order to do that I have to ask questions which may be . . . uncomfortable. Our information says that recently you threatened to shoot Lord Amersham. Is that correct, sir?'

At this, a red flush rose in Danvers' face, rising up from his neck. 'Who's been talking?' he snarled.

'As I said, sir, I regret that information must remain—'

'Damn and blast you!' roared Danvers. He swung away from Stark, his whole body shaking, then swung back again to face the chief inspector. 'My son works for you, doesn't he?'

'Sergeant Danvers is indeed my assistant in this case.'

'He's a loud-mouthed fool!'

'With respect, Colonel Danvers, I must disagree. I have found your son to be hard-working, diligent, very intelligent, and with the greatest of integrity.'

'He's disloyal!'

'On the contrary—'

'Don't you argue with me! I know your kind. I had your sort under me in the army. Barrack-room lawyers. Jumped-up peasants trying to best their betters!'

'That sounds like something Lord Amersham might have said, sir, according to the political statements he made.'

'How dare you!' Danvers burst out. 'Are you equating me with that . . . that . . .'

'With that *what*, sir?' asked Stark, keeping calm, watching Danvers as the colonel clenched and unclenched his fists. *Come on*, he thought. *Punch me, and see what happens. I will hit you so hard you won't know what day it is.*

'Of course, sir, if you insist on refusing to answer, I can always direct my questions to the rest of your household. Your servants, your wife and daughter . . .'

'Don't you dare bring them into this!' stormed Danvers. His face grew tight, and Stark could hear his teeth grinding. 'This is my son who's brought you here, isn't it? Some sort of tale he's told you. Revenge against me.'

'No, sir,' said Stark. 'And I will ask you again. Did you threaten to shoot Lord Amersham following an altercation with him?'

'Yes, damn and blast you! You know I did or you wouldn't be here! Who told you? None of the servants, I'll be bound. They've been with me for years. Except for Millie, and she wouldn't say anything.' He shook his head. 'It's Letitia, isn't it? My daughter. She must have told her brother. She thinks I don't know she goes to see him, but I know!'

'What were the instances that caused you to threaten Lord Amersham, sir?'

'If you know that much, then you know why!' roared Danvers, so furious and so red in the face that Stark worried he might suddenly keel over with a heart attack or a stroke. 'He was chasing my wife, goddamit! The man has – had – no morals! Filthy beast! What women saw in him, I don't know. Well, I knew what he was up to, coming round here when he knew I was out, under the pretence of that Memorial Fund of his. So I warned him.'

'You threatened to shoot him.'

'Yes!'

'Do you have any weapons, sir?'

'Of course I do! I have my hunting guns.'

'What about a pistol?'

Danvers hesitated, then grunted, 'Yes. My service pistol.'

'Might I look at it, sir?'

'No.'

The reply was growled out in fierce but low tones, almost a whisper, so that at first Stark struggled to hear the reply, but the negative response was obvious from Danvers' manner, fists bunched, chin and shoulders thrust forward challengingly.

'I must advise you, sir, that I can obtain a warrant to search these premises if you refuse to cooperate.'

'Then get your damned warrant!' snarled Danvers. 'Now get out of my house! You're not welcome here!'

Stark nodded politely, his manner unmoved by Danvers' histrionics. 'Thank you for your time, sir,' he said politely. 'I shall return with the necessary warrants.' He turned to leave, then stopped and turned back to Danvers. 'I must caution you, sir, that the raising of a warrant can sometimes result in the press being alerted. I will do my best to stop that from happening, but sometimes the staff in a judge's offices have been known to pass on such information in exchange for payment. Once a warrant is applied for, it becomes wider knowledge, and—'

'You dare to threaten me!' roared Danvers.

'In fact, I am doing the exact opposite,' said Stark. 'Because I am sympathetic to your situation, and particularly because my sergeant may become unwittingly involved and exposed to press intrusion himself—'

'Damn you!' roared Danvers again, but more quietly this time. The colonel stood in thought, weighing up his situation.

He is a man being torn apart, Stark decided. *A man desperate for privacy, a man to whom social standing matters almost above all else.*

'Very well,' he said. 'Bridges!' he shouted.

The valet appeared so swiftly that Stark was sure he'd been hovering just outside the library the whole time.

'You called, Colonel?' he asked.

'Take Chief Inspector Stark to the gun room,' growled Danvers. 'Show him my guns.' He hesitated, then added reluctantly, but with an air of final bravado, '*All* of my weapons. Service revolver. Everything.'

'Very good, sir,' nodded Bridges. 'This way, Chief Inspector.'

The gun room was not just for guns; on display were weapons of all sorts, not just ceremonial swords but also spears, assegais and decorated shields made of hide. Mementoes of the colonel's time in Sudan, Stark guessed.

As Stark stood surveying the exhibits, Bridges let out a low and discreet cough, then said, 'If you don't mind, sir, I'd be grateful if you'd apprise me of how Master Robert is. We were always very fond of the young master, Mrs Henderson and I, and we don't wish to trouble Miss Letitia.'

'You can rest assured that young Mr Danvers – Sergeant Danvers – is well and appears very happy in his work. Not only does he seem contented in the police force, it is my opinion he is also very good at it and has an excellent career ahead of him, should he decide to continue.'

Bridges gave a slight bow of his head, with a smile of gratitude. 'Thank you for that, sir. Information about Master Robert has been scarce since he left the house.'

'I will pass on your good wishes to him when I see him later today,' said Stark.

'Thank you, sir,' said Bridges. He looked around to make sure they weren't being overheard, then added, 'The colonel isn't a bad man, sir.'

'You've been with him a long time?'

'I served under him in the army, sir,' said Bridges. 'He was an excellent commander. Brave, and fair to his men. If there was a charge to be led, he was always at the front. When I was wounded and invalided out of the army, he offered me a position with him. He didn't need to. He could have found himself an experienced valet. But, as I say, he's a very loyal man. I know the rift between himself and Master Robert hurts him deeply. I wish they could find a way to reconcile their differences, but they are both very obstinate and headstrong.'

'Sergeant Danvers doesn't strike me as headstrong,' Stark mused. 'On the contrary, he seems quite reserved and thoughtful.'

'He is, sir, but he also has the bulldog determination of his father. Neither of them gives in easily.'

Stark nodded. 'As I said, I will certainly pass on your good wishes, and I will suggest to him that he asks his sister to keep you informed of his situation when she visits him.'

'Better not, sir,' said Bridges. 'I don't wish to cause any problems for Miss Letitia. She is not as emotionally strong as Master Robert.'

'Very well. As you wish.' Stark turned back to the weapons and the glass-fronted gun cabinet, where he could see shotguns and pistols. 'And now, if you will open the cabinets, I can begin the inspection.'

FIFTEEN

Sergeant Danvers sat in the office of Chaim Weigel – the Chief Rabbi, so his old schoolfriend, David, had told him.

'If there's anyone who knows everything about what's going on in the Jewish community, whether Orthodox or not, it's Rabbi Weigel. He's a man with his finger on the pulse. And he won't bore you rigid about religion; that's another good thing about him.'

'So,' said Weigel thoughtfully. 'You think that Lord Amersham might have been shot because of his anti-Semitic views?'

'Which were pretty extreme,' said Danvers. 'He seemed to blame the Jews for everything that had gone wrong since history began, starting with the death of Jesus.'

'Yes,' nodded the rabbi. 'I have read some of Lord Amersham's thoughts on the issue of Jews. Although I note that we were not alone in his negative thoughts. He also seemed to disapprove of people of colour, for example. Negroes. Arabs. Orientals. Muslims. Women. The Irish. The lower classes.' He chuckled. 'It seems to me to require a special talent to insult the number and range of people that Lord Amersham has given offence to.'

'Yes,' agreed Danvers. 'We are looking into other groups of people he has attacked as well. His attacks on the Jews are just one aspect of our investigations. Whether anyone might be so enraged by them as to want to . . . well . . . silence him. Stop that sort of talk being repeated.'

Rabbi Weigel nodded thoughtfully, then he asked, 'How well do you know your history, Sergeant?'

'A bit,' replied Danvers. 'Mainly what I learned at school. Dates. Kings. Wars. 1066. Magna Carta.'

The rabbi nodded. 'In 1290 King Edward the First expelled all the Jews from England,' he said. 'Four hundred years later, Oliver Cromwell asked the Protectorate government to lift the ban on Jews in England, and they refused. Until recently, in Ireland, part of the British Empire, there was the law of De Judaismo, which required all Jews to wear a special yellow badge identifying them as Jews. It was not repealed until 1846.' He shook his head resignedly. 'Throughout history, we Jews have died in our millions as a result of persecution. Look what is happening in Russia as we speak – Jews being forced to emigrate in their thousands.

'The attacks on Jews by Lord Amersham and his like are nothing new. They are part of our way of life. We have been the object of persecution since time began. Believe me, Sergeant, the anti-Semitic verbiage of Lord Amersham is akin to a flea bite on the hide of an elephant. It is insignificant in the whole order of things. He is not worth the bother of killing him. Every Jew knows that to do such a thing would only make matters much worse for every other Jew.

'In short, I think it highly unlikely that your killer is a Jew, prompted by Lord Amersham's virulent views of Jews.' He chuckled and added, 'Of course, you might think I would say that, anyway.'

*   *   *

Stark left the Danvers residence and made for the waiting car.
Sergeant Danvers could be relieved and reassured: there was no
nine-millimetre pistol among the colonel's collection. And the
colonel didn't appear the kind of man who would carry out a
secret ambush and then run off. The colonel was a man of very
public demonstrations of anger. If he'd shot Lord Amersham, he
would have made sure everyone knew he'd done it.

Stark got into the rear seat of the car.

'Back to Scotland Yard, sir?' asked Stan, his driver, starting
the engine.

Stark hesitated before replying. No, there was another call he
needed to make. His conscience nagged at him.

'No,' he said. 'Buxton Street in Stepney.'

'Buxton Street, sir? Near the Communist Party place where
we were the other day?'

'The very same, Stan. There's something there I need to check
on. Some unfinished business.'

He sat back as the car moved off, mulling over the reception
he'd get at the Communist Party offices. Hostile, of course. But
that didn't matter. What they thought of him didn't matter; what
was important was what he thought of himself.

The car pulled to a halt outside the unkempt building in Buxton
Street, and Stark got out.

'Do you want me to come in with you, sir?' asked Stan. 'After
what happened last time, things might get a little rough, depending
on who's in there.'

'No, I can manage, thanks, Stan. There shouldn't be any rough
stuff. If there is, I'll attract your attention.'

'How, sir? I doubt if I'll hear a shout.'

Stark smiled. 'I'll chuck something through their window into
the street.'

'Right, sir. I'll watch out for it.'

'I hope it won't be necessary.'

As Stark made his way up the dank staircase, he hoped he
wasn't being too optimistic about the reception he would receive.
It would depend on who was there when he arrived. Dan Harker,
possibly – continuing his spying operation?

He reached the door and knocked. He heard the familiar voice
of Lady Amelia Fairfax call 'Come in!' and walked in.

Lady Amelia was sitting at the desk in the outer office where the girl, Naomi, had sat on his previous visit. She stared at Stark in surprise, and then her expression hardened.

'You have a nerve coming here!' she snapped.

'Yes, I have,' replied Stark. Before she could embark on a lengthy harangue, Stark said, 'I've come to apologize.'

Lady Amelia stared at him, an expression of bewilderment on her face. 'Apologize?' she echoed.

He nodded. 'I was wrong to threaten you the way I did, but I had a lot of pressure to get to the bottom of this case.'

'And so you decided to go for the ones who can't fight back – the poor, the underclass!' she snapped angrily.

'I was following a definite lead . . . which turned out to be a dead end.'

'And an innocent man was dragged in for questioning and beaten—'

'He was not beaten,' said Stark quickly.

'That's not what he says.'

Stark hesitated, then said, 'I would be careful about anything that Dan Harker says to you, or – more importantly for you – you to him.'

'What's that supposed to mean?' she demanded.

'Just a piece of advice,' he said.

He turned to go.

'No, you don't!' she said angrily. 'If you've got something to say . . .'

He turned back to her. 'I've said it,' he said flatly. 'I came here to apologize, and I did.'

He went towards the door, but she got up swiftly from the desk and beat him to it. She pushed her hand flat against the door, holding it shut. 'Wait,' she said. She studied him, her eyes searching his face, curious. 'You are an intriguing man, Chief Inspector,' she said. 'I made enquiries about you after our last encounter. Opinions vary. The people at the top – those aristocratic connections of my former husband – say you are a pain in the backside.'

Stark allowed himself a small smile. 'Yes,' he said, 'that is the impression I've been given as well.'

'But others – those on the street – grudgingly describe you as honest. I even hear you were a hero during the war.'

'There was nothing heroic about the war,' Stark said tightly, almost angrily.

There was a pause during which she continued to study him as if he was a puzzle.

'Would you like to have dinner with me?' she asked.

Stark stared at her, stunned. 'Dinner?'

She nodded. 'Two people, eating at a table together.'

'Why?' he asked.

'As I said, you intrigue me. I'd like to know more about you.'

'There isn't much else to know about me. I'm a policeman.'

'You are a widower. You have a son.'

Now it was Stark's turn to study her with curious and suspicious eyes. 'You've been asking questions about me.'

'I like to know everything I can about my adversaries.'

'I am not your adversary.'

'You were when you came here last.'

Stark nodded in grudging acceptance.

'So, will you come to dinner?'

'At the moment the British Communist Party are still suspects in the murder. At least, in the eyes of certain people in power. It may be heavily frowned upon.'

'But you went to meet Michael Collins.'

'I went to talk to Michael Collins, not to have a meal with him.'

'And if he had offered you a sandwich, would you have refused it?'

Stark studied her, his curiosity roused. 'How did you know I met with Michael Collins? It wasn't in the papers.'

'Because some sections of the Establishment are keen to pin this murder on the Irish. Either them or the communists. You came here, so it makes sense you would have gone to see the Irish delegation. And Michael is the most prominent.'

'You call him Michael. Does that mean you and he are acquainted?'

'That depends what you mean, Inspector.'

'Chief Inspector,' Stark corrected her quietly.

She smiled. 'Of course. *Chief* Inspector. If you mean, am I sleeping with him, the answer is no.'

'I did not mean that at all, Lady Amelia.'

'Amelia, please. Yes, he and I have met. He and the Irish delegation have been in London for some weeks now, and some of them have met those of us who are interested in, and sympathetic to, their cause. Now, will you come to dinner?'

He thought it over. Her logic was skewed, but impeccable. What better way to discern the inner workings of Churchill's Bolsheviks than to meet with one of the Party's leading lights. At least, that was what he would tell anyone who questioned the wisdom of a meeting: *I am following Mr Churchill's orders.*

Instead, he said, 'Things are a bit fraught at the moment. With this murder investigation, my evenings can be disrupted.'

'Afraid?'

'Of what?'

'Of me?'

'Why would I be afraid of you?'

'Plenty of men are.'

He gave a slight bow. 'No, I am not. And I would be honoured to have dinner with you.'

'Then shall we say tomorrow evening; unless something drastic intervenes?'

He hesitated, then nodded. 'Tomorrow evening. What time?'

'Eight o'clock? My house is in Cadogan Square. Number twenty-three. My cook is a wonder, although she does have a tendency to use too much cream in her cooking. Good for the taste, but very bad for the health.'

This is all happening too fast, thought Stark, doing his best to retain his composure and not letting her see his head was reeling with the sudden switch from being apprehensive about a fraught encounter with an angry communist to accepting an invitation to dine with her at her home. Her regal home in a very upmarket part of London.

'I look forward to it. But, with this case, if something should happen to intervene . . .'

She pointed at the telephone on the desk. 'We have a telephone here. And I will give you my number at home.' She took a piece of paper and began writing the numbers down for him.

She handed him the piece of paper. 'There,' she said. 'But if I don't hear from you, I will see you tomorrow evening.'

'You will,' he promised.

He got back to the car and found Stan looking anxiously up at the building, obviously waiting for some hard object to come sailing through an upper window and crash down.

'Tough reception up there, sir?' he enquired.

Stark nodded, doing his best to hide a smile. 'Yes, Stan, but I think I dealt with it.'

SIXTEEN

Stark found Danvers waiting for him in his office when he returned to the Yard.

'You and your sister can set your minds at ease, Sergeant,' he said. 'Unless your father has another pistol hidden away somewhere, all his pistols are standard British army issue. Not a nine-millimetre one among them.'

'Thank God!' breathed Danvers.

'And his man, Mr Bridges, asked to be remembered to you. He obviously has great affection for you.'

At this, Danvers looked guilty. 'Yes,' he said. 'I feel bad about Bridges. I should have kept in touch with him, but I didn't want to put him in a spot with Father. He served with my father in the army. He's very faithful, very loyal. He was very good to me when I was growing up.' He gave a rueful smile. 'You may not think it to look at him, but he was fun. Well, more fun than Father. He seemed to know what boys liked.' He gave a short derisory laugh. 'I've never been sure that my father was ever a boy himself. I think he went straight from infancy to adulthood.'

'They were a different generation,' said Stark. *Just like my father*.

'Oh, I'm sorry, sir!' said Danvers suddenly. 'Chief Superintendent Benson called in. He would like to see you as soon as you arrive.'

'Any particular reason?' asked Stark.

Danvers shook his head. 'No, sir. He looked concerned.'

'He always looks concerned,' said Stark. 'Have there been any developments I need to know about before I go and see him?'

'No, sir. I went to see the Chief Rabbi, but it looks as if the Jewish aspect will turn out to be a dead end. With all they've suffered through history, the opinions of Lord Amersham don't seem to matter very much.'

'So, you were given a history lesson by the Chief Rabbi.'

'Yes, sir. The persecution of the Jews.'

'Education, Sergeant, a wonderful thing. I'll go and see what the chief superintendent wants, and then we'll take stock of things so far.'

Chief Superintendent Benson was alone in his office when Stark opened the door to the call of 'Come in!' in reply to his knock. No members of Special Branch this time. The chief superintendent was standing by the window and had obviously been looking out at the vista from Scotland Yard – the streets, the tops of the buildings.

'You wanted to see me, sir,' said Stark, coming in and closing the door.

'Yes. Take a seat.'

Stark settled himself down on the chair opposite the chief superintendent's. As Danvers had reported, he did indeed look concerned, but then he always seemed to have a permanent expression of anxiety. Responsibility hung heavily on Benson.

'An update, Stark. On the Amersham enquiry.'

'Yes, sir,' said Stark. 'I regret that at this moment we have no positive line of enquiry. We followed up the suggestions both of Special Branch into the Irish delegation, and of Mr Churchill into Bolsheviks being behind the murder. So far, neither course has shown any positive signs, and our investigation into the British Communist Party revealed that Special Branch have their own operatives working inside that organization, so I think they can be discounted.'

'But not completely, eh, Stark! There is always the lone-wolf Bolshevik!'

'Yes, sir, and that possibility remains at the forefront of our minds. We also need to look into Lord Amersham's private life. There are reports of affairs, and we need to see if any of them could have resulted in . . . say . . . the attack being the result of jealousy or revenge. And there are the other areas of Lord Amersham's political opinions that have caused some anger among certain areas of the population. Sergeant Danvers has been looking into his remarks about Jews, for example—'

'Yes, yes,' interrupted Benson impatiently. 'What you're telling me is that you're no nearer to solving this than when the murder happened.'

'It's still early days, sir,' said Stark.

'And in the meantime rumours circulate and spread! Confidence in the police to keep the streets of London safe falls! And that gives rise to political unrest!'

He's been talking to someone with more power than him, realized Stark. He's being leant on. Benson's next words told him who by.

'I had a meeting with the Secretary of State for the Colonies last night,' said Benson.

So, Churchill again, thought Stark bitterly.

'He is concerned that, as long as the murderer remains at large, it raises concerns about the Irish talks going on at this moment. Lord Amersham was well known for his antagonism to home rule for Ireland—'

'With respect, sir,' cut in Stark firmly, 'I met with members of the Irish delegation, following my meeting with members of Special Branch here in your office—'

'And it was a mistake!' said Benson. 'Mr Churchill has said so, and I agree with him. We need to bring this case to a speedy conclusion to protect those talks.'

'We are doing our best, sir,' said Stark. 'But we have many lines of enquiry to follow—'

'It doesn't matter about lines of enquiry!' burst out Benson. 'What matters is protecting the reputation of the police force, and stopping rumours circulating that could harm these talks. We need a result that brings this case to an immediate conclusion, and without creating serious political problems! The Irish business, Bolsheviks, Jews, adulterous love affairs among the top echelons of society – all of these will only make things worse and give encouragement to our political enemies!'

'What do you suggest, sir?' asked Stark carefully.

'You said it yourself, Stark, that there were rumours about Lord Amersham's . . . about his private life. Isn't it possible that there may have been a situation where a man from the lower orders, possibly a servant, who wrongly believed that his wife or fiancée or sister had been taken advantage of by Lord Amersham, killed Amersham in revenge. I stress *wrongly* believed it, Stark. Lord Amersham must be depicted as perfectly blameless.' Benson nodded. 'It would be so much neater if that were the case. No politics. No scandals involving important people.'

Stark studied the chief superintendent. So this was the solution that Churchill had come up with. Or had it been Benson himself who'd proposed it?

'That could be a possibility, sir,' said Stark carefully. 'But even if we were to discover such a situation and find a possible culprit who fits the description, the evidence would have to be examined at a trial.'

'Unless there was no trial,' said Benson.

Stark regarded Benson warily. 'Could you clarify that for me, sir?' he asked carefully.

'You know what I mean. If the accused died before coming to trial.'

A chill went through Stark as he heard the words, and his anger must have shown in his face as he said through clenched teeth, 'Are you suggesting, sir—'

It was as if he'd hit Benson with a cattle prod. The chief super-intendent sat bolt upright and stared at Stark, shocked. 'How dare you, Stark!' he shouted. 'How dare you think that I would even suggest something like that! We do not kill suspects in this country!'

'No, sir, but—'

'What I meant was find someone who died shortly after Amersham's murder. A suicide. Someone who could use a gun. An ex-soldier would fit the bill. Even better if he had a sister or someone, who also recently died in tragic circumstances.'

'And blame him for the killing?'

'It works, Stark. We can't have this murder remaining unsolved, but we can't afford to stir up the kind of social unrest you are talking about with your investigation. Bolsheviks, Jews, the Irish, the aristocracy. Things are on enough of an edge here, with the war still fresh, and my God, man, any of those could set off a revolution!'

'With respect, sir, without a proper investigation, that would be making a scapegoat of an innocent man.'

'Who may not be innocent!'

'Yes, sir, but—'

Benson held up a hand to silence Stark and fixed him with a firm stare. 'This suggestion has come from a higher authority than me.'

Stark sighed. 'I accept that Mr Churchill wishes to protect the Irish talks . . .'

'Higher than Mr Churchill. He informs me that this suggestion came during discussions with the Prime Minister.'

So, that duplicitous goat, David Lloyd George, was behind this.

'And, further, it has the approval of the Commissioner.' He leaned back in his chair and continued to fix Stark with his firm glare. 'It's an order, Stark, from the highest authority. Find someone who fits the bill. Let me know the details, and I will inform the Commissioner and the press. And by tomorrow. It is vital that we close this case with the utmost urgency.'

Stark held Benson's gaze. He felt rage building up inside him – the same sort of rage he used to feel in the trenches when a particularly stupid order with deathly implications was passed down the line, coming from some general or field marshal safely tucked away far from the action. But he'd learned that questioning such an order was futile – even deadly, because it could lead to a firing squad for 'cowardice'. In this particular case now, to defy such a direct order would be grounds for dismissal. To what point? Another DCI would simply replace him, one who would carry out the chief superintendent's instructions.

'Yes, sir,' said Stark.

As he got up and left Benson's office, he vowed: *I will not be a party to this. I will not blacken the name of an innocent dead man just to satisfy someone's political whims.* But how could he stop it?

'What did the chief superintendent want?' Danvers enquired as Stark stomped into the office. It was obvious to Danvers from the angry scowl on the chief inspector's face that the meeting had not gone well.

'He wants us to frame someone for the murder,' growled Stark.

Danvers stared at Stark. 'You're not serious!'

'I'm afraid I am. The unholy trinity of the Prime Minister, the Secretary of State for the Colonies and the Police Commissioner have instructed Chief Superintendent Benson to order me to find a suitable culprit. The first requirement is that he is already dead, so there will be no trial with awkward questions being asked. Preferably someone who's killed himself since Lord Amersham was shot. Or, if not, someone we can claim killed himself.'

'And what's the motive?'

'His wife, daughter, sister, whatever, was taken advantage of by Lord Amersham. Or, to be precise, he *believed* – but *wrongly* – that she was taken advantage of by Lord Amersham. His Lordship, of course, must be seen as absolutely blameless.'

Danvers shook his head in disgust. 'It stinks,' he scowled.

'Yes, it does,' nodded Stark.

Danvers looked appealingly at Stark. 'We aren't really going to do this, are we, sir?'

'No,' said Stark. 'But we are going to appear to, to keep Benson and the rest of that despicable crowd happy. The problem is that Benson wants us to give him a name by tomorrow. So we have to slow it down, gain some more time.'

'He won't believe it. He'll know we're dragging our heels.'

'Not if we prove to him how methodical we're being. How we are working efficiently to make sure that this ruse of theirs works, and there won't be any awkward questions. And for that, Sergeant, we need lists.'

'Lists, sir?'

'We'll start with a list of working-class men who've killed themselves recently. Then another list of *ex-servicemen* who've killed themselves recently. Then yet another list of working-class women who recently died in tragic circumstances. I'll tell him that all three lists will have to be cross-referenced to find the connection: a man on list A who is also on list B, with a relative or associate who is on list C.' Stark gave a grim smile. 'If he's not happy with our progress, I can always suggest he give the job of cross-checking the three lists to a government department. That should slow the whole thing down to a virtual stop, but it'll be out of our hands.'

Danvers shook his head. 'What happens if we can't find anyone who fits the bill?'

'Sadly, there will be plenty of them,' said Stark. 'Ex-servicemen who couldn't cope with life at home after the war. Couldn't find a job. Marriage fallen apart. Dumped on the scrapheap. There'll be hundreds of them. That's why compiling these lists could buy us the time we need to find the real killer.'

The telephone on his desk suddenly came to life, the ring of its bell startling them both. Stark picked up the receiver. 'DCI Stark,' he said. He listened, then reached for a pen and a piece of paper. 'Where?' he asked. Then, 'Who?'

He wrote a few words down, hung up the phone and turned to Danvers.

'I think the chief superintendent's plot to frame an innocent dead ex-soldier has just died its own death,' he announced. 'There's been another murder. Tobias Smith, MP. One bullet in the face, one in the heart.' He took his overcoat from the hook and pulled it on. 'Come on, Sergeant. This one could give us the connection we've been waiting for.'

SEVENTEEN

Whereas the murder scene at Lord Amersham's house had been notable for the absence of any onlookers and potential witnesses, the shooting of Tobias Smith had attracted a throng of people. Uniformed officers were on guard, keeping back the crowds. The majority of those who'd gathered seemed to be women, although Stark saw quite a few reporters at the front of the mass, open notebooks in their hands, talking animatedly to the people around them and the policemen holding the crowd back. They were all looking for their exclusives, with editorial deadlines hanging over them if they were to get their stories in the next editions, ahead of their competitors.

'No sign of Mr Churchill,' Danvers muttered as they reached the police line stopping entry to the front of Tobias Smith's house.

'Just what I was thinking,' agreed Stark. Would Churchill arrive and take charge, as he had at Regent's Park? Or would the presence of so many reporters make him decide to stay away? Churchill was well known for his talent for self-publicity, but he liked it to be on *his* terms. 'I'm sure we'll hear from him later.'

They walked up the short path from the pavement to the front of the house. It was a large red-brick house, semi-detached, one of a pair, a bay window at the front, a gate at the side leading to the rear of the house. A large front door painted black was at the top of a short flight of four steps. A sheet lay on the steps, covering a body.

A uniformed sergeant moved away from a group of constables and approached Stark and Danvers, saluting them.

'Sergeant Alder, sir,' he introduced himself.

Stark nodded. 'We met last year, Sergeant, at the leaving do for Superintendent Wainwright.'

Alder looked impressed. 'Thank you, sir,' he said. 'We did indeed, but I wasn't sure you'd remember.'

That's another of the boss's talents, thought Danvers. *He remembers everyone. It's as if he's got a camera in his head.*

Alder gestured at the sheet covering the body. 'I left the body where it fell, sir, to give you a chance to look at it before it was moved.'

'Good thinking, Sergeant. Any witnesses?'

'Yes, sir. A Mrs Wiggis. She cleans for the neighbours, and she was in their downstairs front room when she heard the shot. As you'll see, it's a bay window, the same as Mr Smith's downstairs front, so she was able to get a good view. Though I haven't had a chance to talk to her properly yet to find out exactly how much she saw.' He pointed at the next-door house. 'I left her in there to avoid her being bothered by reporters.'

Again, Stark nodded approvingly. He'd keep a watch for Sergeant Alder when it came time for promotions. Being able to control a situation as efficiently as this, especially in an expensive area like Maida Vale, showed a rare talent.

'What would you like to do first, sir? View the body or talk to Mrs Wiggis?'

'Let's look at the body, Sergeant. Then we can get it moved.' He looked towards the house. 'Anyone else at home? Family?'

Alder shook his head. 'Mr Smith was a bachelor, sir. No family. There's a housekeeper – a Mrs Yardley. She's inside, in a room at the back. She's very upset. I've let a neighbour go in with her for the moment to keep her company. Mrs Yardley has a daughter in Kentish Town. I've sent someone to collect her and bring her here.'

Again, good thinking, thought Stark approvingly.

Sergeant Alder gestured to two of the constables. 'Lift the sheet for the chief inspector,' he ordered.

The constables raised the sheet, peeling it back from the body, revealing the shattered face first, then the blood-soaked shirt and jacket.

'One to the head, one to the heart,' said Alder. He gestured at the open coat. 'Powder from the shot on the front of the coat. He must have been close.'

'Indeed,' said Stark. He looked towards the front door and noticed a chip in the brick by the doorpost. 'The bullet went straight through?' he asked.

Alder nodded. 'The head shot. I've left the bullet where it fell. No one's touched it. I'm guessing the other bullet is still in his body somewhere.'

Stark turned to Danvers. 'Sergeant, get the bullet.'

'Yes, sir,' said Danvers. He pulled a clean handkerchief from his pocket and went up the steps to the front door, picking up the bullet carefully with the handkerchief, wrapping it in it and putting it in his inside pocket.

'He was wearing an overcoat. Was he leaving the house or returning home?'

'Returning home, according to Mrs Yardley. He always came home at this time. Regular as clockwork, she said.'

Which is what got him killed, thought Stark. The assassin watched him, noted the regularity of his movements and simply lay in wait.

Danvers rejoined him. 'It looks like a nine-millimetre, sir,' he said. 'Same as the other.'

'I would have bet my pension on that,' said Stark. 'What about the pathologist?'

'He's on his way, sir,' said Alder.

'Good,' said Stark. He turned to Danvers. 'Sergeant, if you take Mrs Yardley, I'll talk to Mrs Wiggis. We'll compare notes afterwards.'

Danvers nodded, headed towards the front door and rang the bell.

Sergeant Alder gestured at the crowd being held back by the police line. 'What do you want me to do about them? There are reporters there.'

'Leave them where they are,' said Stark. 'The crowd will disperse soon enough once the body's gone. The reporters won't hang about too long after that; they'll want to get their copy in. If they want a statement, tell them to get in touch with Chief Superintendent Benson at Scotland Yard.'

Alder did his best to suppress a small smile. 'Will do, sir,' he said.

'Right,' said Stark. 'What's the name of the family next door, where Mrs Wiggis is?'

'Anstruther,' replied Alder. 'But they're all out. Only Mrs Wiggis is in.'

Good, thought Stark. *One less influential crowd of people to worry about upsetting with my presence.* 'Thank you, Sergeant. If you need me, I'll be talking to Mrs Wiggis.'

He headed for the steps to the Anstruthers' front door, and saw that Danvers had already entered the Smith house. Split the work and speed the investigation seemed the order of the day here. With two politicians shot dead, Benson wouldn't be alone in demanding swifter action.

Mrs Wiggis was obviously waiting for someone to call. He caught a glimpse of her through the bay window, and then she vanished. As he reached out to press the bell, a short round woman in her fifties, wearing an apron, opened the door.

'Mrs Wiggis?'

'You must be the inspector they said they'd sent for.'

'Chief Inspector Stark from Scotland Yard. May I come in?'

'Well, I'm not coming out there and talking in the cold,' she said. 'And the family's all out at the moment, so we won't be inconveniencing them.' She stepped aside and let Stark in. 'Feet,' she ordered crisply, pointing at the mat just inside the front door.

Obediently, Stark wiped his feet.

'I don't want any mud tramped into the front room,' she said, leading Stark towards it. 'We're going in there because I'm guessing you'll want to see where I saw anything from.'

A woman used to being very much in charge, assessed Stark, amused, pitying the Anstruther family.

Stark joined Mrs Wiggis by the bay window and looked out at the scene. He saw that the pathologist, Dr Kemp, had just arrived and was being directed by Sergeant Alder to where the body lay.

'Poor Mr Smith,' said Mrs Wiggis, shaking her head sadly. 'He never caused trouble to no one. Who'd want to shoot him?'

'That's what we're trying to find out,' said Stark. 'Did you actually see the shooting?'

She shook her head. 'No. I *heard* it. It's important to get things right.'

'Absolutely,' agreed Stark.

She pointed to a bookcase near to the door. 'I was doing my dusting over there when I heard this bang. Next second I heard another one.'

'So they were very close together?'

'Very close. I went straight to the window and looked out, thinking it might be kids or someone messing about. I mean, it's a good area, but people come here from all different places – all sorts. There was a man standing pointing the gun at poor Mr Smith. I knew Mr Smith was dead straight away.'

'How could you tell?'

'I used to be a cook at an army camp in the war. I've seen people who'd been shot before. There was blood on Mr Smith's face and on his shirt and coat.' He shook her head. 'You don't survive them easily.'

'No you, don't,' agreed Stark. 'And the man who did the shooting?'

'He was short. Thin. Badly dressed. Rough-looking clothes.'

'What about his face? Beard? No beard? Hair colour?'

She shook her head. 'I couldn't see anything of that. He had a scarf pulled up over the bottom part of his face, and a woolly hat on. You know, like seamen wear. Dark blue wool. It was pulled down right over his ears.'

'Did he see you?'

She shook her head. 'Once I'd realized what had happened, I ducked out of sight. I didn't want him shooting me through the window.'

'Quite right,' said Stark. 'That was quick thinking.'

'But I saw him run off.'

'And the gun?'

'He put it in his jacket pocket as he ran.'

'What did you do next?'

'I ran out to see if Mr Smith might be alive, and if there was anything I could do for him. By then, the door of the house had opened and Mrs Yardley – she's Mr Smith's housekeeper – had come out.' She shook her head sadly. 'She went all to pieces. Started screaming. She's very sensitive.

'Anyway, I came in and phoned the police, then I went to take care of her till the police arrived. Luckily, Mrs Hoskins from the Webbs' house on the other side heard all the ruckus and she came out, so she was able to help me with Mrs Yardley until the police came. Sergeant Alder.' She gestured towards the sergeant outside. 'He's good. He used our phone to phone you. I didn't even have to ask him to wipe his feet when he came in. We need more policemen like him.'

We certainly do, thought Stark.

EIGHTEEN

He spent another ten minutes with Mrs Wiggis, going through her account of the attack, and finding out what he could from her about Mr Smith and his household and habits, although Mrs Wiggis was reluctant to 'gossip' as she termed it.

Stark returned to the outside as Dr Kemp was finishing his examination.

'Chief Inspector,' Kemp greeted him.

'Doctor,' nodded Stark. 'What can you tell me?'

'With certainty, he's dead. Everything else will have to wait until I get him on the table.'

'There's a lot of pressure on this one,' said Stark. 'It looks like the same person who shot Lord Amersham.'

'It may be the same weapon,' Kemp corrected him. 'That doesn't mean it's the same person.'

'I stand rightly corrected,' acknowledged Stark.

'I'll let you know what I find as soon as I can,' Kemp promised him. 'They'll be on my back just as much as yours.'

Danvers joined Stark as Dr Kemp supervised the carrying of the body to the waiting vehicle.

'How did you get on with Mrs Yardley?' Stark asked.

Danvers sighed. 'And there was much wailing and gnashing of teeth,' he groaned.

'I didn't take you for a religious man, Sergeant,' commented Stark.

'I'm not really, sir. It's just that the housekeeper was so over-wrought it brought that quotation to mind. School assembly. Fortunately, she had a neighbour with her, who did her best to calm her down.'

'I think we need to get back to the Yard and compare notes,' said Stark. 'Now that the body's gone, there's not much more we can do here. Our job now is to dig into the lives of Mr Smith and Lord Amersham, and see what the common link is. Because that's what got them both killed.'

Stark went over to Sergeant Alder. 'We'll leave you now, Sergeant. But if you can send your men around to canvass anyone who might have seen anything, such as which way the attacker ran off . . .'

'Already under way, sir,' said Alder.

'Excellent work,' said Stark.

As Stark and Danvers walked back to their waiting car, Stark commented, 'That's a man to watch, Sergeant. He's a good copper. Better than many ranked over him. Bear him in mind if you find yourself with a tricky case.'

'Like this one, sir?'

'I'm hoping we don't get another case like this one,' said Stark ruefully.

Back in their office at Scotland Yard, Stark and Danvers exchanged the information they'd received from their respective interviewees. That from Mrs Yardley was the sparsest, and most of it – between tears – was relating what Mrs Wiggis had told her had happened, and how wonderful a man was Mr Smith – no trouble to anyone, hard-working and kind.

'Well, that's one difference about them: their personalities. Tobias Smith, gentle and kind, and Lord Amersham, a pain in the backside to nearly everyone.'

'I recall you said that Lady Amersham told you her husband was universally liked and respected.'

'I'm sure that Rasputin's mother would have echoed the same sentiments about her offspring.' He studied his notes. 'So. A short, thin man wearing poor-quality, rough clothes. Seaman's woolly hat. Scarf.'

'Who is also a deadly shot,' added Danvers. 'It's starting to sound like one of Churchill's Bolsheviks.'

'Yes, well, we'll bear that in mind,' said Stark. 'We'll start by trying to find the common link.'

'Parliament,' pointed out Danvers. 'They were both in the same political party.'

'So are plenty of others. We need to find out what *especially* links them together. Were they on the same committees together? Did they socialize?' He mulled it over, then said, 'Go to the library, Sergeant. See what you can find about them there. See what's in *Who's Who* and *Debrett's*. Any other books or papers they might have with information about them. Bring them all back here and we'll plough through them and find that thread.'

'Bring *everything* back?' queried Danvers. 'With someone like Lord Amersham, there might be quite a bit.'

'Even if it means more than one journey. It's only one floor down, and you're young and fit.'

After Danvers had left, Stark reread the notes he'd made during his interview with Mrs Wiggis. That was a good point Dr Kemp had made about the same weapon being used not necessarily meaning it was the same person both times. That would suggest collusion, a conspiracy rather than one vengeful individual.

We need to double-check the area around Lord Amersham's house, see if there were any sightings of a small, thin man dressed in rough clothes around that time.

His door opening made him look up from his desk. Chief Superintendent Benson stood in the doorway, looking more miserable than ever. He came in, shut the door, then paced around before saying, 'A bad business, Stark.'

'Yes, sir.'

'I've had the Commissioner on the phone. He wants to know if we should be putting bodyguards on the Prime Minister and other members of the government.'

'We're still not sure of the motives for the killings—'

'It's political! That's obvious. Two members of the government.'

'I believe that Tobias Smith was actually a backbencher, sir.'

'He was still an MP and part of the governing coalition! Someone is killing members of this government!'

'That may be the reason for the killings, although we are looking at other possibilities.'

'What other possibilities? There's going to be a public outcry over this!'

'Sergeant Danvers and I are looking into the lives of both men to try to find common ground—'

'We know what the common ground is, Stark! Politics!'

'But we don't know if there may be other issues. In their private lives, for example.'

Benson shook his head. 'That's the last thing we need, Stark. Scandal! The press are only too eager to rake over muck about the great and the good. We don't want any more of that!'

The office door opened and Sergeant Danvers appeared, carrying an armful of books and paper files. He stopped when he saw the chief superintendent. 'I'm sorry, sir,' he apologized. 'I hadn't realized you were in here or I would have knocked.'

'Always knock,' growled Benson. He made for the door. As he was about to leave, he turned to Stark and said warningly, 'Bear in mind what I said.'

With that, he left.

'What was all that about, if I'm allowed to know?' asked Danvers as he put the books down on his desk.

'The chief superintendent is worried that a scandal involving politicians might be revealed,' said Stark. 'I get the impression he is particularly sensitive about any scandal that might involve the Prime Minister.'

Danvers laughed. 'I would have thought there were enough of those already,' he said. 'Shares. Titles being sold for cash. Not to mention all the different women he's supposed to be having affairs with.'

'Rumour and gossip, Sergeant,' said Stark. 'Nothing proven. And it would not be a good idea to utter such things in this building, nor anywhere else where people might pass on what you said to the chief superintendent or others in authority. Promotion is often not just about having talent; it's about knowing when to open your mouth and when to keep it shut.'

'Yes, sir. Sorry, sir. I was just repeating what it says in the papers.'

'Well, take my advice and don't. Now, what have you got?'

For the next hour the two men pored over the reference books and newspaper cuttings Danvers had brought up from the Yard library, checking and cross-checking every reference for Lord Amersham and Tobias Smith.

Both men had been sixty-eight years old when they died. Both had been educated at Harrow. After school, their paths seemed to have diverged: Amersham – then known as Alastair Redding – had gone to Sandhurst to pursue a military career, and Smith to Oxford to study law. Both had entered politics at about the same time, in their fifties. Both had landed safe Conservative seats. Alastair Redding had been made a peer, Lord Amersham, in 1910. There was no mention of enoblement for Tobias Smith.

'We need more than these pages are telling us, Sergeant,' said Stark thoughtfully. 'We need someone who knew both men, and knew them well.'

'I don't get the impression that they socialized much together,' said Danvers. 'Tobias Smith was a bachelor, and very set in his ways. Quite High Church, reading between the lines. I can't imagine him out carousing with Lord Amersham and bedding the maidservants.'

'No, nor can I,' nodded Stark. 'So we'll start with the one point of commonality. Their political allegiance. The Conservative Party.'

'Sir Austen Chamberlain, sir?' asked Danvers.

Stark shook his head. 'Sir Austen Chamberlain may be the leader of the party, but we need to talk to someone who really knows what goes on.' He tapped the open book on his desk and read, 'Sir William Fanshawe. The Tory Chief Whip.'

NINETEEN

Stark and Danvers walked into the cavernous reception area of the Palace of Westminster which housed the two Houses of Parliament, the House of Commons and the House of Lords. *This is where it all happens, and has happened for hundreds of years*, thought Stark: the government of the people. And not just the people of Britain, but the people of the whole British Empire, a quarter of the population of this planet.

The decoration in this huge main hall was meant to be imposing, and it was. The arched dome of the high ceiling, the mixture of styles, mainly Gothic but with Classical references, invoking the great civilizations of the past, as well as stamping the importance of this House on the present. It was contrived to create an atmosphere of reverence, reinforced by the fact that those who spoke did so in hushed tones, whispers, as people did in the great churches and cathedrals.

Stark approached a sergeant-at-arms, dressed in almost medieval clothes: a black frock coat, tight knee breeches, buckled shoes.

'Detective Chief Inspector Stark and Sergeant Danvers from Scotland Yard. We have an appointment with Sir William Fanshawe.'

The sergeant-at-arms gestured towards a lectern at one side, where another equally ornately dressed man stood. *All they need are powdered wigs and we could be back in the eighteenth century*, reflected Stark. He'd brought Danvers with him precisely because they would be entering this institution with its archaic ways, and, as he'd informed the sergeant, 'You know these sort of people better than I do. You'll be able to understand what's *not* being said.'

The sergeant-at-arms repeated the information Stark had given him, and the keeper of the appointment book at the lectern ran a finger down the open page. 'Yes,' he announced. 'Sir William is expecting them. The Rose Room.'

'If you'll follow me this way, gentlemen,' said the sergeant-at-arms.

Stark and Danvers followed him across the lobby, their heels ringing on the marble of the ornately decorated tiled floor. They went through an arch, then along a gloomy corridor until they stopped at a door, above which was a carved rose, painted red.

The sergeant-at-arms knocked at the door.

'Enter!' came the instruction from within.

The sergeant opened the door. 'Detective Chief Inspector Stark and Detective Sergeant Danvers from Scotland Yard,' he announced.

'Do come in.'

Stark and Danvers entered.

The walls of the room were adorned with portraits, most of royalty from the historic past, judging by the dress and regalia portrayed, and some more recent ones of people Stark didn't recognize.

Sir William Fanshawe came from behind his large, dark oak desk and approached them, his hand held out in greeting. He was a tall, thin man in his sixties, grey-haired, worried-looking, with a large grey moustache, not dissimilar to that preferred by Lord Kitchener.

'A bad business,' he said as he returned to his chair behind his desk, gesturing for them to take the two chairs he'd had placed ready for their visit. As they sat, Fanshawe looked at Danvers and said, 'You're Deverill Danvers' boy, aren't you? Robert?'

'Yes, sir.'

'Thought I recognized you. Saw you with your father a couple of occasions. So . . . you're with the police now?'

'Yes, sir.'

Fanshawe hesitated, then said, 'I heard your father wanted you to follow him into the regiment.'

'Yes, sir, he did. But I decided on this path. I thought I could serve society better this way.'

Fanshawe nodded noncommittally. He looked as if he was going to say more on the subject, but instead said, 'You know we offered your father a seat in the House. He'd have made a damn fine MP.' He sighed. 'He turned us down. Too much of an army man. I get the impression he doesn't have much time for politicians.'

I am beginning to like your father more and more, Sergeant, thought Stark. 'What we're looking for is common ground with Lord Amersham and Mr Smith, Sir William,' he said. 'Things they had in common that might give us a clue as to the motive for why they were both killed.'

'Well, there are some links, obviously, both being members of the Conservative Party.'

'We understand they went to the same school. Harrow.'

'Yes, well, so did quite a few of us. Harrow or Eton. A few went to Winchester. Nothing special there.'

'What about their careers? Lord Amersham was in the army . . .'

'And a damn fine soldier!'

'What about Mr Smith?'

'No. Eyesight problem. Virtually blind in one eye. He was more the academic type. Oxford rather than Sandhurst. He went into law. Damn fine lawyer.'

'Clubs?'

'They were both members of the Carlton. Of course, so are quite a few members of the House.'

'Political committees?'

'They sat on some committees together, but they weren't always necessarily allies. Same party, obviously, with the same Conservative loyalties, but on some issues Tobias took a different stance from Lord Amersham.'

'What sort of issues, sir?'

'Well, I suppose it wasn't the issues as such – after all, they were both very loyal to the party. It was more the way they expressed themselves. Alastair could be a bit . . . intemperate in the way he expressed his views. Tobias, on the other hand, was more circumspect. Came from being a lawyer, I suppose.

'The only place they really found a common platform was on the Irish question. Both were fiercely opposed to home rule. They wanted Ireland to stay as part of the Union. They were both on the Committee for the Preservation of the Union.'

'And would you say that Mr Smith was very vocal in that view? More so than, say, on other topics.'

Fanshawe nodded. 'Yes, I think I would. He was a very clever speaker on the issue, both in the House and outside. Alastair was all fire and brimstone, but Tobias was clever. Made his points like a lawyer.' He sighed. 'Not that it did them much good. They were at odds with the government's stance. But that's one of the problems you get when you have a coalition government. Tories and Liberals.' He shook his head sorrowfully. 'Not natural bedfellows. But what choice did we have with Lloyd George riding the crest of wave after the war.'

In the car on their journey back to the Yard, Danvers proffered an opinion. 'From what Sir William said, it looks like the Irish issue is the common one, sir.'

'Yes, but why would the Irish want to kill them?' asked Stark doubtfully.

'Because both men opposed the idea of the Irish Free State and are opposed to the talks going on right now in London?'

'There are lots of people who oppose the idea of the Irish Free State.'

'But those two were prominent men in positions of power.'

'Yes, I suppose so,' acknowledged Stark.

They got back to the Yard and checked on whether there had been any recent developments, but there had been none. There was a message from Chief Superintendent Benson asking for an update, but nothing from Churchill or Special Branch.

'I think they've decided to keep their communications with the chief superintendent and avoid talking to us,' commented Stark.

'Which is a good thing,' observed Danvers.

'Yes, and no,' said Stark. 'It means they think we're not getting anywhere, and they don't want to be seen to be tainted with our failure. Two dead members of parliament. Serious questions will be asked, and careers will be at risk.'

'Yours and mine, sir?'

'Most definitely mine. If you keep your wits about you, you should be all right. When the blame game starts, blame me. Everything you did was only acting on my orders.'

'I wouldn't do that, sir.'

'No, Sergeant. I don't think you would. But I would strongly advise it.'

'Do you think they might take us off the case, sir?'

'Not at the moment. If no culprit is found, they'll need a scapegoat. I can't see anyone else wanting to take on this case right now; it's a real poisoned chalice.' He looked at the clock. 'Seven o'clock, Sergeant. It's been a very long day. Time for us to depart. I'll give you a lift to Russell Square.'

'There's no need, sir. I can walk.'

'I'm sure you can. But just for once allow me to give you the luxury of letting a police driver take you home. It's on the way to Camden Town.'

The car let Danvers off at Russell Square, and then proceeded onward to Stark's home. As the car carried him, Stark let his mind wander to Lady Amelia and tomorrow night's dinner date. He wondered what he should wear. Not that he had much choice. He had two suits: his day-to-day working one, and a charcoal grey one for 'special occasions' – weddings and funerals.

He still hadn't cleared it with Henry and Sarah. Not that he needed their permission, but he needed to keep their goodwill as far as Stephen was concerned.

The car pulled up.

'Here we are, sir,' said his driver.

'Thanks, Tom.'

'Goodnight, sir.'

'Goodnight, Tom.'

The car drove off and Stark made for his front door. He was reaching into his pocket for his key when he heard a sound behind him. He started to turn around, and as he did so something heavy crashed down on to his head, sending him tumbling to the pavement.

TWENTY

A boot smashed into his ribs, sending pain coursing through his body. He doubled over on the ground, rolling, trying to protect himself, but another kick caught him, this time on the side of the face. He felt the warmth of blood splash out on to his skin. He kicked out, and his foot connected with someone. Through blurred vision, he saw a man stumble. But then he realized someone else was there, another man, and this one was armed with a knife, because he saw the light from the street lamp glint on the blade.

Suddenly, light flooded the scene, and he heard his father's angry shout of 'What's going on?'

A last kick was aimed at him, hitting him in the shoulder, and then the two men ran off into the darkness.

Stark struggled to sit up. His head ached and he felt sick.

Henry crouched beside him. 'Son! What was that about?'

'I don't know,' Stark managed to mutter. His voice felt strange and thick to him.

'Can you stand?'

Stark pushed himself up from the ground and nearly fell, but his father caught him.

'Let's get you in and seen to.'

'I'm all right,' said Stark, pushing himself free. He stumbled towards the light of the passageway, and crumpled against the doorpost.

'You don't look it,' said his father.

'I'll be OK,' insisted Stark.

'Dad!' Stephen had appeared and was looking at Stark in shock and horror.

Sarah stood behind Stephen, a look of bewilderment on her face. Then she swung into action. 'Get him into the kitchen,' she ordered. 'I'll get a kettle on.'

Stark allowed his father to support him down the narrow passage to the kitchen.

'Who did it?' asked Stephen, his voice anxious.

'Two men,' said Henry. 'Help me get his coat off.'

'I'll be all right,' said Stark, but he let Henry and Stephen take his overcoat and jacket off, although his moan of pain as his jacket was removed prompted his mother to order, 'Get his shirt and vest off as well. He might have cracked something.'

Slowly, painfully, they peeled Stark's shirt and vest off him, and then settled him on a chair by the table.

Sarah had put a bowl on the table and was pouring hot water into it. 'Get the iodine from the cupboard, Stephen,' she said.

She began to wipe the blood from Stark's face with a warm cloth, and then the dirt that had been thrown on to his face when he'd fallen to the pavement.

'It's not too bad,' she declared. 'You're going to have a black eye and a big bruise on the side of your face, but the cut isn't as bad as it looks. It's just over your eyebrow. I'll have to sew it.'

'Maybe we should get a doctor,' suggested Stark.

'Doctors?' echoed his father scornfully. 'With the money they charge! Your mum can do just as good a job at stitching as any old sawbones!'

'Stephen, go and get my sewing box,' said Sarah.

Stark sat and let his mother attend to him. She selected a needle and put it in boiling water to sterilize it, then selected a reel of thick black cotton.

'Does it have to be black?' complained Stark.

'It's all I've got,' his mother retorted.

'Be thankful your mum's a sewer,' put in his father.

Stark gritted his teeth while Sarah pushed the threaded needle into the flesh above his eyebrow and pulled the wound closed, then tied it off. She'd already dabbed the open cut with iodine, which had brought tears of pain to Stark's eyes.

'Now let's look at your ribs,' she said.

'I need to go to the police station and report it,' said Stark.

'You're in no fit state to go anywhere,' said his father.

'They need to start investigating who might have done it before the trail goes cold,' insisted Stark.

'In that case I'll go and get a copper,' said his father.

'If we had a phone, we could call the station,' said Stark.

'I've told you before, we don't need one of them things in this house,' said his father, putting on his coat. 'It'd only unsettle your mother.'

At this moment, Sarah Stark looked the least unsettled of them all as she examined her son's ribs, prodding gently with her fingers and registering when he winced with pain.

'I don't think there's anything big broken,' she said. 'One of 'em may be cracked, but I think it's mostly bruising. I'll wrap a bandage round and we'll see how it goes.'

First thing tomorrow I'm going to see the doctor at the Yard, vowed Stark.

His mother gently applied a foul-smelling liniment to his side, then asked Stephen to help her wrap the long bandage around his father's ribs, more to give Stephen something active to do and stop him from being too worried than because she really needed his help.

By the time she was finished and Stark had his vest and shirt on once again, Henry had returned. 'I had to go all the way to the station,' he said.

Stark saw that he had an old acquaintance of his, Charlie Watts, with him. He and Charlie had been young constables together years before. Now he was a DCI and Charlie was a station sergeant.

Watts took off his helmet as he came into the kitchen, a concerned expression on his face. 'I hear you were attacked, sir,' he began.

'Forget the "sir" business, Charlie,' he grunted. 'For one thing, I'm off duty, and for another, we've known one another too long for that.'

In as much detail as he could remember, Stark filled Watts in about the attack on him. 'Trouble was, I didn't see much of them. All I can say for sure is there were two of them, and one of them had a knife.' He looked at his father. 'I don't know if you got a better view of them, Dad?'

Henry shook his head. 'It was all too quick. I heard this

crashing about outside and went to see what was going on, and there was this bloke kicking Paul. There was another one there with him, but they ran off when I opened the door.'

'Any description at all, Mr Stark?' asked Watts, his pencil poised over his open notebook.

'No. It was dark.' Henry thought it over. 'One was taller than the other. About my height. Big bloke. Broad shoulders. He was the one doing the kicking. The other one was small and thin-looking.'

'Faces?'

Henry shook his head. 'It looked as if they had scarves or something pulled up over their faces. And I'm pretty sure they both had caps on. You know – flat caps.'

'Did you see which way they went when they ran off?'

'Towards Camden Street,' replied Henry. 'I think they turned down it, towards Crowndale Road.'

Watts nodded, put his pencil into his pocket and closed his notebook. 'Thank you, Mr Stark. That gives us something to go on.' He put his helmet back on. 'I'll get some constables on it, asking questions.' He looked enquiringly at Stark. 'Any reason you can think of why they might have attacked you?'

Stark shook his head. 'No idea,' he said. But inside he thought: *Plenty. Maybe I'm getting too close to something over these murders.*

After Watts had taken his leave, his father said, 'That's what you should have done, Paul. Stayed at the local station, like Charlie Watts there. Good pay. Regular hours. Not far from home. Maybe then you wouldn't have been done over like you were.'

'Being a local copper is just as dangerous, even more so,' countered Stark. 'Charlie's had his share of injuries on Friday nights, dealing with the drunks.' *But not anyone who was intent on killing him*, he thought, remembering the light glinting on the knife blade.

TWENTY-ONE

When Stark arrived at Scotland Yard next morning, his first port of call was the mortuary in the basement.

Dr Kemp was sitting at a desk, going through some papers, and he looked up with a weary sigh as Stark walked in. 'If you've come for the report on Tobias Smith, I sent it up to your office first thing,' he began, then he stopped when he took in the damage to Stark's face. 'My God, what happened to you?'

'I was attacked.'

'That is a serious bruise around your eye. Were you badly hurt?' Kemp got up and came over to peer closely at Stark's face. 'Concussion?'

'That's what I'd like you to find out. Would you give me a once-over?'

Kemp shook his head. 'I don't do living bodies any more, Chief Inspector. Now, if you were dead, I'd be prepared to take a look at you.'

'Very funny.'

'Why didn't you go to your doctor? Or go to the hospital?'

'I don't have time. I've got a murderer to find.'

'I can't treat you.'

'I don't want you to treat me; I just want you to check me over. Tell me if anything's broken.' As Kemp frowned, puzzled, Stark added, 'I got kicked in the ribs.'

'OK,' nodded Kemp. 'Take off your top clothes.'

As Stark removed his overcoat, jacket, shirt and vest, Kemp said, 'Who bandaged you up?'

'My mother.'

Kemp undid the pin holding the bandage in place, and unwrapped it from Stark's torso, revealing a livid yellow and purple bruise one side. 'He must have been wearing heavy boots,' he commented. 'That is a nasty bruise.'

Stark sat down on a chair, and Kemp probed and poked around the bruise, gently at first, working his way in to the bruise itself, making Stark wince.

'I don't think there's anything broken,' the doctor said thought-fully. 'Nothing that could puncture a lung or anything. But I think one of your ribs might be cracked. It'll heal, but it'll take time. And it's going to hurt when you laugh.'

'I rarely laugh,' said Stark.

'Yes, that's true,' agreed Kemp. The doctor leaned forward and examined the cut above Stark's eye. 'Whoever stitched that did a professional job. It's very neat, and there's no sign of infection.' Dr Kemp nodded approvingly. 'I can still smell traces of iodine.'

'My mother did it,' said Stark. 'She also confirmed your diagnosis about my ribs: one might be cracked, but not seriously.'

Dr Kemp regarded Stark, curious. 'Did she have medical training? Was she a nurse?'

'No,' said Stark. 'She had seven brothers, and two of them were prizefighters. Her father taught her how to sew them up.'

'Tell her if she wants a job, I can find one for her here,' said Kemp. 'My current assistant is better suited to working in a butcher's.'

'You wouldn't object to having a woman working for you?' asked Stark.

'Not at all,' said Kemp. 'During the war women did most of the work, however heavy it was. Munitions. Driving lorries. I've never understood why women are capable of doing all types of labour when war has taken most of the men away, but once the men return they are considered unfit and too genteel.'

'I agree with you,' said Stark, putting on his clothes. 'Unfortunately, most don't. Including my father. And what he says goes. So the likelihood of my mother coming to work here is remote, to say the least.'

Stark headed up the stairs to his office, leaving the smell of decaying flesh and disinfectant behind in the basement. He found Danvers already there.

The sergeant leapt up from behind his desk as Stark came in. 'They said you were attacked, sir!' he exclaimed, his tone urgent, worried.

'Who said?' asked Stark.

Danvers hesitated, then said, 'I can't remember, sir.'

I know, thought Stark. *My driver this morning, who would have told one of his colleagues, who would have told the duty*

desk sergeant, who would have passed it on. The bush telegraph.
'Yes,' he said, taking off his overcoat and hanging it up. 'I've just been for a check-up with our good pathologist. He says he's sent up the report on Tobias Smith.'

'Yes, sir,' nodded Danvers, pointing to an open file on his desk. 'I was just reading it. It confirms what we thought. One bullet to the head, which went straight through his skull; the other stayed in the heart. Nine-millimetre ammunition, from the same gun as killed Lord Amersham.' He looked questioningly at Stark. 'Do you think the attack on you is connected?'

'I don't know, Sergeant. I can't think of anyone I've offended enough to want to kill me. Mind you, I've put a few people away in my career, and had a few hanged for their crimes, so some kind of revenge could always be a possibility.'

'Did you see who attacked you?'

'There were two of them. A big man, tall, muscular. The other was short and thin.'

'A short, thin man. Same description of the man who shot Tobias Smith.'

'I'm afraid there are an awful lot of short, thin working-class men in London,' said Stark. 'Malnutrition and poor living conditions don't help. Also, the man who attacked me had a knife, not a gun. And he wore a flat cap, not a seaman's woolly hat.'

'So you don't think it's connected?'

'I don't know,' admitted Stark. 'They must have been lying in wait for me, so it was deliberate and personally aimed at me, not some random mugging. And, apart from this case, I haven't exactly been in the public eye.' *And I wouldn't have been in the public eye over this case if Churchill hadn't decided to further his own ends by using my name in the papers*, he thought bitterly.

The ringing of the phone on his desk interrupted them.

'Chief Inspector Stark,' he said.

'Sergeant Watts from Camden Town here, sir,' said the voice. So, formal again. Both on duty, and there would be people at Camden Town nick listening.

'Good morning, Sergeant,' said Stark. 'And I'd like to thank you again for your support last night.'

'Always ready to help if I can, sir,' said Watts. 'I'm phoning because we might have a lead on the men who attacked you.'

'Oh?'

'Yes, sir. One of my men spoke to a witness who said two men ran past him last night at about the time you were attacked. He said they came rushing round the corner into Crowndale Road from Camden Street, and nearly knocked him over. The description tallies with what your dad – sorry, sir – Mr Stark reported. Flat caps. Scarves pulled up over the bottom part of their faces. One a big bloke, the other short and thin.'

'Well done, Sergeant. Can he add anything else?'

'Yes, sir. That's why I'm calling. He said they were Irish.'

'Irish?' Stark was immediately alert. 'Is he sure?'

'Yes, sir. He says he heard one of the men shout to the other, "We'll get the bastard next time", and the other said, "We will indeed!" and they both had Irish accents. Then they ran off.'

'Which way?'

'Towards St Pancras Station.'

'Do you have the name of this witness?'

'Yes. He's called Pete Stamp. He lives at the back of Mornington Crescent.'

'Known to the local police?'

'No, sir. Nothing on record, anyway.'

Stark thought it over. A real lead or a red herring? 'I'd like to talk to him myself, if that's all right with you, Sergeant,' he said. 'Is there any chance of getting hold of him today?'

'I don't see why not,' said Watts. 'We've got his address. I'll round him up and phone you to let you know when he's coming in.'

'Thanks, Sergeant,' said Stark. 'I appreciate that.'

He hung up and looked at Danvers, who was waiting expectantly. 'That was Camden Town nick,' he said. 'They turned up a witness who reckons he saw the men who attacked me. According to him, both men had Irish accents.' He gave a wry smile. 'Mind, that's not unusual in Camden Town. About half the population there is Irish, or second generation.'

The phone rang again.

'We are in demand today,' commented Stark drily as he picked up the receiver. 'Chief Inspector Stark.'

'Main reception, sir. We have a Mr Collins who'd like to see you.'

'A Mr Collins?' repeated Stark, puzzled.

'A Mr Michael Collins.' There was a pause, then the duty Sergeant added, 'He's an Irish gentleman, sir.'

Stark smiled. 'Sergeant Danvers will be down right away to collect him and bring him up,' he said. He hung up and looked at the waiting and curious Danvers.

'The Irish issue intercedes even more today. Not just a report about blaming a pair of Irishmen as my attackers, but now we have none other than Michael Collins himself in reception to see me.'

'*The* Michael Collins, sir?'

'In person. You are about to meet a legend, Sergeant. I would appreciate it if you would go and bring him up here. And then engage yourself in some activity that will give him and me privacy for our discussion.'

'This isn't going to please Mr Churchill, sir,' Danvers warned.

'Very true, but if I am asked about this by Mr Churchill, I will point out that Mr Collins came here to see me, not the other way round, and it could have been detrimental to the talks if I had refused to see him. Not to mention very discourteous.'

TWENTY-TWO

S tark was at his desk, pretending to study some reports, when he heard the footsteps stop outside his door. He wanted to appear busy when Collins arrived, but the truth was he felt both bewildered and intrigued. Why had the big Irishman decided to come here – to Scotland Yard of all places – to see him?

The door opened and Danvers appeared. 'Mr Michael Collins, sir,' he announced.

With that, Danvers stepped back and let Michael Collins enter. If he felt uneasy about being here, the big man didn't show it. He smiled as he took Stark's outstretched hand.

'Welcome to my office, Mr Collins,' Stark said. He turned to Danvers. 'Thank you, Sergeant.'

'Yes, sir,' said Danvers, and pulled the door shut.

Collins studied Stark's face, then gave a grin. 'You look like someone's given you a bit of a pasting, Inspector.' He settled on a chair and looked round the room, then gave a light laugh. 'Jaysus, who'd have thought the day would come when Micheál Ó Coileáin would walk voluntarily into this place! It wasn't so long ago there was a price on my head! Good money would have been paid to get me in here.'

Stark sat down and nodded, waiting.

'Anyway, I thought I'd call on you here rather than invite you to Cadogan Gardens, or anywhere else. This way we can be assured Ned doesn't burst in on us.' The big Irishman smiled. 'Ned's a fierce fine patriot, but he's very strong in his dislikes, and it can sometimes get in the way of clear thinking.'

'I'm guessing your visit isn't a social occasion,' said Stark.

'If it was, we'd have a bottle on the table,' said Collins. He leaned forward and looked at Stark firmly. 'The word is that you were given a going over by some compatriots of ours.'

Stark studied Collins suspiciously. 'Word travels very fast,' he said. 'I've only just been told they were Irish a few moments ago.'

'We like to keep our ears to the ground,' said Collins. 'And, as you know, there are an awful lot of folk from the old country here in London. Yourself included, granting your granny's permission.'

'I'm sure she'd give it,' said Stark.

'Did she talk much of Banteer?' asked Collins.

Stark shook his head. 'I think her memories of that time were . . . difficult.'

Collins laughed, only this time his laugh was harsher, angrier. 'Difficult!' he echoed. 'The bodies of the starving lying by the roadside. Too many to bury.'

'Thousands,' nodded Stark.

'Die or leave,' said Collins. 'The coffin ships to America. As a result there are more Irish in Boston than in Ireland itself.'

'Not all the fault of the British,' said Stark carefully. 'There were Irish landlords who could have done more.'

'Irish!' spat Collins angrily. 'West Britons!' Then he seemed to take control of his rage, because suddenly his angry features changed as if a switch had been thrown, and he gave Stark a rueful smile. 'But I didn't come here to talk politics. I have had enough of doing that every day since I've been here. I'm here to tell you no one connected with the Irish delegation attacked you. I don't want what happened to you clouding the issue of the talks.'

'The witness said one of them had an Irish accent.'

'There are lots of Irish in London.' Bitterly, he added, 'And not all of them like what we're doing, or why we're here.'

'Ulster Protestants.'

'Not just them.' The big man hesitated, then looked about him as if to check who might be listening, before he leaned forward and said quietly, 'There are a few of our own kind who think we're traitors to Ireland by being here.'

'The Oath of Allegiance. Twenty-six counties instead of thirty-two.'

Collins looked at Stark with a new respect in his eyes. 'You've been doing your homework, Mr Stark.'

Thanks to the reports about the talks, and those taking part, that Special Branch had given me to read, thought Stark. 'That's my job,' he said.

'Checking up on us?'

'Checking up on everyone who may have had reasons for not liking Lord Amersham or Tobias Smith.'

'I didn't like either of them, but there was no reason for us to kill them.' With that, Collins stood up. 'I'd better be off. I'm expected at the talks.'

'I'll walk you down to reception,' said Stark.

'Making sure I leave the building?' asked Collins mischievously.

'Well, it wouldn't do if you decided to blow Scotland Yard up while you're here. That would get me in a whole lot of trouble.'

Collins laughed, and walked alongside Stark along the corridor and down the stairs. All the time, Stark was aware of faces of the people in the corridors and on the stairs turned towards them, watching. *They've come out of their offices to catch a sight of the famous Michael Collins*, thought Stark.

Stark escorted Collins across the main reception area to the double doors to the street. 'Do you want me arrange a taxi?' he asked.

Collins shook his head. 'Your government's laid on a car for me. It's waiting outside.'

'In that case, thank you again for calling,' said Stark. He held out his hand to Collins, who shook it.

'It's been a pleasure meeting you, Chief Inspector.'

'And you, Mr Collins.'

As Collins was about to walk out through the door, Stark added, 'The last time we met, at your hotel, I felt you knew I was coming. And why.'

Collins hesitated, his hand on the door handle. 'That's an interesting observation,' he said.

'So either British Special Branch has someone in your group, or you have someone in here,' said Stark.

Collins grinned, a genuine, friendly, relaxed grin. 'Or maybe it's a bit of both,' he said. 'Remember what they say: keep your friends close, but your enemies closer, providing you can tell the difference. I'd say, trust no one.'

'Not even you?'

Collins gave his relaxed shrug again. 'That's up to you, Inspector.'

Collins left, and Stark headed back upstairs to his office.

Danvers was waiting for him, agog with expectation. 'What did he want?' he asked.

'To let me know that my attacker wasn't anything to do with the Irish delegation,' replied Stark.

'Was that all?' said Danvers, disappointed. 'That's a bit odd, isn't it, coming here just to say that?'

'Yes, it is.' He frowned. 'Why would Collins make a special trip here, of all places, just to tell me it wasn't one of their associates who attacked me?'

'Maybe because it was?'

Stark sighed and shook his head. 'I don't know, Sergeant. But it does look as if every new step seems to point us back to the Irish situation. The talks. The trouble is, all the information we've got about them has come from parties with their own special interest to protect. Special Branch. Michael Collins. Sir William Fanshawe represents the official government line. Churchill refuses to admit this has anything to do with the Irish talks at all. We need someone with a neutral view. Someone who'd give us the candid truth.'

'Not many of those around when it comes to Ireland, sir,' said Danvers. Then a new thought obviously struck him, because he added, 'Although there might be someone.'

'Oh?'

'My Uncle Edwin. Sir Edwin Drake.'

'*Sir*?'

Danvers nodded. 'He's my mother's brother. He used to be at the Colonial Office. He was knighted for his ambassadorial services.'

'Why didn't you mention this before?' demanded Stark.

'Well, we weren't sure if the murders were definitely connected to the Irish business,' said Danvers defensively.

'For God's sake, Sergeant!' exploded Stark. 'It was one of the key points!'

'Yes, sir, I'm sorry, sir. I suppose the truth is I hadn't really given much thought to Uncle Edwin lately.'

The phone ringing stopped Stark from chastising his sergeant any more. 'DCI Stark,' he said.

It was Charlie Watts from Camden Town. 'That witness we were talking about, sir. Pete Stamp. He's coming in.'

'When?'

'My man says in half an hour.'

'Any difficulty getting him to come in?'

'No, sir. He seems very keen to talk.'

'Right, I'll be along.'

Stark hung up. A keen witness. He was always suspicious of that. Too often it meant they had a secret agenda of their own, someone they wanted to get into trouble. Still, it was a lead.

'That was Camden Town. They've got the witness who saw the men who attacked me. I'm going along there now.'

'Do you want me to come with you?'

'Right now I want you to tell me about your Uncle Edwin. You said he *used* to be at the Colonial Office.'

'Yes, sir. He . . . er . . . retired. That was the official line. Although within the family it's said that he resigned. I believe he had differences with Winston Churchill. We didn't see a lot of him; he and my father never really got along. My father preferred the company of men of action. He wasn't fond of politicians. But he knew about Ireland. He lived there for a while.'

'Married?'

'Widowed. No children.'

'What does he do now?'

'He stays at home and reads and paints. He's seventy-something. Nice old chap.'

'In that case, I'd like you to get in touch with him and see if you can arrange for us to visit him to pick his brains. And soon. Everyone's going to be on our backs now, from the Prime Minister down.'

TWENTY-THREE

C harlie Watts was waiting at the reception desk when Stark arrived at Camden Town police station.

'He's in interview room two,' said Watts.

'Has he been here long?'

'No, he walked in about five minutes ago.'

'How does he seem?'

'Chatty. Cheerful.'

'Odd for someone coming in to a police station,' mused Stark.

'Not if they're innocent,' pointed out Watts.

'I don't know,' said Stark. 'I've noticed that even some innocent people get a bit edgy when they come into a police station.'

'You've been in the job too long,' grinned Watts. 'Makes you suspicious of everyone.'

Stark followed him out of the reception area and along a corridor to a room with a large figure two on it. Watts opened the door, then stood aside for Stark to enter. A man was sitting at the table in the room. Apart from the table and two chairs, the room was devoid of furniture of any sort.

The man stood up as Stark walked into the room, a confident, relaxed smile on his face.

Why is he so cocky? wondered Stark. One thing was for sure, though: he wasn't either of the two men who'd attacked him the night before. This man was of average height, average build. He had the appearance of almost every other man in the area: slightly unshaven, grey woollen jacket and trousers, not quite matching enough to be a suit, collarless shirt.

'This is Detective Chief Inspector Stark,' Watts told the man.

The man nodded in greeting.

'I'll leave you to it,' said Watts, and he left.

Stark sat down in the chair opposite the man, taking out his notebook and pencil, which he put down on the table before him. 'Thanks for coming in,' he said.

'Just doing my public duty,' said the man, putting on a serious expression.

'Indeed, and it is much appreciated,' said Stark. He flicked open his notebook, checked something in it, then asked, 'Mr Stamp? That right?'

'That's me.'

'The sergeant tells me you saw the two men who may have taken part in an assault last night.'

Stamp nodded vigorously. 'The two Irishmen!'

'You're sure they were Irish?'

'Oh yes! I lived next door to an Irish family for years. I'd know that accent anywhere!'

'According to the report, they bumped into you in Crowndale Road, having just come out of Camden Street.'

Again, Stamp nodded energetically. 'That's right!' He leaned forward and asked enthusiastically, 'Is there a reward? If they get caught?'

'There might be,' said Stark carefully. 'That usually depends on the outcome.'

'Oh,' said Stamp, obviously disappointed. 'You mean if they don't get caught, there isn't.'

'Sometimes there is,' said Stark. 'It depends on the circumstances. Can you describe them?'

'Well, it's like I said to the copper: one was big and the other was little. They both had flat caps on, and both had scarves pulled up, so I couldn't see their faces.'

'And then they rushed off in the direction of St Pancras station?'

Again, the energetic nod. 'That's right.'

'And they didn't say anything to you?'

Stamp frowned, puzzled by the question. 'I don't get you. Why would they talk to me?'

'Because they'd just bumped into you. Did they apologize? Say sorry?'

Stamp's face brightened. 'Oh yes! I see what you mean!' Again, he nodded. 'Yes, that's right. He did, now you come to mention it. "Sorry," he said.'

'The big one or the little one?'

'I think it was the big one,' Stamp replied after some thought.

Stark looked down at his notebook. 'And did one of them say "We'll get the bastard next time", and did the other one say "We will indeed!" before or after he'd said sorry to you?'

Stamp looked bewildered. 'How do I know?' he demanded.

'I'm just trying to get the picture of what happened,' explained Stark gently.

'Oh, I see,' said Stamp, but the uncertainty in his voice and his face showed that he didn't. Or that he did and he was wary.

Stamp frowned thoughtfully for a short while, then announced, 'They said it after he'd said sorry to me. The big one, that is.'

'And who said what after that? Which one said: "We'll get the bastard next time"?'

'The little one.'

Stark nodded, then smiled appreciatively and rose to his feet, holding out his hand to Stamp. 'Thank you, Mr Stamp,' he said. 'You've given us invaluable information; and if there is a reward, I shall see that you get it.'

'Thank you,' beamed Stamp, getting to his feet and shaking Stark's hand. 'Hope you catch 'em!'

Stark waited until Stamp had left the station, then he went to the desk where Sergeant Watts stood on duty.

'Well?' asked Watts. 'What do you think?'

'Can you do me a favour?' asked Stark. 'Can you put a watch on him? Nothing obvious.'

'Sure,' nodded Watts. 'What do you want to know?'

'Who he sees. People he goes for a drink with.'

'You think he's lying?'

'I think he made some of it up. I'd be curious to find out a bit more about him, especially his regular companions.'

'Leave it to me,' said Watts. 'When I get anything, I'll phone you at the Yard. Or, if it's after hours, I'll pop round to Plender Street.'

'Thanks, Charlie.'

Watts grinned. 'Your dad still won't let you have a phone in at home?'

Stark sighed wearily. 'He's still living in the nineteenth century. Thinks modern things like the telephone are some instrument of the devil.'

'My dad was the same,' said Watts sympathetically. 'But it

must be hard for them at that age – all these modern things they don't understand.'

Sergeant Danvers was going through witness statements when Stark returned.

'Did you see him?' Danvers asked.

Stark nodded.

'And? Was he able to describe anybody?'

'In detail. Except for their faces.'

Danvers frowned. 'You don't seem convinced,' he said.

'I'm not,' said Stark. 'Either he's lying or he's exaggerating. The idea that two men, on the run, bump into him and say sorry, and then proceed to stand there and say things like "We'll get the bastard next time" and "We will indeed!" before rushing off is like something out of a bad stage play. I've asked Sergeant Watts to keep a bit of eye on him. See who he meets up with, in case there's something else going on with him.'

'But why would he lie?'

'That's what I want to find out. He might be protecting someone.'

'If that's the case, surely it would have been easier for him if he hadn't come forward to say anything at all.'

'Unless he wants us to follow a false trail,' said Stark. 'The Irish accents, for one thing. Which brings us back to your Uncle Edwin.'

'I telephoned him and he says he'll be delighted to help,' said Danvers. 'He's invited us to call on him this evening, if that's all right. We're invited to dinner.'

Dinner! thought Stark. *Damn!* 'Is that necessary?' he asked.

'It would make him happy,' said Danvers. 'I don't think he gets get much company. And I am family. I think he'll be pleased, and he'll talk more easily.'

'Fine,' nodded Stark. *Bang goes my dinner with Lady Amelia Fairfax. At least now I don't have to tell my parents about it.*

This is ridiculous, he scolded himself. *You are a grown man. You have a son. You fought in the war. You won medals for bravery, yet you're acting like a small boy who's afraid of admitting to something he knows his parents won't like. Behave like a grown man, for God's sake!*

Why was he so reluctant to tell them he was going to dinner?

Because he knew what his father thought of Lady Amelia. Every time she appeared in the papers, going on about social injustice or anything at all, his father's usual disgusted comment about her was 'That Jezebel's in the papers again!'

'What time?' asked Stark.

'Eight o'clock.'

'Where does he live?'

'Knightsbridge.'

'In that case, we'll meet here at half past seven and get a car to take us. We can always get a taxi back.' He looked at the clock, which showed a quarter to five. 'Let's call it a day, Sergeant. After all, we're working tonight on unpaid overtime.'

'The meal will make up for it,' said Danvers. 'Uncle Edwin's housekeeper is a very good cook.'

'I hope so,' said Stark.

The promise of two good meals tonight, he thought. Lady Amelia's and Uncle Edwin's. Lady Amelia would have to wait.

TWENTY-FOUR

Stark waited until Danvers had left the office, then phoned the offices of the Communist Party. He was told that Lady Amelia had left for the day.

He telephoned her house at Cadogan Square. She was in.

'I've been expecting you to call,' she said. 'It's off for tonight, isn't it? I heard about Tobias Smith.'

'I'm afraid so,' said Stark. 'A line of enquiry has come up that I have to follow this evening.'

'What line of enquiry?'

'I can't tell you.'

'He wasn't as bad as some of them,' she said. 'Tobias Smith. He was even talking about supporting votes for women.'

So that's what Sir William Fanshawe had been referring to when he'd said that Smith and Amersham held different views on some things.

'Although I hope this isn't just an excuse,' she said.

'No, I will definitely come and have dinner with you.'

'When?'

'Tomorrow evening.' The words were out of his mouth before he'd even thought about it properly. 'Tomorrow evening at eight.'

'Unless someone else gets shot,' she said.

'At this stage, I'd rather not joke about that,' said Stark.

'No,' she said. 'Tomorrow evening, then.'

He went downstairs to the car pool and found his allocated driver for the journey home. It was someone new, someone he didn't know, so he had to give him directions. His parents expressed surprise at seeing him home so early.

'I haven't got supper ready yet,' his mother said. 'I didn't expect you at this time.'

'Don't worry,' said Stark. 'I won't be staying.'

'Huh!' snorted Henry.

Stark looked down at Stephen and gave him a smile. 'Stephen, would you pop up to your room for a moment? I need to talk to your grandparents about something.'

'What?' asked Stephen, and Stark saw his son's face tighten, fear in his eyes. *He's suffered so much in his short life*, thought Stark. *He's lost so much, he's worried he'll lose more.* 'It's nothing serious,' Stark assured him. 'Nothing about us. It's . . . adult talk. Work talk. It won't take long, I promise.'

With a feeling of relief, he saw the tightness in Stephen's face relax. *I have to play this business about Lady Amelia carefully for Stephen's sake. I don't want him getting the wrong impression. It's only a dinner – nothing else, nothing more – and I want to make sure he knows that.*

'I'll be up and see you in a minute, son,' he said.

'All right, Dad,' said Stephen. He headed up the stairs to this bedroom.

As soon as Stephen reached the landing, Henry turned on his son accusingly. 'What's going on?' he demanded suspiciously. 'What can't you say in front of Stephen?'

'It's about the case,' said Stark. 'I don't want Stephen to get worried when I talk about it, especially after what happened last night.'

'What?' asked Sarah apprehensively.

'I've got to go out with Sergeant Danvers this evening. That's why I'm back early now. There's a lead we're following and I might be back late. Will you look after Stephen?'

'We always look after Stephen,' snapped his father irritably.

'I know, but I'm asking because I don't want you to think I take you for granted,' said Stark.

'Of course it'll be all right,' said his mother quickly, before Henry could continue the argument. 'What about your dinner?'

'That's all right, the sergeant and I will look after ourselves.'

'He doesn't look like he eats much,' said his mother. 'He's very thin.'

'That's because he's young,' said Stark. 'He burns it off. And he walks everywhere.'

'You're not going to get yourself beaten up again?' asked his father.

'I hope not,' said Stark with a smile. 'Don't worry, Sergeant Danvers will be with me.'

'Are you going anywhere dangerous?' asked his mother, still doubtful.

'Knightsbridge,' replied Stark.

Henry sniffed. 'Very upmarket. Very posh.'

Now's the time, thought Stark. 'Actually, talking of upmarket and posh . . .' he began tentatively, and then stopped.

'Yes?' prompted his mother.

'Would you look after Stephen again tomorrow night for me?'

'Of course,' said his mother.

'What is it? Another investigation?'

'Not exactly,' said Stark. 'I've been invited to dinner.'

'Dinner?' echoed Henry, suspiciously.

Sarah looked at him and smiled broadly. 'It's a woman, isn't it!' she said. 'I can tell! I could always tell with you, Paul!'

Am I that transparent? Stark cursed himself. 'Yes, it is,' he said.

'Who is it? Someone from work?'

'No. It's . . . it's Lady Amelia Fairfax.'

His father stared at him, mouth open. 'That Jezebel?' he stammered at last.

'Dad, just because the papers say those things about her . . .'

'But . . . she's a married woman!' said Sarah, distressed.

'Divorced,' said Stark.

'Absolutely not!' snapped Henry indignantly.

Stark nodded. 'Fine,' he said. 'I'll ask Mrs Pearce next door. She's always offered—'

'No!' said his mother.

Henry glared at his son. 'This woman's that important to you, is she?' he demanded.

'No,' replied Stark. 'But I've been invited to dinner by her, and I'd like to go.'

'Dinner!' sneered his father.

'Yes, *dinner*,' emphasized Stark. 'If you remember, it was only a couple of days ago you were telling me I ought to get married again.'

Sarah stared at him, shocked. 'You're not thinking of marrying her?'

'No, of course not! But say I did meet someone and wanted to go out with her, I can't if we're going to have this sort of situation every time.'

'This is different and you know it,' said Henry. 'I was talking about someone of our own sort. Our own type.'

'But not divorced. A woman who's never been married.'

'You're twisting my words!' growled his father. 'There are plenty of widows around. Nice women. Women of our sort.'

'Our class? Working-class women?'

'What's wrong with that? Me and your mum are working class. *You're* working class. Don't look down your nose at your own, boy, just because you got some high and mighty job at the police. You're no better than Charlie Watts, so don't think you are!'

'I don't think I'm better,' insisted Stark. 'All I'm saying is, why do we all have to stick to our own class?'

'Because that's the way it is,' said Henry flatly. 'That's the way it always has been.'

'The rich man in his castle, the poor man at his gate,' quoted Stark bitterly. He'd always resented the sentiments of that hymn, 'All Things Bright and Beautiful': *The rich man in his castle, the poor man at his gate, God made them high or lowly and ordered their estate.*

'That's right,' nodded his father. 'It's the natural order of things.'

'Not for me, it isn't,' said Stark. 'I had enough of the high and mighty during the war. Most of them couldn't tie their own shoelaces without help. Anyway, I'm going out to dinner tomorrow evening at Lady Amelia Fairfax's, and if you don't want to look after Stephen for me—'

'We will!' said Sarah quickly. 'You know we will, Paul.'

Stark stopped and looked apologetically at his mother. There was no need to take out his anger at his father on her. 'Yes, I know, Mum,' he said. 'I'm sorry. That was very unfair of me. I apologize.'

Henry glared at him, sniffed angrily, then disappeared towards the kitchen.

'You promised Stephen you wouldn't be long,' Sarah reminded him.

'Yes, I did.' Stark reached out and hugged her close. 'The last thing I want to do is upset you and Dad. But I've got to have a life of my own, and what I want to do and the way I want to live it won't suit Dad.'

'I know,' she said. 'But don't ever take Stephen away from us.'

'I never will,' Stark assured her. 'I promise.'

TWENTY-FIVE

Stephen was sitting on his bed, looking at a book about aeroplanes, when Stark came in.

'More planes?' he said.

Stephen nodded. 'When we've finished the Sopwith Camel, me and Grandad are going to make an Avro.'

'Great,' said Stark. He sat down on the bed next to Stephen. 'The reason I asked you to go upstairs while I talked to your grandad and grandma was because I thought that one of the things I was going to tell them would make your grandad upset.'

Stephen hesitated, then said quietly, 'I heard him getting angry.'

'The thing is, Stephen, I am going out on work tonight. I have to see a man who might have some information that will help me with the case I'm on. But tomorrow night, I shall be going out for dinner with someone your grandad doesn't like.'

'A woman?'

'Yes,' nodded Stark.

Stephen hesitated, then looked at his father and asked directly,

'Is she going to take you away from us? Is that why Grandad's upset?'

'No,' said Stark firmly. 'No one's going to take me away from you, I promise. The thing is that Grandad has his own views about the kind of people he wants me to mix with.'

'Like he says to me about not playing with Terry Smith?'

Terry Smith, the same age as Stephen, and one of the enormous Smith clan who lived a few streets away and were noted for their criminality.

'Yes,' said Stark. 'Like that.'

'Is this woman like the Smiths?'

'No,' replied Stark, smiling at the comparison. 'This woman is called Lady Amelia Fairfax, and she lives in a very nice house in a very nice part of town.'

'Lady?' queried Stephen. 'A real lady, like you see in the papers?'

'A real lady, like you see in the papers,' agreed Stark. 'And she's invited me to dinner tomorrow night, but your grandad thinks I shouldn't go.'

'Why did she invite you to dinner?'

That's a very good question. Stark had been asking himself the very same since she'd invited him. 'I think she felt a bit lonely and wants someone to talk to,' said Stark.

'Hasn't she got any friends?'

'I'm sure she has, but maybe she wanted to talk to someone different for a change. Anyway, that's where I'm going tomorrow evening.'

'Will you be back?'

'Absolutely,' nodded Stark.

'Grandad says you ought to get married,' said Stephen suddenly.

'Perhaps one day I will. But I'm not planning to do anything about it any time soon.' He looked into his son's eyes, so Stephen could see into his own and know he was being sincere. 'I'm not going to do anything that divides us up. I don't spend enough time with you as it is.'

'Because of work,' said Stephen.

Stark nodded. 'Yes,' he said. 'And once this case is over, I'm going to make sure I spend a lot more time with you. We'll do whatever you want. Go places together. Do things.'

'I like doing things with Grandad as well. Making models.'

'I know,' said Stark. 'And you'll still do that.' He looked at his watch. 'I've got to go.'

'This man you've got to see about work?' said Stephen.

'Yes.'

'Are they very dangerous people, the ones you catch?'

Stark hesitated. 'They can be,' he said. 'But luckily I don't do it on my own.'

'You were on your own when they hurt you the other night.'

'Yes, but that was rare. That's never happened before.'

'Will they come back again and try to hurt you?'

Stark saw that Stephen's lower lip was trembling. He reached out and put his arm around his son, cuddling him to him. 'Not a chance!' he said determinedly. 'No one's coming here again like that!' And he vowed: *When I catch the bastards who did it, who've frightened Stephen in this way, I shall rip their hearts out.*

The meal at Danvers' Uncle Edwin's was excellent. Four courses: leek and potato soup to start, followed by lightly steamed haddock, steak with all the trimmings as the main course, and a rice pudding for dessert. *I won't need to eat again for a month,* thought Stark. Then he remembered that he would be facing another meal the following evening. *This is not a style of living you can allow yourself to get used to,* he warned himself. *Not on a chief inspector's pay.*

Sir Edwin Drake was someone who had allowed himself to get used to the finer things in life: food and wine especially, to judge by his expanded waistline. Not that Drake bulged too obviously, but then his clothes had been made for him by the best tailors. During the meal they kept light conversation going, mainly social, which meant reminiscences between Danvers and his uncle about family members. For Stark, it was an insight into the world his sergeant inhabited, one very different to his own.

For his part, Sir Edwin Drake was very pleasant company: charming, engaging, occasionally telling humorous stories about public figures he'd come into contact with, such as Lloyd George and Churchill. Although, Stark noted, he avoided mentioning any of the Irish politicians he must have met – de Valera and Collins and the rest.

After the meal, Drake invited Stark and Danvers to join him

in the library for cigars and brandy. As they left the dining room, two servants entered and began clearing the dining table.

If my parents could see me now, thought Stark. *Dad would accuse me of being too big for my boots, and Mum would just be terrified.*

They settled down into large and luxurious dark leather armchairs in the library, Stark and Danvers both refusing the offer of a cigar but accepting the brandy.

'Thank you for not bringing the reason you came this evening into the conversation at table, Chief Inspector,' said Drake. 'I do so enjoy good food, and I like to treat it with delight, rather than as background to serious talk.' He lit his cigar and waved away the smoke, then said, 'So, Bobby tells me you want to know about Ireland.' He smiled. 'It's a big subject.'

'I'm interested in your view of the present situation,' said Stark. 'The talks going on in London at the moment.'

Drake nodded. 'It's complicated,' he said. 'Of course, nearly everything about Ireland is. People think there are just two political factions in Ireland. The mainly Catholic population in the south, who want home rule, and have agitated for it for many years. And the mainly Protestant faction in Ulster who want to remain part of Britain. Actually, it's not that straightforward, and these talks that are going on in London have brought home the divisions in the home rule faction.' He looked enquiringly at Stark. 'How much do you know about the talks? The terms being discussed, that sort of thing.'

'That Ireland is to become a self-governing dominion of the British Empire, the same status that Australia, Canada, New Zealand and South Africa have,' said Stark.

'Good,' nodded Drake. 'And the head of state?'

'The Irish Free State will be able to elect its own president, but the King will remain the head of state. Members of the new Irish Free State's parliament will have to take an oath of allegiance to the Irish Free State, and also take a secondary oath to be faithful to His Majesty King George, his heirs and successors by law, in virtue of common citizenship.'

'I congratulate you on your sharp memory, Chief Inspector,' Drake nodded. 'There are many involved in the current talks who would not be able to quote from the treaty document so accurately.'

'The wording struck me as being memorable, sir,' replied Stark.

'It is,' agreed Drake. 'The rest of the terms?'

Stark called to mind the documents he'd been given by Special Branch to read in Benson's office. 'Northern Ireland will have the option of withdrawing from the Irish Free State within one month of the treaty coming into effect. If Northern Ireland chooses to withdraw, a boundary commission will be constituted to draw the boundary between the Irish Free State and Northern Ireland.'

'And there you have the two sticking points at the heart of the issue, Chief Inspector. The King as head of state and the related oath of allegiance to the British royal family, and the loss of Northern Ireland. One faction is prepared to accept those terms as the best option available, hoping to get improvements on them later.'

'Michael Collins and the others who are in London.'

'Yes. The other faction resolutely opposes the oath of allegiance to what they see as a foreign invading power, Britain, and also the loss of Northern Ireland. They want an independent and united Ireland of all four provinces: Munster, Leinster, Connacht and Ulster.'

'By "the other faction", I assume you mean de Valera?'

'Exactly. And that is why de Valera is not with the delegation in London.'

'I understood it was because he is too busy running the Irish Free State as its president, and that the delegation are here acting on his behalf.'

'That's the official reason. The real reason is that de Valera knows that this treaty is the best the Irish can get at this stage. And when it's voted on in the Irish Parliament – the Dáil – de Valera will oppose it. But he can't do that if he's been seen to support it in London.'

'So what do you think will happen?'

'I think the treaty will be signed after long discussions, and taken to Dublin to be ratified by the Irish Parliament. De Valera and his faction will vote against it.'

'And who will win?' asked Danvers.

'I think initially the treaty will be passed by the Dáil, but by a narrow margin. But then . . .' Drake paused, and a look of deep unhappiness came into his face. 'But then I think it will lead to civil war in Ireland as de Valera urges his followers to fight against the terms of the treaty, and the treaty-ites against those who want a free and independent united Ireland. Unfortunately, I foresee bloodshed in Ireland even worse than the War of Independence we've experienced so recently. Brother against brother. Mother against sons.' He shook his head. 'It will be carnage.'

'Is there a way to stop it?' asked Danvers. 'What if Collins and his colleagues refuse to sign the treaty?'

'Then the state of war between Britain and Ireland will continue.' Drake sighed. 'Whichever decision is taken in London, I fear it will lead to war of one sort or another.'

TWENTY-SIX

In the taxi that took them home, Stark patted his stomach. He still felt bloated. 'I don't think I'm going to need to eat again for a week,' he said. 'Four courses!'

'Uncle Edwin entertains so rarely; that's why he splashed out tonight,' said Danvers. 'But it was good food, wasn't it?'

'Excellent!' agreed Stark. 'I think we'll have to find ways to ask your Uncle Edwin's advice more often.'

'What did you make of what he told us?'

Stark hesitated. Then he leant forward to make sure the glass partition between them and the taxi driver was securely shut, before saying, 'I think the Irish business is a dead end, as far as these murders are concerned.'

Danvers looked at him, puzzled. 'But you said there was a connection. The business of them both being against home rule.'

'Yes, but it doesn't make sense about them being killed over it. Think about it from the point of view of a possible assassin. Amersham and Smith and their Union group are out of the loop as far as the government is concerned. They have no power and no influence. So what's the point in killing them? The pro-treaty crowd, the Irish delegation in London, have no interest in killing them. It wouldn't benefit them; it could only make their bargaining position worse.

'The anti-treaty Irish, the de Valera faction, they also have no real interest in killing them. They know that this group are outside the seat of power; they have no impact on the talks. Amersham and Smith and their like shout and rant about keeping Ireland British, but that's all they can do. They are not a threat. Lloyd George and Churchill have set their minds on getting a deal. So why kill Amersham and Smith? It doesn't make sense.'

'The man who attacked you had an Irish accent.'

'So the witness said, but I'm not a hundred per cent sure of that.' Stark shook his head. 'There *is* something going on here involving the Irish talks, but I don't think the murders are connected to it. I think that Special Branch used the murder of Lord Amersham to try to undermine the talks. There *is* a faction inside Britain that wants these talks to fail, and they are more powerful than mavericks like Lord Amersham and Tobias Smith. And I'd bet my pension that some of the people in Special Branch are connected with them.'

'The two you saw?'

'Chief Inspector Burns and Inspector Rogers,' nodded Stark grimly. 'They had those files all ready for me. They wanted me to come to the conclusion that there was a split between the pro-treaty delegates, and de Valera and the anti-treaty brigade, and put suspicion on de Valera.'

'Why?'

'To undermine the talks. Churchill was right. He said to me, "There are powerful people in Whitehall who want these Irish talks to fail. They will do anything to stop the talks succeeding." We need to look elsewhere for our murderer.'

Stark's mother was still up when he arrived home, sitting in the kitchen by the range, darning a hole in one of Stephen's socks. He looked at the clock. Eleven.

'You needn't have waited up,' he told her.

'You know your dad, he likes to make sure everything's locked up for the night and the door bolted. I told him I'd make sure. He had to go to bed. He was tired.'

Stark nodded, choosing not to comment about his father. 'Did Stephen get to sleep all right?' he asked.

Sarah nodded.

Stark hesitated, then said, 'I'm likely to be home late tomorrow night, Mum. I'd prefer it if you didn't wait up.'

Sarah opened her mouth as if she was about to say something, then changed her mind and just nodded.

This was always going to be difficult, Stark groaned silently to himself. 'You go on up, Mum. I'll bolt the door.'

'I'll just finish this,' said his mother, gesturing at the partly darned sock in her hands.

'All right,' said Stark. 'I'll see you in the morning.'

He went to the front door and slid the bolts into place, then headed up the stairs. Quietly, he opened the door of Stephen's room and looked in. Stephen was fast asleep, his hands clutching at the sheet, pulling it up around his face.

'Goodnight, son,' Stark whispered, then gently pulled the door closed and went to bed.

TWENTY-SEVEN

Next morning, Stark was up and washed and dressed before anyone else. He was boiling a kettle to make tea when his mother appeared.

'You're up early,' she commented. She turned away from him as she added, 'Your dad's feeling a bit under the weather this morning. So he's staying in bed for a bit.'

He can't face me, thought Stark. *He can't even bear to be in the same room as me*. 'In that case, maybe I can take Stephen to school this morning?' he suggested.

Sarah shot him a puzzled glance. 'I thought you had to get to work? Isn't there a car coming for you, like usual?'

'Yes, but he won't mind waiting. It won't take me long.'

The school, Richard Cobden, was just a couple of hundred yards down Camden Street. It had been Stark's old school, a place of fear and dread for many, with teachers whose philosophy seemed to have been to beat learning into children with the aid of a cane and anything else that came to hand. It was no wonder that quite a few children had left school unable to read and write properly, and many with stammers in their speech. By all accounts, things had improved since those days. And, fortunately for Stephen, he was a bright boy for whom reading and writing and arithmetic were a pleasure.

'I'll go up and tell him,' said Stark. *And maybe I'll bump into Dad on the landing*, he thought as he climbed the stairs.

There was no chance of that: the door to his parents' bedroom remained firmly closed.

Stark went into his son's bedroom and found Stephen just stirring. 'Morning, son,' he smiled. 'How are you this morning?'

'All right,' yawned Stephen, pushing himself up from the covers.

'I thought I might take you to school this morning,' said Stark. 'What do you think?'

'With Grandad?' asked Stephen.

'Your gran says your grandad is feeling a bit poorly this morning, so he's going to stay in bed for a bit longer.'

Immediately, he saw a flash of alarm in Stephen's eyes. 'He's not ill, is he?' he asked.

He's suffered too many people dying in his short life, thought Stark. He shook his head and made sure Stephen saw his reassuring smile. 'No, no,' he said. 'Nothing like that.' He winked and lowered his voice to a whisper as he said, 'If you ask me, it's because he's getting on a bit. He needs more rest. But he won't admit it. You know your grandad.'

Stephen smiled back.

'So, is that all right, me taking you to school?'

Stephen nodded, a big smile on his face. 'Yes! That'll be great!'

A loud banging on the front door stopped Stark before he could say any more. He looked at his watch, puzzled. Quarter past seven. It was far too early for his car to arrive.

They heard the sound of the front door opening, his mother's voice and a man's, then his mother called up the stairs, 'It's a policeman, Paul! For you!'

Stark groaned. *What now?* He gave Stephen a smile. 'I'll go and see what he wants. I'll be back in a moment.'

Ted Post was standing on the doorstep, in uniform, looking apologetic. 'I'm sorry to call so early, sir,' he said. 'But Chief Superintendent Benson insisted.'

Stark stared at Ted, stunned. 'Benson's in at this hour?' he queried.

'On his way, sir,' said Ted. 'He phoned the Yard and left a message for the duty driver to come and get you.'

Stark hesitated, torn. 'Are you sure it can't wait, Ted? I promised my son I'd take him to school.'

'The message said it was very urgent, sir.'

'Another murder?' asked Stark, his heart sinking at the thought.

'I don't know, sir,' said Ted. 'All the message said was to come and get you and take you to the Yard, urgent. Orders of Chief Superintendent Benson.'

Stark sighed and nodded. 'I'll get my coat.' He turned to look enquiringly at his mother, who'd been standing listening to this exchange with a worried look on her face.

She nodded. 'I'll take Stephen to school,' she said.

'I'll just go up and tell him,' he said.

Stephen was out of bed and pulling on his clothes when Stark returned.

'I'm afraid I've got to go, Stephen,' he said unhappily. 'Scotland Yard have sent a car for me. They need me urgently. So I'm afraid I won't be able to take you to school this morning after all.'

For a moment, Stephen's face registered his disappointment. But then he forced a smile. 'That's all right, Dad,' he said. 'Another time will do.'

Yes, thought Stark bitterly, *it's always going to be 'another time'*. He kissed his son and said goodbye to Sarah.

As the car raced through the streets, he thought about his relationship with his son. The truth was, they hardly really saw one another. He did his best, but working late often meant that Stephen was in bed by the time he came home, and because crime didn't work office hours, Saturdays and Sundays too often were spent at the Yard or questioning people.

I need a proper job, he thought. *One with regular daytime hours, where I can spend proper time with Stephen, helping him as he grows up, enjoying doing things with him.* Stephen was eight years old and the years seemed to fly by more quickly than ever. Soon Stephen would be nine, then ten, then twelve, then fourteen, and leaving school to go to work. *And I'll have missed his childhood.*

TWENTY-EIGHT

When he got to the Yard, Stark found Sergeant Mason on duty at the reception desk.

'I hear there's a flap on,' he said. 'What's happened? Another murder?'

Mason shook his head. 'I don't think so,' he said. 'No one's said anything about it to me if there is. All I know is the chief super came in in a terrible temper. He asked if you were in yet, and when I told him you were on your way, he flew up the stairs.'

So it was serious, but not another murder, reflected Stark. *We can be thankful for that, at least.*

He went up the wide, ornate marbled staircase to the first floor, and along the corridor to the chief superintendent's office. Benson was standing by his desk, glaring at a leaflet clutched in his hand. He glowered as Stark came into his office. 'You should be on the telephone, Stark!' he snapped.

'I got your message, sir,' said Stark.

'A message isn't good enough! This is the twentieth century, not the Dark Ages! We need faster reactions!'

'Yes, sir. I believe something has happened?'

'Yes!' Benson thrust the leaflet at Stark, who took it. It was badly printed on cheap paper, but the message was clear:

Who are the real murderers?
Lord Amersham and Tobias Smith MP are dead.
Who's next?
We're coming for you.
The Hand of Justice.

'These were stuck up on walls in the most expensive areas of London during the night,' said Benson. 'Knightsbridge. Maida Vale. Kensington. Hampstead. And this was pushed through the letterboxes of most of the daily papers. Luckily, it was too late for them to print for this morning's editions, but it'll be in the later ones.'

He handed Stark a letter. Like the leaflet, it was badly printed on cheap paper. Stark read it.

> To the Editor.
>   The poor of this country have suffered too long. Millions gave their lives during the war and their reward has been even greater poverty for their families they left behind. The real murderers are those who grow rich on the poor who died. The slum landlords. The profiteers.
>   Now the people are rising up and throwing off their oppressors. Proper wages and proper living conditions have been denied to the poor of this country for too long. Now we are taking those rights by force. The first move is to clear away the scum who keep the poor down and stop them having their rights. Lord Amersham and Tobias Smith are just the start. Others will follow.
>   The Hand of Justice.

Churchill's Bolsheviks, thought Stark.

'The Prime Minister's secretary telephoned me at home at a quarter past six this morning! That's how important this is, Stark!'

'Yes, sir,' nodded Stark, putting on an appropriate expression of deep concern. Inwardly, he thought angrily, *And for this I gave up taking Stephen to school! Another hour would have made no difference at all to this situation.*

Benson was still talking. 'A meeting to deal with this has been convened at Ten Downing Street. You're to go.'

'With the Prime Minister, sir?'

'The Home Secretary, Edward Shortt, will be chairing it. You will represent Scotland Yard. Special Branch will be there.'

'Who else, sir?'

'At this stage, I don't know. It's short notice.' He pointed at the leaflet. 'This could be the biggest threat we've faced since the war, Stark. Insurrection!'

'What time is this meeting?'

'Nine o'clock. You'd better get along there now. Better early than late. We don't want to show ourselves up, not at Downing Street.'

'No, sir.'

Stark took the leaflet and the letter and hurried up the stairs to the next landing and his office. Danvers was already there, studying a copy of the same leaflet.

'They roped you in as well?' asked Stark.

Danvers shook his head. 'Uncle Edwin phoned me. They stuck one of these on his gatepost. I thought it might cause a fuss, so I came in.'

'Cause a fuss is right,' grunted Stark. 'The Prime Minister's summoned a conference to deal with it. The chief super has ordered me to attend, representing Scotland Yard.'

'Congratulations, sir,' said Danvers, impressed.

'I'm not sure if congratulations are in order,' commented Stark doubtfully.

'But a conference at Downing Street . . .' persisted Danvers.

'Politicians do not necessarily make good policemen, Sergeant,' said Stark. 'Our primary job is to stop crime, and apprehend the criminals when it happens. Their agenda is driven by political survival.'

'What do you want me to do while you're out, sir?'

'Carry on digging into the lives of Lord Amersham and Tobias Smith. There has to be something else besides the Irish issue that links them.'

In the car on the way to Downing Street, Stark weighed up this new development: the threat from the Hand of Justice. Was it a new development or a red herring? It had certainly set the cat among the pigeons as far as the ruling classes were concerned, but could it be that was its sole aim? To rattle the ruling elite? Or were they really behind the two killings?

Stark also reflected on the fact that *he* was being sent to this conference. A chief inspector. Why hadn't Chief Superintendent Benson opted to go himself? Or, at least, detail one of his superintendents? Instead, Benson was sending a detective chief inspector – a senior officer, but not *that* senior.

His mind went back to the conversation the previous evening with Sir Edwin Drake, and the reason why de Valera wasn't in London. Because de Valera knew the talks would be seen as a failure in Ireland and he intended to distance himself from them. Collins had been sent as his emissary, but also as his scapegoat. When the blame game began, the finger would be pointed at Collins, not at de Valera.

Is that the case here? thought Stark. *Benson knows that this investigation seems to be failing so far.* The defence that it was early days in the investigation would cut no ice with the politicians, those who felt threatened and might consider themselves as the next targets. Being selected to attend this conference as the representative of Scotland Yard, the investigating team, was a poisoned chalice as far as Stark was concerned. This conference was not just to move the investigation forward; it was to start pointing fingers, to begin allocating blame. Two high-profile people from the establishment had been murdered and no one was yet in custody. Threats had been made against the rest of the ruling elite. The politicians were afraid, not just for their lives but about their careers. They needed the confidence of the electorate if they were to hang on to their jobs. They needed to show people that they were on top of this threat, and to do that, they needed someone to blame. A scapegoat.

Michael Collins and I have more in common than just our birth dates and military experiences, thought Stark ruefully. *We're both going to be hung out to dry.*

TWENTY-NINE

The faces around the long, shiny, dark oak table in the conference room inside 10 Downing Street were grim. Stark was at one end, sitting next to Chief Inspector Burns and Inspector Rogers of Special Branch. At the other end were various high-ranking uniforms representing the army: two field marshals and a brigadier. *So martial law is a possibility*, thought Stark. In between were various civil servants, all dressed in identical dark clothes, some making notes even though the meeting had not even begun. Near to them sat Winston Churchill, glowering and glaring, shifting on his chair as if he was just bursting to start making his points.

The Home Secretary, Edward Shortt, took pride of place at the centre of the table. Shortt looked very much an old establishment figure, dressed formally in dark suit and tie, the monocle he habitually wore giving him the air of a Victorian aristocrat.

In fact, Stark knew that this was appearance only. Shortt did not come from a titled family; his father had been a vicar in Newcastle upon Tyne. He'd gained his degree at Durham University, rather than Oxford or Cambridge, and after a career as a barrister he'd entered politics on the Liberal ticket, entering parliament as the member for Newcastle. He'd been appointed Chief Secretary for Ireland at the same time as Ireland had the seen rise of republicanism, and he'd been promoted to Home Secretary in 1919, right in the middle of a strike by the police. Both appointments had been seen as poisoned chalices, positions no one wanted at those particular times, but Shortt had carried them off with aplomb and a minimum of fuss. He'd managed to settle the police strike to the satisfaction of both sides, and had actually ended up gaining the support and respect of most rank-and-file police officers.

Because Shortt did everything in an understated and non-dramatic style, he'd gained the reputation – unfair in Stark's opinion – of being lazy and lacking in energy. In this he was the polar opposite of Churchill, who seemed to bristle with high energy even when he was just sitting down. This became apparent as soon as Shortt tapped the badly printed leaflet in front of him, and said, 'Well, gentlemen. What do we make of this?'

That was the cue that Churchill had been waiting for. He immediately pointed a stubby finger at Stark and growled accusingly, 'I told you this was Bolsheviks, Stark!'

'You did, indeed, Mr Secretary,' nodded Stark. 'And we investigated the known Bolshevik organization, the British Communist Party.' He looked pointedly at Burns and Rogers. 'With the cooperation of our colleagues in Special Branch.' *Who are already deep inside the BCP*, he thought.

It was Burns who moved in to cover Special Branch. 'Yes indeed,' he said smoothly. 'And we have continued our investigations into them.' He tapped the leaflet in front of him. 'Whereas this apparent organization, the Hand of Justice, has yet to be proven.'

'What do you mean, Chief Inspector?' asked Edward Shortt.

'For all we know, they may not even exist as an organization. They may be just a few radicals exploiting the tragic deaths of Lord Amersham and Mr Smith for their own ends.'

Shortt looked at the leaflet and nodded thoughtfully.

'Yes, that's a good point,' he said. 'In which case, we will have been made fools of.' He looked around the table. 'What does everyone else think? Has anyone heard of this Hand of Justice?'

There was a shaking of heads.

'However,' spoke up Stark, 'it is worth pointing out that these leaflets appeared on walls in the more affluent areas of London, all some distance apart, in a very short space of time.'

'What's your point?' demanded Churchill.

'To stick these up on walls in places as far apart as Knightsbridge, Hampstead, Maida Vale, Westminster, St James's, and all at the same time, means a lot of people and efficient coordination. Which suggests an organization rather than a few radicals.' As his words sank in, he added, 'However, I agree with Chief Inspector Burns. That does not necessarily mean they are connected with the shootings. They may well be taking advantage of them for their own political ends.'

'What is the situation regarding the murders?' asked Shortt. 'Do we have any viable suspects?'

Stark felt all eyes on him. 'We are still pursuing various lines of enquiry,' he said. 'At the moment we are trying to establish what might have connected Lord Amersham and Mr Smith. We believe there will be a link as the same person killed them both.'

'The link is Bolshevism!' roared Churchill. 'They were both in Parliament!'

'True,' nodded Stark. 'But there may be other issues.'

He looked towards Burns and Rogers, waiting for them to bring up the issue of Irish home rule, but both men kept their eyes averted from him and their heads down, apparently studying the leaflet and letter to the press from the Hand of Justice, resolutely making sure they could not be accused of bringing the issue of Ireland into the discussion.

One of the field marshals tapped his copy of the letter to the press and announced, 'I think one of the first things to do is put out a government notice, stopping the newspapers from printing this. We've got to make sure we don't have revolutionaries running riot in the streets. This letter is the sort of thing that could trigger that.'

'Too late for that, I'm afraid,' said Shortt. 'In fact, the mid-morning editions will be on the streets already.' He sighed. 'These people knew what they were doing, with the timing.'

'Our first duty is to protect the King and Queen,' said Churchill. 'We can't have a repeat here of what happened in Russia.'

Burns nodded. 'Steps have already been taken,' he assured the meeting. 'Extra security officers have been assigned to the royal family, and we have looked at their timetable of forthcoming public engagements.'

'We also feel that the situation here in England is very different to the events that tragically happened in Russia,' added Rogers. 'There, the political situation encouraged the murders of the Romanoff family. Here, we believe the majority of the public support the King and Queen and actively wish to protect them from harm.'

'At the moment!' thundered Churchill. He thumped his fist on the leaflet. 'That could soon change if these people have their way! Riot! Revolution!'

And so it went on: the same things, the same sentiments being repeated over and over again around the table. It was Special Branch who made a suggestion to counter Churchill's and the army's fears of insurrection breaking out when the letter from the Hand of Justice became public.

'I suggest we cast doubt on the Hand of Justice being a real political force,' suggested Burns. 'Expose them as a fraud, a bunch of would-be radicals who actually have nothing to do with the tragic murders. Discredit them and their awful press releases.'

'How do we do that?' asked the brigadier.

'We put out a statement from someone who was a member of this so-called organization, giving the truth about them. That they are useless idiots, mentally unstable, who are just using these tragic murders for their own ends.'

'We could add that they are also known sexual perverts,' added Rogers. 'The public hate that.'

'So you'd be making it up?' asked the brigadier.

'We'd be true to the reality of the situation,' said Rogers.

'Very well,' nodded Shortt. 'See what you can do.' He turned to look at Stark. 'But I'm sure you agree, Chief Inspector, that the best way to stop any such threats from these people – real or imagined – is to catch the perpetrators of these crimes.'

'I do indeed, sir,' said Stark.

*　　*　　*

Stark's first act on returning to the Yard was to call on Chief Superintendent Benson to report on the meeting, but he learned from Benson's secretary that he was out for the rest of the day, 'on important business'.

Distancing himself from me and anything to do with me to avoid his career being tainted, decided Stark.

He went to his office, where he found Danvers waiting for him.

'How did it go, sir?' asked Danvers.

'Exactly as expected when politicians organize anything,' said Stark. 'It was a talking shop with everyone covering their own particular areas of responsibility. The one thing everyone agreed on was that it's up to us to find the killer.'

'So we're being held responsible?'

'We are the lowest notch on the totem pole, Sergeant. Of course we're going to be the ones.'

'What do they think of this Hand of Justice organization?'

'Special Branch are sure they don't actually exist as a viable organization, and they're going to do their best to discredit them enough so that the general public won't believe in them either.'

'Do you think they're right?'

Stark frowned. 'I think that any outfit that can stick these leaflets over half of the richer areas of London in a very short space of time, without anyone getting caught doing it, shows coordination and organization. Personally, I wouldn't rule them out. But then, I'm suspicious of everyone. What's happened here?'

'Sergeant Watts from Camden Town phoned. He asked if you'd call him as soon as you got in.'

'Did he say if he'd learned anything?'

Danvers shook his head. 'He said he'd talk to you.'

Stark shrugged. 'Charlie always was a bit tight-mouthed,' he said. 'His mantra is "Knowledge is power".'

'Bacon,' nodded Danvers.

'Who?' asked Stark.

'Francis Bacon – 1561 to 1626,' answered Danvers. 'From his *Sacred Meditations*.'

Stark looked impressed. 'I must admit, I can't see Charlie Watts reading Francis Bacon. Pulp thrillers and cowboy books are more in his line. Anyway, let's see what he's found.'

Stark dialled the number and heard Charlie Watts' voice say, 'Camden Town police station. Sergeant Watts speaking.'

'DCI Stark here, Sergeant,' said Stark. 'My sergeant, Sergeant Danvers, said you called.'

'Yes!' said Watts enthusiastically. 'I think we might have something on those blokes who did you over.'

'Oh?'

'We put a discreet tail on Pete Stamp, like you asked, and he's been seen in close company with a couple of blokes who fit the description: one big, muscular bloke and one small, thin bloke.'

'Have you got names?'

'The big bloke's called Joe West, the small one's Eddie Saunders. Ring any bells?'

'They do indeed, Sergeant. Especially Eddie Saunders.'

'Yeah, I thought it might. It's a long time ago, though.'

'Some people don't forget.'

'What do you want me to do about them?'

'Pick 'em up. All three of them. On suspicion of attempted murder.'

'Attempted murder? You sure?'

'I am at this moment, and we need something strong to keep them in custody. Do you think you'll be able to lay hands on them?'

'No problem. We know where they are. I can have them here inside the hour.'

'Fine. In that case, I'll be along. I'll bring my sergeant with me so I can introduce him to you. He's a good bloke; you can trust him. One thing: when you bring them in, put Pete Stamp in a different cell from the other two.'

'You got it,' said Watts. 'See you soon, Chief Inspector.'

As Stark hung up, Danvers burst out, 'They've found them? The men who attacked you?'

'Oh yes,' nodded Stark.

'How can you be so sure?'

'I'll tell you in the car on the way to Camden Town,' said Stark. 'It'll be good for you to meet Charlie Watts. He can be a very valuable asset, especially if you want someone to keep an ear to the ground as you move on upwards in this job.'

'You think I will?' asked Danvers.

'Yes, I do,' said Stark. 'And, what's more, you think so, too.'

THIRTY

They took a car from the motor pool, with a driver Stark was unfamiliar with. As they drove north from Scotland Yard, Stark made sure the glass panel between them and the driver was firmly shut before he started recounting the story behind the attack on him, and the reason he was so sure that they'd caught the guilty men.

'It goes back to before the war. To 1910. I was twenty-three years old, and I hadn't long got into the detective division as a DC. Before that I'd been a uniform with a beat in Camden Town. Charlie Watts was a beat copper out of Camden Town at the same time, too, and wasn't yet a sergeant. A little girl had been raped and killed. Annie Angel. She was five. Local gossip pointed to it being a tearaway called Wilf Saunders, but we didn't have any evidence against him.'

'Wilf Saunders? Relation of this Eddie Saunders we're going to talk to?'

'Wilf was Eddie's older brother. Wilf was eighteen. Eddie would have been about twelve. Anyway, I went to talk to Wilf Saunders, and he pulled a knife on me. We struggled, and during the struggle the knife went into his throat. Cut the jugular vein. I did my best to save him, but he died.'

Danvers looked at him, shocked. 'He died?'

Stark nodded.

'But . . . it wasn't your fault!'

'That was what the enquiry said,' Stark nodded. 'They even gave me a commendation. But Eddie wasn't convinced it was an accident. I remember he came up to me after the inquest and shouted at me: "You did Wilf! I'm gonna have you for that!"'

'But that was ten years ago!'

'I know, but for someone like Eddie, that feeling of revenge is something you carry with you for ever.'

'But why attack you now?'

'Maybe because my name got into the papers over these murders, and it provoked him to put his threat into action. Who knows? But I'm sure that Eddie and this Joe West character were the ones. And once I get Pete Stamp talking, we'll nail them and put them away. And that's why I need you with me, Sergeant. So that when we question Pete Stamp, you're there to see that there are no threats from me of physical violence, no coercion. I don't want some sharp lawyer getting this case thrown out and Eddie walking around free to put my family at risk. Because that'll be his next target: my son or my parents.'

As he saw Danvers settle back on the seat, the bewildered expression on his face showing that he was struggling to take in this information about his superior officer, Stark's mind went back to that time: 1910, a year and a half before he met Susan. When he was still carrying a torch of sorts for Eve Angel, even though she'd been married for seven years to one of his best pals, Ben.

He remembered he'd told her he loved her once, when she was still Eve Adams, just before she got engaged to Ben Angel. He'd had to have a drink to work up the courage to tell her, and she'd laughed and told him not to be so silly, so he'd made a joke of it, pretended he hadn't really meant it, just a piece of fun. But he had meant it, and it had broken his heart when Ben and Eve told him they were going to be married, although – again – he'd put a brave face on it, made lots of jokes about it, and had forced himself to smile throughout their wedding.

There was no doubt that Ben and Eve were happy. Baby Annie had arrived a year later. And for the next five years, Stark had eased his pain by throwing himself into work. He'd studied for exams and worked hard, building up a good reputation in the force, and then applied for the detective division.

DC Paul Stark. That had been in 1910. In that same year, little Annie, then aged five, had vanished. She'd been waiting in the street while Eve had gone back indoors to get something. Eve swore she'd only left Annie alone for two minutes. Maybe three. But when she went out, Annie was gone.

At first, Eve thought that Annie was playing a joke on her, hiding, or maybe she'd wandered around a corner. After Eve had searched and hunted high and low around the nearby streets, and knocked on neighbours' doors, the awful truth sank in: Annie was gone.

Her body was discovered later that day on a patch of waste ground. She'd been raped and stabbed.

Questions asked suggested that a young man called Wilf Saunders was the most likely. He'd been warned off by other parents to leave their daughters alone. Some little girls reported that he'd offered them sweets to go with him, but none of them had done so. The more questions the police asked, the more the answers pointed to Wilf Saunders. But there was one problem: Wilf claimed he was helping his mum at home all that day, and his mum backed him up in his story.

The fact that Mrs Saunders had a reputation as a liar and a drunk, and was also fiercely protective of her sons, cut no ice with Stark's superior officers. Saunders had an alibi; there was nothing that could be done.

What was the point at which Stark had decided there was something that could be done? He guessed it was when he saw Wilf Saunders' smirk as he asked him again about this alibi. Yes, it was that smug smirk that had done it.

Had Stark actually gone in search of Saunders to kill him, knowing that they would never get justice in a court of law? Or had he, as he'd always told himself, just gone to have a private talk with Saunders, man to man, to try to force him into confessing? He knew that Saunders was guilty. Saunders knew he knew. And Saunders knew that there was nothing Stark could do about it.

Stark closed his eyes to bring the scene to his mind. A hut by the canal where he'd found Saunders. No, not found him; he'd *followed* him. This hut was Saunders' private lair, and Saunders had reacted with anger when Stark had pushed open the door to find him. Angry words. Both of them shouting. Who'd struck the first blow?

I did, Stark told himself. A punch into that smug, self-satisfied face, blood spurting from Saunders' nose.

That was when Saunders had produced the knife. Was it the one he'd used to stab little Annie to death?

Stark remembered Saunders lunging for him, and grabbing Saunders' arm. Then the struggle, both of them fighting to get hold of the knife, and realizing that this was it; this was the end for whoever lost.

The knife sliding into Saunders' neck. The gush of blood.

Could he have stopped it happening? Could he have disarmed Saunders? Had he really wanted to disarm Saunders?

The aftermath. The inquest. The enquiry. Exonerated, except in the eyes of the Saunders family. Not that Mr Saunders got very much involved in the condemnation of him; Bill Saunders had never been much of a father, away most of the time. No, the hatred towards him had come from Mrs Saunders and young Eddie.

'You killed our Wilf!' Both of them had shouted it at him.

He'd ignored them. The police inquiry into Wilf Saunders' death cleared him of blame. He was even given a commendation for bravery for tackling a man armed with a knife. On the streets of Camden Town there seemed to be tacit approval for what he'd done. The dangerous thug who pestered their daughters was gone. The streets were a bit safer.

For Eve and Ben, nothing was good. The death of Wilf Saunders wouldn't bring their beloved daughter back.

Eve took to wandering the streets, sometimes in her nightdress, talking to little girls who would have been about Annie's age, but her appearance – her desperate smile and staring eyes – frightened the girls and they called for their mothers, who chased Eve away. Finally, Eve took Ben's cut-throat razor one day and slit both her wrists. And then, just to make sure she did the job properly, she slit her throat.

Ben found her body when he came home from work, and the neighbours talked for days afterwards about the horrific animal howling they heard from the house when he found her.

That was the end. Ben moved away, unable to cope with the constant memories the area presented to him. Some said he'd gone up north; some said he'd gone to sea.

Stark had made an attempt to find him, but life caught up with him. He was promoted at work, he met Susan, Stephen was born, and after that there was just looking forward. Although he never forgot what happened, never forgot Eve and Ben, or Wilf Saunders, other things took precedence. And then there came the war, and everything he'd experienced before, all the horrors, were eclipsed during those four years. Wilf Saunders was in the past.

Until now.

THIRTY-ONE

S tark and Danvers sat across the table from Pete Stamp. They were in the same interview room where Stark had questioned Stamp before, but now the atmosphere between them was very different. Stamp was worried, Stark could tell. His confident swagger of their earlier interview had gone; now he was a man brought in for questioning, arrested, trapped. His whole manner was that of someone who was trying to keep his frightened desperation from showing, and failing.

'You see, Pete, we've got an issue here,' said Stark, his tone concerned. 'As you know, we've picked up Eddie Saunders and Joe West, and they tell a very different story to yours. According to them, it wasn't just that you came up with the idea of telling us that story about the two Irishmen; you were the one who came up with suggesting the attack on me.'

Stamp shook his head. 'No, no.'

'Well, that's where we've got a problem, Pete. You see, that's two against one. Which, when it comes to court, will carry more weight with a jury. Especially when the charge is attempted murder. That's twenty years inside, hard labour.'

Stamp stared at Stark and Danvers, horrified. 'Attempted murder?' he repeated.

'Assault with a bladed weapon,' nodded Stark. 'That's attempted murder. Stabbing.'

'I don't know anything about that!' protested Stamp.

'But you admit you made up the story about the Irishmen?'

'No! That was Eddie's idea!'

'What was Eddie's idea?' asked Stark.

'Me saying they was Irish blokes.'

Stark nodded thoughtfully, his eyes on Stamp the whole time. 'Maybe you'd better tell us the whole story, from your point of view.'

'It ain't just my point of view, it's the truth!' insisted Stamp. 'Eddie come to me and said him and Joe were in a bit of bother. They'd had a run in with a bloke and the police might be looking for them. If I went to the police and said I'd seen the two blokes running away, and said they was Irish, that'd let 'em off the hook.'

'And did they tell you who this bloke was they'd had a run-in with?'

Stamp shook his head. 'No! If I'd known it was you, Mr Stark, I'd never have done it!'

Inwardly, Stark smiled to himself at the lie. 'And the business of seeing them in Crowndale Road . . .'

'That's what Eddie told me to say. He said to tell the police I saw these two blokes come running out of Camden Street and into Crowndale Road, and say I heard 'em talking, so that's how I knew they was Irish.'

As Stamp was led back to his cell, Charlie Watts put his head into the room and asked, 'Who do you want next?'

'We'll have Joe West,' said Stark.

Joe West was indeed a big man. Well over six feet tall, wide muscular shoulders, thick arms, and a face that looked as if it had been hit many times, with a flattened nose and thickened ears. A boxer, thought Stark. No, a bare-knuckle prizefighter.

He sat in the chair, his face grim, scowling at the two detectives.

'The thing is, Joe, there's a good reason why we've brought you in over this assault,' said Stark quietly, almost apologetically. 'We've got a witness who can identify you. A woman who lives in Camden Street, just round the corner from Plender Street. There's a street light just outside her house. And she says your cap fell off as you were running past it.'

'My cap never fell off!' snorted West indignantly. And then he realized what he'd said, and it was as if a wall came down between them: his mouth set in a grim line, his jaw clenched, he looked past them instead of at them, turning on himself. From that moment, if he heard what they said, he showed no sign of it, made no comment of any sort, didn't even acknowledge their presence.

'So you admit you were in Camden Street with Eddie Saunders on the night in question?'

No reply.

'Was the purpose of the attack just assault, or was it attempted murder?'

No reply.

'How long have you known Eddie Saunders?'

Again, no reply.

After a further ten minutes of no response of any sort, Joe just sitting rigidly still on his chair, his eyes fixed on a spot in the wall behind and just above Stark and Danvers, Stark got up and went to the door of the interview room. 'You can take him back to his cell,' he told the uniformed officer on duty outside. 'Then bring us Eddie Saunders.'

After the door had closed on the constable and Joe West, Stark said to Danvers, 'Right, you take the questioning of Eddie Saunders.'

'Me?' said Danvers, surprised.

Stark nodded. 'It'll be good experience for you, and it won't be what Saunders is expecting.'

The door opened and Saunders was escorted in. Whereas Joe West had been obstinate, like a block of stone on legs, and Pete Stamp had been nervous and apprehensive, Saunders swaggered. He had a cocksure smile on his face. He didn't wait to be invited to sit; he took hold of the back of the chair and sat himself down on it, then shuffled it around so that he was directly facing Stark, a look of aggressive hatred and a challenge in his eyes.

'Edward Saunders,' began Danvers, 'I am Detective Sergeant Danvers and this is Chief Inspector Stark. We have received information that you and Joseph West, in conspiracy with one Peter Stamp, were engaged in an assault on DCI Stark on the evening of the twelfth of October outside a house in Plender Street, Camden Town.' He looked at Saunders. 'What do you say to that?'

Saunders said nothing. Instead, he smiled at Stark.

'Your silence can be taken as an admission of guilt,' continued Danvers calmly. 'Which may be mitigated if you would advise us of your whereabouts on that evening.'

Stark could see that Danvers' calm manner, the long words, his way of speaking in quasi-legal language unsettled Saunders slightly. This wasn't what the man had been expecting.

'What's that mean?' he demanded. 'Mitigated?'

'To tend towards vindication,' said Danvers. 'Extenuation.'

The wonders of a good education, Stark smiled inwardly to himself.

Saunders looked bewildered, none the wiser, exactly as Danvers had intended. He shot a look at Stark, who remained silent. In fact, Stark turned away from Saunders' look and gazed absently at a stain on the wall.

'The question is,' continued Danvers, 'was the attack by you and Joseph West on Detective Chief Inspector Stark simply an assault, or was it attempted murder?'

Saunders shot a look of hate at Stark, who remained impassive, ignoring him, looking around the interview room, seemingly studying it in some detail.

'Why doesn't he talk?' hissed Saunders.

'Was the idea of informing the police that the men who attacked DCI Stark were Irish yours or Peter Stamp's idea?'

'I'm saying nothing!' snapped Saunders; and again he glowered at Stark.

Stark remained silent, his manner deliberately casual, almost indifferent. He looked casually around the room, seemingly bored by the questions Danvers was putting to Saunders. Saunders' angry glare was fixed on Stark, and he kept it on the DCI as Danvers asked, 'What was the motive for your attack?'

At that, Stark turned his attention to Saunders and smiled, a smug smirk of triumph.

It was the smile that did it.

'He knows why!' shouted Saunders, and he leapt to his feet, his chair falling back and tumbling to the floor. He was shaking with anger, his finger pointing at Stark. 'He killed my brother!'

The sound of the shout and the chair falling over had brought a uniformed constable into the room. Danvers held up a hand to tell the constable to return outside. When the door had closed again, he looked at Saunders. 'So the motive for your attack was revenge for the death of your brother,' he said.

'He killed him!' hissed Saunders. 'Murdered him! And he thought he'd got away with it!'

Still Stark didn't speak, but now the smile had gone and been replaced by a cold implacable stare at Saunders. Danvers shot a questioning look at Stark, asking, *Shall I continue?* Stark nodded.

'Edward Saunders, you have admitted the attack on Detective Chief Inspector Stark, along with your accomplice, Joseph West. As you were armed with a knife, the charge will be attempted murder.'

'Yes, I wanted to kill the bastard!' hissed Saunders. 'If his old man hadn't come out, I'd have done it as well.'

'Did Joseph West know that you intended to kill DCI Stark?'

Saunders hesitated, then shook his head. 'No. Joe just thought we was going to teach him a lesson.'

'And Pete Stamp?'

Again, Saunders shook his head. 'He was just to tell a story to put you lot off the scent.'

'Why Irishmen?' asked Danvers.

Saunders shrugged. 'Cos there's a lot of 'em in Camden Town.'

Later, when Saunders had been returned to his cell, Stark gave Danvers an approving nod.

'That was an excellent touch,' he said. 'The pseudo-lawyer approach, with a mouthful of words calculated to confuse.'

'But all accurate,' said Danvers. 'I always enjoyed reading dictionaries at school.'

'No wonder you and your father have difficulties,' murmured Stark.

Danvers looked as if he was about to make a retort of indignation about this comment on his family life, but then, instead, he smiled. 'There may be something in what you say, sir,' he admitted. He gestured at the door. 'What about Saunders? Do you think he was telling the truth about Joe West? That West didn't know Saunders was planning to kill you?'

'I don't know,' admitted Stark. 'He could well be protecting West from a charge of attempted murder, which shows some kind of loyalty. The main thing is, we've got them. And they'll be off the street.'

THIRTY-TWO

Stephen and Sarah were sitting at the kitchen table eating supper when Stark arrived home.

'Where's Dad?' asked Stark.

He looked at the table, at the third plate, almost empty, and realized that his father must have got up and left the table when he heard his son's key in the lock.

'He's out in the yard,' said his mother. 'He's measuring.'

'Measuring for what?'

'He's thinking of keeping chickens,' said Stephen. 'He's going to build a run for them, and he said I can help him.'

'Fresh eggs,' nodded Stark approvingly. 'And a chicken for the table now and then. It's a good idea.' He turned to Stephen. 'How was school?'

'All right,' said Stephen. 'We did the seven times tables today. I remembered it all. I got a gold star in my book.' He looked hopefully at Stark. 'Will you take me to school tomorrow?'

'Your dad's going out tonight,' said Sarah. 'He might not be back.'

'I'll be back,' Stark promised. 'Yes, of course, Stephen.' He looked at his mother. 'I might be back late tonight, but I'll definitely be back.' He gestured at the back door to the yard. 'I'll just go and see Dad.'

'He . . . he might be busy,' said his mother awkwardly. 'With the measuring.'

'I want to tell him we caught the men who attacked me the other night.'

'Who was it?' asked Sarah, suddenly alert, as was Stephen.

'A couple of local men,' replied Stark. 'They felt they had a grievance for something that happened a long time ago. It's nothing to do with the case I'm working on.'

'Did you lock them up?' asked Stephen.

'We did,' nodded Stark. 'They're safely under lock and key. They won't be bothering me again.' He headed for the back door. 'I'll see you in a minute.'

Henry was standing outside in the yard. If he was doing any measuring, he was doing it by eye because there was no sign of a ruler. But then, when Stark had watched his father at work at his carpentry, much of the measuring appeared to have been done by eye.

Henry scowled as he saw his son. 'I'm not talking to you,' said his father.

'No, I got that impression,' said Stark. 'And that's fine. I just wanted to let you know we caught the men who attacked me. That's all.'

He turned and headed back towards the house, but a shout from his father stopped him. 'Wait! Who were they? And why?'

Stark retraced his steps towards Henry. 'Joe West and Eddie Saunders.'

'Saunders? A relation of Wilf Saunders?'

Stark nodded. 'His younger brother.'

Henry stood, silent, letting this sink in. 'After all this time.'

'He didn't believe what happened was an accident.'

'It was, though, wasn't it?'

Stark felt a sense of anger rising in him as he observed the questioning look on his father's face. '*You* have to ask me *that*?' he demanded.

'I didn't mean . . .' began Henry, equally angry, but defensively so.

Stark shook his head. 'Maybe it's a good thing we're not talking,' he said.

He turned on his heel and walked off, fuming with silent rage. Of all people to think he had deliberately killed Wilf Saunders, he hadn't expected it from his own father.

Stark took a taxi to Cadogan Square and Lady Amelia Fairfax's house. As he stood at the imposing front door, beneath the stately portico arch of the porch, he looked down at himself, at his suit. His best suit. Yet here, in these surroundings, it looked somehow very second best. The previous night, dinner at Danvers' Uncle Edwin's, it hadn't bothered him. He hadn't been there to impress Sir Edwin. But he suddenly became aware that he wanted to impress Lady Amelia. Here he was, standing there looking like someone's poor relation.

It was too late to flee now and telephone with some excuse. He'd already rung the bell.

The door was opened by a stoutish woman in her fifties.

'Good evening,' he said. 'I'm Chief Inspector Stark. I believe Lady Amelia is expecting me.'

'Yes indeed, sir,' said the woman. 'I'm Mrs Walker, the housekeeper.' She opened the door wider for him to step into the hallway. 'May I take your coat?' She took his coat and hung it on an ornamental coat stand. 'If you'll follow me, Lady Amelia is in the drawing room.'

Stark followed her along the hallway to the drawing room,

where Lady Amelia was standing waiting for him. She looked stunning. She wore a long dress of pale blue, a necklace made of small pieces of amber. Her reddish hair was pulled back and curled atop her head, making the beauty of her face even more devastating.

Stark felt even shabbier in his so-called best suit.

'Lady Amelia,' he said.

She held out her hand to him, and he took it gently in his. 'Good evening, Chief Inspector.' She smiled. 'Look, I can't keep calling you Chief Inspector all evening. Can I call you Paul?'

'Far better. And . . . Amelia?'

She nodded.

'Will it be all right for me to serve the first course in fifteen minutes, m'lady,' said Mrs Walker.

'Thank you, Mrs Walker. That will be fine.' Lady Amelia released Stark's hand and went to a sideboard where drinks were set out. 'Sherry?' she asked.

'Sherry will be perfect,' replied Stark.

This was a different woman from the one he'd encountered at the Communist Party offices. There, she'd been challenging, defensive, tigerish almost. Here, on her own territory, she was . . . She was simply gorgeous, thought Stark. But the tiger in her could still be seen in the way she moved, as she returned from the sideboard with their glasses of sherry. She handed him one, then gestured at the chairs. Just as at Sir Edwin Drake's: large, opulent leather. *Do the upper classes all go to the same furnishers?* Stark wondered.

He sat down and they raised their glasses to one another in a polite toast before sipping.

The sherry was delicious. A different drink altogether to the sherry his family sometimes had at Christmas.

'I was worried that you might have to cancel again, when I read the news,' she said. 'This Hand of Justice, claiming they killed Lord Amersham and Tobias Smith. Are they responsible?'

'We're looking into it,' said Stark. 'Have you ever heard of them before?'

'In my role as a radical Bolshevik?' she asked, amused.

'If you like,' said Stark. 'Although I was thinking more in your role as an organizer of the British Communist Party.'

'You don't consider them to be one and the same?'

'When it comes to politics, I've noticed that there are more divisions among those who should be on the same side than there are between those they are supposed to be opposing. The Russian Revolution is a case in point: Leninists against Trotskyites, with Mensheviks against both of them. Like Ireland, with the talks going on at the moment. The home rule Republicans split between the pro-treatyites and the anti-treaty faction.'

'You're very politically aware.'

'Aware enough to know to keep my distance.'

'Actually, I'm not an organizer of the BCP. As I told Bobby Danvers that first time he came to interrogate us . . .'

'Interrogate?'

She laughed. 'All right, talk to us. As I told him, I was just in the office doing a favour for Sylvia Pankhurst.'

'But you believe in the cause?'

'Of course I do! Otherwise I wouldn't be there!'

'Back to my original question: have you ever heard of the Hand of Justice?'

'Am I being interrogated?'

'We can talk about the weather, if you'd prefer. Or the latest fashions.'

'Do you know much about fashion?'

'Not a thing.'

'No,' she said. 'I've never heard of them. But that doesn't mean they don't exist. There are lots of organizations that have sprung up, especially since the war, to try to make this a fairer society.'

'There's the Labour Party.'

She scoffed. 'Fine for people who belong to a trade union, but what about the others who live at the bottom of the social heap? Women. The unemployed. The disabled who can't work. Former soldiers who've come back blind, or their bodies wrecked.'

'The Labour Party held seats in the War Cabinet. There is talk of it winning a majority at the next election, especially since women have been given the vote.'

'Women over the age of thirty who are property owners. Men can vote at twenty-one Where's the fairness in that? Are you a Labour Party man?'

Stark shook his head. 'As I said, I keep my distance. If pressed, I'd describe myself as non-political.'

She laughed. 'And as I said, on the contrary, you are one of the most politically aware people I've met.'

'The two are not the same,' he pointed out.

'Have you read Karl Marx?' she asked.

'No, nor Lenin or Trotsky. My reading of late has been the Police Manual.'

'I can lend you a copy of *Das Kapital.*'

He smiled and shook his head. 'Thank you, but I'd rather stick to the Police Manual.'

There was a discreet cough from the doorway. Mrs Walker was standing there, now wearing an apron. 'Dinner is served, m'lady,' she announced.

The meal was excellent. It was hard to choose between the food served here and the dishes he'd eaten the previous night at Sir Edwin Drake's. Soup again as the starter, a mushroom soup this time, followed by small pieces of fried cod, then roast lamb with mint sauce and roasted vegetables, and rounded off with a delicious apple tart. *I mustn't allow myself to get used to this quality of food and cooking*, Stark warned himself. *These two meals are it for the year, possibly for longer. Even the annual meal for senior officers at Scotland Yard didn't taste as good as this.*

For Stark, tonight's meal was the preferred one. The food may not have been any better than that served at Sir Edwin's, but Lady Amelia was far more desirable as company. She was amusing, offering anecdotes that pricked the pretentions of many of her social class, encouraging Stark to be scurrilous about the top brass at Scotland Yard, something he tactfully avoided. However, he told her tales of criminals he'd caught where their excuses or the situations in which they'd been apprehended had a humorous aspect, like the unfortunate burglar who'd trapped himself when a sash window had fallen down on him while he was exiting a house, and had been left dangling upside down, his trousers caught in a window catch, until the young Stark, then a beat constable, had come along and found him.

'He claimed he'd been hired to remove the valuables we found in his sack by the owner of the house, but hadn't been able to do the work until two o'clock in the morning because he'd been held up. He then expressed great surprise when the owners of the house woke up and came to the window, and declared they'd never seen him before in their lives. He told me he had obviously got the wrong house.'

'And you believed him?'

'Of course,' smiled Stark. 'My sergeant, however, didn't, and he got six months.'

Their talk flowed easily as they ate and took sips of a delicious wine, although they both avoided topics that might be too personal. There was no talk from her about her former husband. There was none from him about Susan, and neither questioned the other about their private lives.

There was talk of politics, including the Irish situation, but not in any depth – more anecdotes about their respective encounters with Michael Collins and Ned Broy and Erskine Childers.

'Such a fine novelist,' said Amelia of Childers. 'Have you read *The Riddle of the Sands*?'

'I have indeed,' said Stark. 'I thought it was excellent, and it gave me great pleasure to tell Mr Childers so.'

It wasn't until the last mouthful of the delicious apple tart had been finished and their plates pushed to one side that she posed a personal question, when she asked him, 'Aren't you rather young to be a chief inspector?'

'Dead men's shoes, I'm afraid,' replied Stark.

'The war?'

'Just so. When I came home, there was a marked shortage of officers in the detective division. Plenty of them were killed in Flanders. And so I took the opportunities that were offered.'

'Did you have a bad war?'

'Despite people bandying that phrase about, no one had a good war. The best you could hope for was to survive intact. Only a few of us managed that.'

Mrs Walker appeared. 'Will there be anything else, m'lady?'

'No, thank you, Mrs Walker. The meal was excellent. I hope it was to your satisfaction, Paul?'

'Very much so.' He smiled at the housekeeper. 'Thank you very much, Mrs Walker. You are a creator of culinary marvels.'

He saw the housekeeper blush.

'Thank you, sir,' she said. 'Well, if there's nothing else, m'lady, I shall be away to my bed. I shall clear up in the morning.'

'Thank you,' said Amelia. After the housekeeper had left the room, she said to Stark, 'And you are a terrible flatterer.'

'Good work deserves appreciation.'

Amelia looked at the used dishes and glasses left on the table.

'Mrs Walker is being very discreet,' she said. 'Usually, she would clear everything away and wash everything spotless, rather than let things congeal, as she says.' When Stark didn't respond, she asked, 'Are we going to bed?'

'I hope so,' he replied.

She hesitated, then said awkwardly, 'It's been a long time since I've been with anyone. Despite the salacious rumours the papers print about me.'

'The papers print nothing about me,' said Stark, 'but it has been a very long time for me, too. I may disappoint you.'

She looked at him. 'Do you know how rare that is in a man?' she said. 'To even *think* of pleasing the woman.'

He rose and took her hand, and she stood up and lifted her other hand to stroke his face.

'You have beautiful eyes,' she said.

'And you are the most stunning and exhilarating woman I have met in far too long a time.'

She kissed his fingers gently, caressingly, then led him out of the room and towards the stairs.

Their first time was awkward, two people discovering each other's body, but then they became unified as they moved to the same rhythm, slow to begin with, then gaining urgency, quickening, until they both came with loud cries before he collapsed on her.

The second time was slower as they luxuriated in one another, kissing, stroking, caressing, her scent on him, on his fingers, on his tongue, her lips moving over his body in butterfly kisses before he entered her again and they poured into one another.

Afterwards, as they lay there, arms around one another in the tangled sheets, she asked, 'Will you stay?'

'No. I want to, but I want to be there for my son when he gets up in the morning.'

She hugged him closer. 'Do you know how very rare you are, Chief Inspector Stark?'

'No, Lady Amelia Fairfax, but I'd be delighted to have you tell me.'

She smiled broadly at him. 'I've found your flaw!' she announced. 'Vanity!'

He smiled gently back at her. 'I have yet to find yours,' he told her.

She put her arms around him, then pushed him gently on to his back. 'Mine is a great appetite,' she said.

And she climbed on top of him, her legs straddling him, and her mouth found his again.

THIRTY-THREE

S hooting. Guns firing, the sound deafening . . .

Stark jerked his head up from the pillow. He was in his bed, not the trenches.

The sound was from downstairs, from the street door. He pulled on the light and looked at the clock. Six o'clock.

Hastily, he pulled his trousers on and, barefoot, went out of his room on to the landing. His mother was already there, her dressing gown wrapped around her, a worried expression on her face.

'I'll go,' said Stark.

As he went down the stairs, his first thought was that it was one of the Saunders clan, come to exact revenge again, this time for the arrest of Eddie. He stopped by the front door and called out, 'Who is it?'

'Sergeant Danvers, sir!' came the shout.

Stark unbolted the door.

Danvers was standing there in the dark. 'Sorry to wake you up, sir. The chief super telephoned me at half past five. He sent me to get you, urgently. There's been another shooting.'

'Where? Who?'

'Regent's Park. Walter Parrot, the owner of the *Daily Bugle*.'

'I'll get dressed and be with you.' He saw the taxi standing by the kerb. 'No cars in the motor pool?'

'A taxi was quicker, sir. And he did say it was urgent.'

Stark nodded, closed the door and hurried back inside. Sarah had come down the stairs and was looking anxiously at him.

'It's Sergeant Danvers,' Stark told her. 'There's been another killing. I've got to go. Will you explain to Stephen?'

'Of course,' she said. 'Who is it?'

He hesitated. 'Some newspaper owner,' he said. 'I haven't got all the details yet. I'll tell you when I get back.'

With that, he hurried into his room and pulled his clothes on. *I should wash*, he thought. *I still have the scent of her on me.* But there was no time. He would wash when he got to Scotland Yard, later. Right now, getting to the scene of the latest crime was more urgent.

He hurried out to the street and joined Danvers in the back of the taxi.

'Park Square East, Regent's Park,' Danvers told the driver.

As the taxi moved off, Danvers said to Stark, 'The chief super also said I should ask you to get a telephone installed at home.'

'Or did he say you should *tell* me to get one put in?'

'It would be wrong for me to tell a superior officer anything.'

'So, what do we know about the shooting?' asked Stark.

'Apparently, the butler heard the doorbell at five o'clock. He answered it, and a small man was there who said he had to see Mr Parrot.'

'At five o'clock in the morning?'

'It seems that Mr Parrot is a very early bird. He likes to be at the *Daily Bugle* in Fleet Street when the London editions roll off the press at six. It seems he usually leaves the house at about quarter past five.'

'Suggesting the gunman knew his routine.'

'Yes, sir.'

'It still seems odd: a stranger turning up at his house at that time of the day, and someone like Walter Parrot seeing him. I presume he did, or did the man burst into the house?'

'No, Mr Parrot went to the door to talk to the man.'

'Why?'

'According to the butler, the man said he knew who the killer was.'

'Well, he got that right,' said Stark wryly.

'Mr Parrot went to the door, and when he got there, the man pulled out a pistol and shot him. One shot in the chest, one in the face.'

'Description of the man?'

'Same as the others. Small, thin.'

'Where was the butler when the actual shooting took place?'

'He'd gone back into the house. He was making coffee for Mr Parrot when he heard the shots.'

'So it was the butler who called in the killing?'

'No, that was a Miss Agatha Redford. She's Mr Parrot's private secretary. She was . . . er . . . staying the night. Because she'd had to work late. She made a point of telling the duty officer that.'

Stark nodded. 'Was Parrot married?'

'No, sir. He was, but he's divorced.'

Regent's Park, reflected Stark. The scene of the first killing, of Lord Amersham. Surely that couldn't be the connection? Some neighbourhood dispute? No. The second murder had occurred in Maida Vale. What did a newspaper proprietor have in common with a peer of the realm and an MP?

He thought about the *Daily Bugle*. A so-called newspaper that spat out propaganda on behalf of the right wing of the Conservative Party. So that would put Walter Parrot in league with Lord Amersham. But not with Tobias Smith who, by all accounts, tended towards the more liberal wing. But there was a connection here and, with this third shooting, they were getting close to finding it; he could sense it.

The house in Park Square East was large, detached, clearly expensive, but there was no obvious security. No gates, just an open drive to a large garage at the side of the house. In the darkness of pre-dawn, Stark saw police examining the steps of the house and the grounds immediately in front of it, searching for clues: footprints, signs that would point to the killer.

We already know the killer, thought Stark. *He's the same man who killed the other two. We know his height, his build, the clothes he wears, and that he's a deadly and accurate shot with a pistol. What we don't know is who he is, and why he's doing it.*

Stark sought out the officer in charge, Sergeant Jed Roberts from the nearby Regent's Park station.

'A bad business,' sighed Roberts. 'That's two here in a short space of time. We'll be getting a bad reputation.'

'Where's the body?' asked Stark.

'Taken away already,' said Roberts. 'I'll do a report on how the scene looked before they took it. It was blocking the door, see, so we had to get shot of it.'

Stark nodded. 'Miss Redford and the butler?' he asked.

'In the house. The butler's name is Hoskins. He's pretty shaken up. Miss Redford seems to be coping better, but I wouldn't bet on that lasting.' He hesitated, then added quietly, 'I think her and Parrot were more than just businessman and secretary, if you get my drift. I don't want to spread gossip, but it might be worth being aware of that when you talk to her.'

'Anyone else in the house beside them?'

'Housekeeper, two maids, a boy who does the boots,' said Roberts. 'They were all up when it happened, working below stairs. It's an early start for everyone in this household.'

Stark and Danvers headed for the house and rang the bell.

A police constable opened the door. 'Morning, sir,' he said, recognizing Stark. 'I'm just here because the butler's a bit shook up at the moment.'

'Understood,' said Stark. 'Where is he?'

'In the kitchen, with the housekeeper, a Mrs Holmes. They're feeding him brandies to keep him steady.'

'I heard the bell!' A woman's voice made them turn to see a smartly dressed woman in her early thirties approaching them, an anxious look on her face.

'Miss Redford, sir,' whispered the constable.

'Thank you, Constable,' Stark murmured. He made a slight bow of his head towards Miss Redford.

'Miss Redford, I'm Detective Chief Inspector Stark and this is Detective Sergeant Danvers.'

He could see she was working hard to hold herself together. She was a tall, slim woman, her dark hair cut short in a bob, attractive features highlighted by a touch of make-up and lipstick. Although she appeared outwardly collected, the rapid blinking of her eyes and the way she unconsciously twisted her hands together betrayed the fact that she was battling to stop herself from breaking down, at least in this immediate moment.

'I'm sorry to trouble you at this difficult time, but we need to get as much information as we can, as swiftly as we can, in order to try to apprehend the culprit.'

'I understand,' she said.

'You were his private secretary?'

'Yes. Not just for the newspaper, but for his political activities. He trusted me.'

'His political activities?' queried Stark.

'He sat on various committees.' She shook her head unhappily. 'I know he was worried after what happened to Lord Amersham and poor Tobias Smith . . .'

'Was he involved with them, politically?'

'Well, not really, but he chaired one of the committees they were both on. Although Mr Smith wasn't actually on it, officially, he had attended a session—'

'Which committee was this?' asked Stark, suddenly alert.

'The Passchendaele Memorial Fund Charitable Commission. Walter – Mr Parrot – was chairman of the committee. I acted as secretary at most of the meetings because Mr Parrot knew I could be trusted to keep an accurate record of what happened. You know, minutes and keeping the committee informed. You'd be surprised at how lax some of these committee secretaries are. Anyway, after poor Mr Smith was shot, I said to Mr Parrot that he ought to go to the police, that there might be a connection. But he dismissed it. He was so brave! So dismissive of his own safety! He had enemies, you know, because of the attitude of the paper.'

The Passchendaele Memorial Fund Charitable Commission!

'But we checked Mr Smith's background, the various committees he served on, and there was no mention of him being on that particular committee.'

'No, as I told you, he wasn't officially on the committee. It just so happened that a benefits board was due to meet to hear applications, and Walter invited Mr Smith to sit in for that one session. I think he was hoping to persuade Mr Smith to join the board.'

'What happens at the benefits board?'

'People make applications for funds, which are heard by the committee. The committee then takes the decisions on allocating money.'

'Who else was on the board?'

'Brigadier Wellesely, Lord Thomson, Sir Edward Hinds. They made up the five committee members, along with Mr Parrot and Lord Amersham.'

'So at the benefits board when Mr Smith took part . . .'

'That's why Walter – Mr Parrot – invited Mr Smith to sit in, through Lord Amersham. Because the brigadier, Lord Thomson and Sir Edward weren't available for that particular meeting – they are held quarterly – and Mr Parrot liked there to be at least three members on the board to hear the applications. It made it . . . fairer. Less as if it was just Mr Parrot and Lord Amersham making the decisions.'

'When was this particular meeting?'

'In August. The next board is due to meet next month, November.'

'May I use your telephone?' asked Stark.

Miss Redford led him and Danvers to the library and pointed him to the telephone. Stark dialled the Scotland Yard switchboard.

'Put me through to Chief Superintendent Benson,' he said. 'Either in his office or at his home. It's Chief Inspector Stark. It's very urgent.'

A few seconds later, he was talking to Benson at his home.

'I think I've found the connection between the murders, sir. All three victims sat on a meeting of the board of the Passchendaele Memorial Fund Charitable Commission, allocating funds. My suspicion is that someone took revenge after being turned down.'

'Why on earth would anyone do something as drastic as that, just for being turned down?' asked Benson, shocked.

'That's what Sergeant Danvers and I are going to look into,' said Stark. 'But if I'm right, then I think that others associated with the charity could be at risk, especially those on the board. I'm telephoning you immediately because I think it's worth putting police protection on the three remaining members: Brigadier Wellesely, Lord Thomson and Sir Edward Hinds.'

'I'll see to it at once,' said Benson. 'I'll also tell the Home Secretary we've found the motive.'

'At the moment it's still a theory, sir,' said Stark warily. 'But the evidence does seem to point to it.' Stark hung up and turned to Miss Redford. 'Just to make sure I've got it right: there was a meeting in August of the benefits board at which people put in applications to the charity for funding, and at that meeting the board consisted of Mr Parrot, Lord Amersham and Mr Smith?'

'Yes,' nodded Miss Redford.

'No one else was on the board at that meeting?'

'No.'

'Was anyone else in attendance in any other capacity?'

'Well, me, obviously, because I took the minutes.'

'No one else?'

She shook her head.

'Miss Redford, I don't wish to alarm you unnecessarily, but I believe it would be best for you to have a police bodyguard, just until we've apprehended the person who committed these murders.'

'Do you think that's necessary?' asked Redford.

'There were four people at that board meeting. Three of them have been killed.'

'But all I did was take the minutes. I didn't even speak at the meeting. It was the board members who asked the questions of the applicants and made the decisions.'

'That may be the case, but I'm not taking any chances. We'll station an officer on duty outside your home. There'll be more than one of them, working in shifts. We'll also put officers on duty at your office.'

'Won't they cause inconvenience?'

Not as much as shooting you dead, thought Stark. Aloud, he said, 'They will be experienced officers, Miss Redford. Rest assured, they won't cause any more inconvenience than is necessary. Right now, I'd like a copy of the minutes of that meeting in August, along with a list of the people who applied for funding.'

'Of course. They're in Mr Parrot's study. I'll get them.'

As she headed for the door, Stark added, 'Until we get your protection formally arranged, please do not leave this building.'

She nodded and left the library.

'What next, sir?' asked Danvers. 'Talk to the butler, Hoskins?'

'You do that, Sergeant. Get as much of a description as you can. I'm going to go through the minutes of this charity board meeting. That's where our killer will be.'

'You really think it's that simple?' asked Danvers. 'Someone who was turned down?'

'This Passchendaele Memorial Fund is the only concrete link we've found between the three victims.'

'Yes, but killing them because they turned someone down is a bit of an extreme reaction,' said Danvers.

'That depends on how extreme the need for funding was,' said Stark. 'Desperate people do desperate things.'

'Yes, but this is a charity!' protested Danvers. 'What sort of person takes revenge on a charity?'

'That's what we're going to find out,' said Stark, as Miss Redford returned with a box file.

'Here,' she said. 'These are the minutes of the meetings, and the applications that were received before the meeting in August.'

'Thank you,' said Stark, taking the box file from her.

'Will there be anything else?'

'Not at the moment, but we may need your help later on.'

'If you need me, I'll be in Mr Parrot's study,' she said. 'It's just down the hall.'

She left, and Stark sat down at a table, opening the box file.

'If you want me, sir, I'll be in the kitchen with the butler,' said Danvers.

Stark opened the paper file marked *Minutes of Board Meeting 12th August 1921*. As well as the typed minutes, there were about half a dozen letters of application, and other documents, some written, some typed.

'I shall be here, Sergeant,' said Stark, and he began with the minutes of the meeting.

There had been seven applications for funding at that meeting. One familiar name on the list caught his eye, a name from the past that hit him hard and caused him to catch his breath. Rennick. Alice Rennick, widow of Ted Rennick.

Ted and Alf Rennick. Brothers from Bethnal Green, Alf the oldest, Ted two years younger. They'd been in Stark's unit, Privates Alf and Ted Rennick to his Captain Stark. Stark had been next to Ted when he had been shot through the heart. Stark could see him now, his body falling to lie half in and half out of the mud that clung to them all.

Stark sorted through the papers in the file until he found Alice Rennick's letter of application for charitable funding. It was brief and to the point, written in the large awkward lettering of someone who wasn't used to writing.

Dear Sirs.

My late husband, Ted Rennick, was killed at Passchendaele while fighting for King and Country. We have two sons, John and Jeff. They are both aged seven, being twins. They are both very ill and the doctor says they need special

medicines if they are to get better. We do not have the
money for these medicines. The doctor says if they do not
get the medicine they will die. Please can you let me have
the money so we can get these medicines that will save my
two sons. Their father died at Passchendaele and I know
you are a Charity for people who gave their lives for this
Country at Passchendaele.

    Yours faithfully

    Alice Rennick.

Against Alice Rennick's name on the list was the word *Rejected*.

Then Stark realized that against six of the applicant's names,
that same word had been written. Out of the seven, the only
application that had been granted was one from the Watling Street
Memorial Committee, asking for funding towards the erection
of a statue of General Sir Hubert Gough.

Gough!

As Stark read through the documents relating to the other
applicants, a feeling of outrage rose inside him. As well as Alice
Rennick, the other five who'd been rejected were all from indi-
viduals who had written because they were suffering hardship.
There was only one other who had a connection with the Third
Battle of Ypres, a man who claimed to have fought in the battle
and been so badly wounded that he was unable to work. Unlike
Ted Rennick, Stark didn't recognize the name, Arnold Lane. But
there had been thousands and thousands of them engaged in that
battle. The casualty figures had been staggering: 310,000 Allied
casualties alone at that Third Battle of Ypres, 28,000 of them at
Passchendaele. It was a wonder anyone had survived.

Stark ran his finger down the list of the other rejected
applicants.

The mother of a sailor who'd been killed at the Battle of
Jutland.

Two separate applications from women whose husbands had
been killed at the Battle of the Somme in 1916. Remembered as
the bloodiest day in British military history, reflected Stark, with
60,000 British casualties on the first day of the battle, 1st July.
A bloodbath.

The final application was from the sister of a navvy who'd
died while digging the tunnels at Messines.

Five women and one man had applied for money. All had been rejected.

The return of Sergeant Danvers made him look up from the papers.

'I've spoken to the butler and got his statement,' Danvers said. 'It wasn't easy. He's still in a state of shock. That, coupled with the brandies, made it hard for him to focus. But I've got enough to confirm it's the same bloke.'

'Did he get a sight of the man's face?' asked Stark.

Danvers shook his head. 'He said the man was wrapped up against the cold. He had a scarf pulled up.' He gestured at the open box file. 'Get anything, sir?'

'Seven applications for funding were made at that August board meeting,' said Stark. 'Six were rejected. The only one that was accepted for financial assistance was from the Watling Street Memorial Committee, who asked for funding towards erecting a statue of General Sir Hubert Gough.' He shook his head in obvious disgust. 'The man was arrogant and useless. Why on earth would anyone want to erect a statue to him?'

'He did launch the first offensive at Passchendaele, sir,' pointed out Danvers. 'With the Fifth Army.'

'His attitude – his arrogance – led to the slaughter of too many British soldiers. Even Haig recognized that, which was why he had him removed from command.'

'I didn't realize General Gough was removed from his command,' frowned Danvers.

'All right, not *officially*,' said Stark. 'Haig did it by moving Gough and his Fifth Army to a lesser position and putting Plumer and the Second Army in the key offensive role.' He let out a sigh. 'Trust me, Sergeant. I was there.'

'At Passchendaele?'

Stark nodded. He looked at the list of applicants. 'All these other people who applied – families of ex-soldiers, ex-sailors, all of whom I'd bet are in desperate need – and they turn them down and give the money towards a statue of Hubert Gough!' He shook his head. 'Unbelievable! It's no wonder someone shot the bastards.'

'Sir!' Danvers stared at his inspector, shocked.

'You're right, Sergeant,' Stark apologized. 'That remark was uncalled for and inappropriate.'

'Anyone stand out as likely?' asked Danvers.

'Five of the applicants are women; only one from a man. So, unless our killer is a crackshot woman, it's either the one man or a close relative or friend of one of the women.'

'Who's the man?' asked Danvers.

'His name's Arnold Lane, and according to his letter he was badly wounded at Passchendaele. Whether he's our man or not depends on the sort of wound he suffered. If he's missing an arm or a leg, or been blinded, we can count him out. I suggest we split the list. I'll take three of the names, you take three. That way we can speed things up. We need to identify our killer quickly and get hold of him before he kills any more.' He selected three letters of application, which he passed to Danvers. 'You take these. Arnold Lane, the wounded survivor of Passchendaele, and Mrs Victoria Nelson and Mrs Ellen Gates, both of whom lost their husbands at the Somme. I'll take the other three. You'll find their addresses on their letters of application.'

THIRTY-FOUR

Arnold Lane and his wife, Elsie, lived in a tiny terraced house in Hoxton. Lane was in his thirties, according to his letter of application, but he looked much older. He was bald and very overweight, possibly the result of being unable to get around easily. He had one leg missing, cut off just above the knee. In no way did he resemble the description of the assassin.

'I'm here,' said Danvers, after he'd introduced himself to the couple, 'to investigate recent events involving the Passchendaele Memorial Fund.'

They were sitting in the small kitchen, Lane's chair drawn up close to the open fire.

'Them bastards!' spat Lane angrily.

'Arnie!' said his horrified wife.

'Bunch of crooks! Arrest the lot, that's what I say. Obtaining money under false pretences!'

'Arnie, you ought to be careful what you say,' cautioned his wife. 'This is a policeman!'

'I know he's a policeman, which is why I say he should arrest 'em!'

'I understand you applied for a grant from them—'

'Applied!' interrupted Lane, his anger clearly getting the better of him. 'Didn't get it! Was never going to, as I found out! Bastards!'

'Arnie!' his wife reprimanded him again, but he ignored her, obviously gearing up to launch into a further angry tirade to vent his fury.

'You attended a board meeting in August . . .'

'At the offices of the *Bugle*. It turned out that's where they held their meetings because the editor or owner of the paper was chairman of the fake outfit.' He spat into the grate. 'I've never opened that paper since, or allowed it into this house! It was the stories they ran about that so-called charity in the paper that made me think of applying!' He pointed at the stump that was all that was left of his right leg. 'I lost this at Passchendaele, so when I read about the good works they were supposed to be doing, and saw what they were called, I thought: Them's the people for me! Things have been a bit of a struggle for Elsie and me, see, since I come back from the war, what with losing me leg.

'So I sent off a letter applying, and I got a letter back inviting me to attend this meeting at the offices of the *Bugle* in Fleet Street. Well, I was cock-a-hoop! But it was no easy journey, I can tell you, getting all the way there with just one leg. That crutch they gave me plays hell on me arm!'

'It does,' agreed Elsie, deciding to add her voice to her husband's sense of outrage.

'I put on me best suit,' continued Lane.

'His only suit,' added Elsie.

'No need to tell the sergeant all our details, love,' Lane reprimanded her primly. Then he continued his tale. 'I put on me medal, the one I won at Passchendaele. I thought: That'll clinch it.

'Three of them, there were. And a woman keeping notes.'

'Can you remember who they were?' asked Danvers.

'I'll never forget 'em!' snorted Lane. 'That Lord Amersham,

the one who was shot, he was there. And that MP bloke, Tobias Smith.' He calmed a bit as he added, 'He wasn't too bad. Didn't say much. It was the other two as did most of the talking. That Lord Amersham bloke, and Walter bloody Parrot.' He hesitated, then said, 'Someone shot that Smith bloke as well, didn't they?'

'They did,' nodded Danvers.

'Well, if you ask me, they shot the wrong person. The one who deserved shooting was that Walter Parrot! Bastard! It was his name on the letter that got me to go all the way over there, and finally, at the end, they said no.' He shook his head in disbelief.

'What was your response?' asked Danvers.

'What d'you think it was!' burst out Lane. 'I was gutted! "Why?" I asked 'em. "I was at Passchendaele. I lost me leg there. I won a medal there!"'

'Careful, Arnie, you'll give yourself one of your attacks,' warned his wife.

Lane nodded and stopped, then began breathing in deeply to calm himself down.

'What did they say to that?' asked Danvers.

'They said the fund was about raising money to put up memorials to commemorate the war. Plaques on walls. Statues. War memorials. So I said if that was the case, why did they drag me all the way there when they knew the answer was gonna be no? Then this bloke Parrot says it was because they had to be seen to be fair.' He let out a laugh that was a mixture of outrage and incredulity. '"Fair!" I said to him. "What's fair about making a man with one leg suffer the pain of coming all the way here to be spat at like this!" I told 'em: I said the biggest memorials were the people who'd come home without legs and arms, or blind. That's where the money should be going!'

Stark sat in the front room of the neat little house in Holloway, within the shadow of the prison. It was in a poor area, but the house had been kept spotless by Beatrice Plum, the sister of Fred Plum, the navvy who'd died digging tunnels at Messines.

'Do you know about the mines of Messines?'

'I was there,' said Stark.

She looked at him, astonished. 'At Messines?'

'I was nine miles away when they went off.'

Near enough to be thrown to the ground and deafened for hours after by the biggest explosion ever, so loud it was heard a hundred miles away in London. Six hundred tons of explosives spread across twenty tunnels, dug out of the Flanders clay by hand, by miners and navvies, deep beneath the German front line. It was reckoned that 10,000 German soldiers had died instantly as the explosives were detonated beneath them.

'Fred, my brother, was a navvy. He'd worked on the London underground railway, digging tunnels out of London clay, deep down, so he knew what he was doing. Anyway, if you was there, you know they sent as many diggers over to France as they could to dig those tunnels. Miners. Navvies. All blokes who were used to digging underground. And because the Germans were above 'em, they had to do it all by hand, because if they'd used machines the Germans would have heard.'

Stark nodded, the memories coming back. The sight of hundreds of men, armed with picks and shovels, wheeling barrels of clay out of the tunnels. Thousands and thousands of tons of the stuff, wet and heavy and stinking.

Six shillings a day, the diggers were paid. When news of their wages spread among the troops, the soldiers were outraged, because the soldiers were paid just one shilling a day. There was even talk of mutiny unless the soldiers were paid the same rate. Some soldiers offered to be diggers instead of carrying on the fighting, but that sort of talk died down, especially after some of the tunnels collapsed, burying the diggers, suffocating them alive.

'Fred was one of the first to go out there, in February 1917,' continued Miss Plum. 'He was there right up until just the day before they went off on the second of June, digging the whole time.' She stopped and her face clouded over as the bitter memory came back. 'The telegram said he'd been killed on the first of June. Some of his mates told us later the tunnel he'd been working on had collapsed. The struts had sunk in the clay and the roof had come down. They said it was because they was working fast near the end, because they had to get all the tunnels finished on time for the big attack, and maybe someone wasn't doing their job properly of checking the struts.

'Anyway, Fred died. He was one of ten who died in that particular roof cave-in. Without him and what he did, we wouldn't have won the war.' She shook her head. 'We deserved that money to help us. I still don't know why we got turned down.'

The tale that Mrs Victoria Nelson told Danvers was depressingly similar to that he'd heard from Arnold Lane. She'd applied because money was so tight that sometimes she went for three days without eating, unable to afford food. Once she'd fainted in the street, right in front of her neighbour's front door. After the embarrassment of trying to pretend to her neighbour, Mrs Fox, that she was just ill, Mrs Fox had discovered her larder was bare and had persuaded her to apply to the charity for help.

'That's what they're there for, Mrs Nelson,' Mrs Fox had said. 'After all, your Horace gave his life for this country.'

And he had. Horace Nelson had been one of those 60,000 British casualties on the first day of the Battle of the Somme, 1st July 1916.

Like Arnold Lane, she'd trudged across London, on foot because she was unable to afford the bus fare, and faced the panel.

'And they turned me down, Sergeant,' she said, her voice plaintive and still puzzled. 'That's what I thought was cruel. Making me go all the way there just to turn me down. They could have written a letter saying no, couldn't they? It would have saved me a lot of bother.'

'Our son, Bill, was killed on the *Chester* at Jutland,' Mrs Conway told Stark, sitting in the front room of her small house in Leytonstone. 'He was part of a gun crew. The thing that got us was all we had was this telegram telling us he'd died, but no one told us about how, or what happened at the battle. It was only after the war we found out. There was nothing in the papers at the time, nothing. Not till they had that big funeral for Jack Cornwell.'

Jack Cornwell VC, at sixteen the youngest winner of the Victoria Cross, and a member of one of the gun crews on the *Chester*, the same ship Bill Conway had served on. Stark wondered if Bill Conway and Jack Cornwell might have both been part of the same gun crew.

'My Ernie said afterwards it was because so many were killed, if people found out they might lose their . . . their . . . something . . .' She struggled for the right word.

'Morale,' prompted Stark gently.

'Yes, that was it. Lose their morale.' She shook her head. 'People were more concerned about losing the ones they loved.'

Stark remembered the details. The Battle of Jutland in 1916 had been the biggest sea battle ever. Bigger than Trafalgar, bigger than the Spanish Armada. And with it came the massive loss of life. Six thousand British sailors killed. Hundreds wounded. Three British battlecruisers sunk, along with three armoured cruisers and eight destroyers. Two and a half thousand German sailors dead, hundreds wounded. The Germans had lost one dreadnought, one battlecruiser, four light cruisers and five torpedo boats. On paper, comparing the losses, it had been a German victory. But after the battle the German navy had retreated back to German waters and stayed there for the rest of the war. So, a British victory, but at enormous cost.

'Where's Ernie?' enquired Stark.

She dropped her head. 'He died,' she said. 'He was never right after he came back from the war. His lungs, you see. He was gassed. He died last year.'

'How did you find out about the Passchendaele Memorial Fund?'

'It was my friend, Muriel. She gets the *Bugle* and she'd read in there about this charity and what good work they were doing, and she said I ought to ask for help, having lost both my husband and my son to the war.' She looked appealingly at Stark as she added, 'Things haven't been good, and a war widow's pension doesn't stretch far.'

'No,' said Stark sympathetically.

It was the same story he'd heard time and time again since coming back from the war. Widows bringing up children alone, with very little money, and the children getting into trouble with the police for crimes such as theft, shoplifting, burglary.

'You must have felt very angry when they turned you down,' said Stark.

'That's what Muriel said,' sighed Mrs Conway. 'But I didn't. It's what I've come to expect. You don't get anything in this life. Nothing good, anyway.'

'If I had my way, I'd castrate them!' snarled Mrs Gates to Danvers.

After the quiet resignation of Mrs Nelson, Mrs Gates was as angry as Arnold Lane had been. No, angrier.

'Shoot the bastards? That's what you're here to find out, isn't it?'

'Well . . .' began Danvers awkwardly.

She didn't let him get any further. 'Not only would I have shot the bastards, I'd have castrated 'em and cut 'em up like a butcher's shop! And danced on the pieces! My Joe died at the Somme, gave his life so them pieces of shit could wallow in luxury! When I read in the paper they'd been shot, I cheered! If I could, I'd shake the hand of the person who shot them!'

It was Stark's last call, the one he'd been putting off, but the one he knew that *he* had to make rather than give it to Danvers.

He knocked at the door of the tiny terraced house in Bethnal Green. The door opened and he looked down at the face of Mrs Rennick, the widowed mother of Alf and Ted. It had been two years since he'd last knocked at this same door. She'd looked old then, aged by the news of the death of her youngest son. The intervening years had aged her even further.

'Good afternoon, Mrs Rennick,' he said.

She looked at him in surprise. 'Captain Stark!' she exclaimed.

'Not any more. I'm with the police now.'

'Yes, I heard. I saw your name in paper.'

'May I come in?' asked Stark.

She hesitated. 'The house isn't at its best . . .' she began.

'I promise I won't take up much of your time,' Stark said, doing his best to reassure her.

She opened the door wider to let him in. 'Front parlour's best,' she said. 'But I ain't dusted lately.'

Stark followed her into the front parlour. Like the front room at his parents' home, the room was kept for special occasions, special visitors. It was drab and gloomy, the furniture dark, more of a museum than a room to live in. On the mantelpiece he saw a photograph of Alf and Ted, standing proudly to attention side by side in their uniforms, ready to go to war. Only Alf had come back.

'The person I came to see is Alice,' he said as they sat down. 'Is she in?'

'Alice?'

Mrs Rennick looked at him, and Stark saw the anger and hurt in her face, and realized he'd made a big mistake.

'I'm sorry, I realize I've just said something wrong . . .' he began to apologize, but she cut him off.

'She's dead,' she said, the words curt.

'I'm very sorry,' said Stark. 'I hadn't realized. How did she die?'

Mrs Rennick carried on looking at him, silent, obviously torn up by inner turmoil. The death had to be recent, thought Stark. She had been at the charity board meeting just a few weeks ago.

'We don't talk about it,' said Mrs Rennick, her lips pursed, protecting and hiding a bad memory.

'I understand,' nodded Stark. 'Is Alf around?'

She shook her head. 'No,' she said. Then she dropped her head, averting her eyes from his. 'I'm sorry, Captain Stark. We were always very appreciative of what you did, coming round to tell us about Ted. Alf had told us, but it meant a lot, you coming. But I've got things to do.'

'Of course,' said Stark, getting up. 'I'm sorry to have upset you, Mrs Rennick. If I'd known about Alice, I'd never have troubled you this way. But would you ask Alf to give me a call. He can find me at Scotland Yard. Detective Chief Inspector Stark. If I'm not there, just leave a message.'

She nodded. 'I'll tell him when I see him.'

With that, she walked him back to the front door and let him out.

The local nick, he decided. *If they don't know what happened, they'll know who to ask.*

He ordered his driver to take him to Bethnal Green police station, where he found the sergeant on duty at the front desk studying the horses in the racing pages of the paper.

'DCI Stark, Scotland Yard,' he said, showing his warrant card.

'Yes, sir,' said the duty sergeant, suddenly standing up straight at the arrival of this DCI from Scotland Yard, at the same time hastily pushing the paper beneath the desk.

'Do you know the Rennick family?' asked Stark. 'Hazelton Street. Alf Rennick. His late sister-in-law Alice. Alf's mother, Mrs Rennick.'

The sergeant frowned and shook his head. 'Sorry, sir,' he apologized. 'They don't come to mind. But then the only ones we really know are those who are trouble.'

'The Rennicks are law-abiding,' nodded Stark. 'Can you do

me a favour? Can you find out when Alice Rennick died? And how?'

'Certainly, sir. I'll have a word with the officer who has Hazelton Street as his beat. He's bound to know if there's any sort of talk.'

'Can you get hold of him today? We need this as a matter of urgency.'

'I'll make sure I do, sir.'

Stark handed the sergeant his card, with the phone number of Scotland Yard on it. 'Telephone me when you've got the information. If I'm not there, give the information to my sergeant, DS Danvers. If we're both out, leave a message and I'll get back to you.'

THIRTY-FIVE

Danvers was already in the office, going through the notes of his interviews, when Stark returned to Scotland Yard. 'How did you get on?' asked Stark. 'Did you see them all?'

Danvers nodded. 'I think we can rule out Arnold Lane, sir. He's very angry about being rejected, but he's severely disabled. One leg, and very overweight. There's no way he's our gunman.

'Similarly, Mrs Nelson. Not just the fact that she's a woman, she didn't seem to have the same anger about being rejected that the other two had. She seemed to take it as her lot in life, just one more thing to deal with and bear up under.

'Mrs Gates, on the other hand, is a candidate. OK, not herself. She's tall and not particularly thin. But she is very angry about the rejection, and she may have relatives who are good with a gun whom she might have persuaded to carry out the shootings.

'What about yours?'

'My gut feeling is that we can rule out both Miss Plum and Mrs Conway. Although they may have relatives or friends who feel much stronger about the rejection than they did, so we might have to look into that. But the one I'm waiting to find out about—'

The phone ringing interrupted him. Stark picked it up. 'DCI Stark,' he said. Suddenly, he was alert. He mouthed the words 'Bethnal Green' at Danvers, then listened, making notes. Finally, he said, 'You're sure of that?' Then, 'Thank you very much indeed. Pass on my thanks to Constable Harris.' He hung up and said, 'That's the call I was waiting for. I think we have the most likely candidate. Alf Rennick. Brother-in-law of Alice Rennick.'

'Oh?' queried Danvers.

'Apparently, about a month after her application for help was rejected, Alice Rennick's twin sons died. A few weeks later, she killed herself. She slashed her throat with a razor.' *Just like Eve Angel*, he thought bitterly.

'And this chap, Alf Rennick?'

'Ted's older brother,' explained Stark. 'I knew them both. They were in my unit during the war. Ted was killed. Alf fits the bill too, as far as the description goes. And he was an excellent shot.' He was also a man who cared deeply about his family, Stark remembered.

'So we need to get hold of him,' said Danvers.

'We do,' nodded Stark. Then he added, 'But if I know Alf, I think he'll get hold of me.' He looked at the clock. 'Five o'clock, Sergeant. You've had a long day. Time to get home.'

'What about you, sir?'

Stark hesitated. 'I'm concerned about Alf Rennick. If he is our man, then he might strike again tonight.'

'Against whom? He's killed the three men who were on the panel that day.'

'There's still Miss Redford.'

'You think he might go for her next?' asked Danvers.

Stark shook his head. 'No. Killing women isn't Alf's style. But just in case I'm wrong, I think I'll check with the local station and make sure they've still got a guard in place on her.'

Danvers left, and Stark made the call. He was reassured by the duty sergeant that there was still a police guard on Miss Redford, one inside the house and one outside in the street. Reassured, he went down to the motor pool and caught a car home.

Fog had started to come down, thick, peas-soupery green tendrils of fog, which slowed the progress of the car on its way towards

Camden Town. Time and time again lately, the thick fog had come down to envelop London, especially in the early evenings, when the coal fires had just been lit and the smoke belched out from thousands of chimneys to mingle with that from the factories, the railway stations, the traffic. If there was a wind, it sometimes helped to lift the smoke up, but on an evening like this when the barometer showed heavy cloud pushing down, mixing with the thick smoke, it was as if the streets of London were filled with slow-moving walls of evil-smelling, foul-tasting green.

It was six o'clock before the car finally pulled up outside 61 Plender Street.

'Goodnight, sir,' said the driver. 'Usual time in the morning?'

'No,' answered Stark. 'Tell the roster sergeant to have me picked up at nine o'clock. I've got something to do first.'

'Very good, sir.'

Stark shut the car door, and the car moved off slowly, apprehensively, into the fog.

Tomorrow morning I shall take Stephen to school, he promised himself.

He went to his front door and was just taking his key out when he heard a metallic click, a noise he hadn't heard in a long time.

'Evening, Captain Stark,' said the muffled voice.

Alf Rennick.

'Evening, Alf,' he said, keeping his voice casual, although he didn't feel it. Where was Alf? It was always difficult in fog to get a precise location, even when listening for sounds.

'I've got a gun,' said Alf.

'Of course you have. Come to shoot me as well?'

'No. Providing you don't do anything. I just want to talk. Let's go for a walk.'

'On a foggy night like this?'

'It suits me. If you try anything, I can shoot you and just disappear. But I hope you don't. I always liked you. So did Ted.'

'Where are we going?'

'Just round the block. That'll do me. You go first.'

Stark nodded and set off along the street. As they passed a street lamp, the light cut momentarily through the clouds of fog and Stark turned his head. Alf was just a few paces behind him, dressed the same as the description of the shooter: working clothes, cap pulled down, scarf over his mouth. Stark could see the glint of light on the metal of the pistol in Alf's hand.

'I'm warning you, Captain. Don't try anything. I'm good with this. You know that. I was good with a rifle, and even better with a pistol.'

'I do indeed, Alf.'

'Been a long time.'

'It has,' said Stark. 'We'll be getting to the end of the road soon. Any particular way you want me to go?'

'Turn right,' said Alf. 'That'll keep us going nicely in a square.' There was a pause, the sound of their boots on the pavement echoing back to them in the fog. Then Alf said, 'I knew you were on to me when Mum said you'd called round.'

'Yes. I'm sorry to have disturbed your mum. I didn't know about Alice.'

'No reason you should,' said Alf bitterly.

'What happened?'

'Alice didn't do so well after the war. She had the nippers, the twin boys, John and Jeff, and things were hard. With the men coming back from the war, she got kicked out of her job in the factory. They wanted men again, see. I won't bore you with the details, but things got tougher, and this year the twins got sick. Not just ordinary sick, but they needed special doctors. Special medicines. Of course, we hadn't got that kind of money. It was made worse 'cos Alice didn't even get a war pension, like a lot of widows did. They asked her for her marriage lines before she could qualify. Well, you know that not everyone in our class does things like that. I mean, weddings cost money, and it don't mean you're any more together just 'cos a vicar says a few words over you. But they were a real couple, Ted and Alice. A proper couple. More so than plenty who've got all the proper marriage lines. Know what I mean?'

Stark nodded.

'Like I say, things were bad. Then we heard about this charity that had been set up. The Passchendaele Charity something or other. "That's it," says Alice. "Ted was killed at Passchendaele fighting for his king and country." There's no one more deserving of that sort of charity than Ted's family, his kids. So she went for it. She got the paperwork to apply and put it in all proper, although me and her mum had to help her with the writing and spelling. Writing was never Alice's best point. And she got this letter telling her to report to this board, where her application would be heard.

'She was so positive when she got that letter! "We're gonna get it!" she said. "We'll get the money and my kids will be saved!" Because by now things for the twins was getting worse. They looked really bad. *Really* bad.

'And off she went to this board, and they turned her down.

'When she come back, she was like a dead woman. She had their names, the three blokes who'd turned her down. All toffs. Water Parrot, he was the chairman. Lord Amersham. And an MP, Tobias Smith. There was some woman there as well, but she was just the person who kept notes of what was said. It was the three blokes what took the decision.

'Anyway, a month later the twins died. John died first and Jeff died the next day. That was about the middle of September. A week later, Alice did herself in. Slit her throat with Ted's old razor. I don't know why she'd kept it, but she'd kept a load of his old things. Mementoes. She couldn't handle the twins dying like that, not when she'd been so sure she was gonna get the money.'

'Everyone who applied that day got turned down,' said Stark. 'Well, almost everyone. They gave money for some people who wanted to put up a statue of General Gough.'

Alf stared at him. 'A statue of Gough!'

'That was my reaction too, when I read the minutes of the meeting.'

'So that's what the money's for? Statues?'

'I assume so,' said Stark. 'I'm not on their committee. But that's what it looks like. I've gone through the minutes of other meetings, and money seems only to have been given out for statues and memorial plaques.'

'No relatives got anything? What about soldiers who were there and got injured?'

Stark shook his head.

'Bastards!' spat Alf.

'So, you killed them.'

'Yeah.' Alf nodded. 'I think I went sort of crazy. I thought of Ted dying the way he did. And how everything was unfair for Alice and his kids after the war. And when I thought of those three toffs, none of whom had actually been in the war, sitting in judgement on Alice and killing her the way they did. Because that's what it amounted to. They served a death sentence on the twins and on her when they did what they did. That money was collected for those of us who suffered at Passchendaele. That was what they called the charity: the Passchendaele Charity.'

'The Passchendaele Memorial Fund Charitable Commission,' Stark corrected him.

'Same thing,' growled Alf.

Stark shook his head. 'It's a *Memorial* Fund,' he said. 'That's what it says in the title. To raise money for memorials.'

Alf scowled. 'It's a cheat!' he snapped. 'I bet you people who gave to it didn't think the money was going to put up statues and things.'

'You may be right,' said Stark.

'Anyway, it all came over me, and I thought, *It ain't right.* They killed her by what they did. The twins died because of them not paying out like they should have done. They were sick kids, for Christ's sake! What sort of person lets sick kids die! And it wasn't even their money!

'So, I decided to have revenge. Proper revenge. I still had a pistol I brought back, like lots of blokes. I don't know why I kept it. Keepsake, perhaps. Or thinking that if I needed some ready cash, I could always sell it. I bet you kept a gun?'

Stark shook his head. 'No,' he said. 'I vowed after the war I'd never touch a gun ever again.'

'Yeah, well. You was always a bit different. But not too different. One of us, but not one of us. That's why we respected you. You wouldn't take a chance on our lives, not like some of the officers.'

'I just followed orders, like everyone else,' said Stark.

'Yeah, but you *interpreted* them,' said Alf. 'That's what Ted told me one day. I didn't know what he meant. He used to love big words, did Ted. He was always the clever one of the pair of us. He told me what that meant.' He nodded. 'If we'd had a different captain, a lot more of us would have died.'

'Too many of us died as it is,' said Stark bitterly.

'And for what?' asked Alf. 'I got talking to this bloke when I was weighing up what to do about them three toffs. I wanted to kill 'em, I knew I was gonna kill 'em, but I was like . . . hesitating.'

'It's one thing to do it in war, but it's another back home,' said Stark.

'Exactly,' nodded Alf. 'Anyway, like I say, I was talking to this bloke, expressing all my anger over what these three toffs had done to Alice, how they'd killed her, and how I wanted to kill them, and he said, "Why don't you?" And then he said about how we'd all been cheated. How we'd gone off to war on a promise of coming back to a place fit for heroes. Proper houses for everyone. Fair wages. Jobs for all. But what had happened? For us, nothing. For the nobs at the top – the politicians, the generals and field marshals, the aristocrats – everything. The ones who made money out of the war were the ones who owned the factories that made the guns and bullets, not the soldiers who fired 'em, or the workers who made 'em.

'You know yourself, Captain, the thousands of men who came back from the war blind, missing arms or legs, or their lungs choked from poison gas. Did they get any help? No. They were left to beg in the street for handouts.' He shook his head, angry at the images of the ex-soldiers he talked about.

'Who was this man?' asked Stark. 'The one who told you about this?'

Alf gave a smile as he shook his head. 'No, no, Captain,' he said. 'You don't catch me that way. Anyway, I already knew what he was saying. I'd seen it with my own eyes. And, after what had happened to Alice, it just made me more sure than ever he was right: we'd been cheated.

'The three that I killed, they're just the start. We're going for them all. The industrialists who made money out of the war and haven't given anything back. We know who they are. The generals and such who're living high on the hog, while ordinary soldiers rot in the streets.'

'That sounds like a revolution,' commented Stark. 'Shades of Russia. You going to kill the King and Queen?'

Alf shook his head. 'No, it ain't their fault they're who they are. And they ain't bad. It's the others, those who take advantages. Landlords who earn their fortune from houses and rooms that are unfit for a pig to live in.'

Churchill's Bolsheviks, thought Stark. 'So, this Hand of Justice outfit . . .' began Stark.

Alf nodded. 'That's just a name, though,' he said. 'You gotta call it something or no one takes any notice. Though they'll take notice once we start clearing the scum out.'

'We?' queried Stark.

'Me, I'm just the start,' said Alf. 'I'm the blue touchpaper that sets it off. There's more to follow. Angry ex-soldiers who feel the same way I do. Who've been kicked out of their homes, their jobs. And we've all been well trained in weapons, Captain.' He looked hopefully at Stark. 'You ought to join us.'

Stark shook his head. 'Not me, Alf,' he said. 'I'm on the other side of the fence. I'm a copper.'

'That's just it: you ain't on the other side,' insisted Alf. 'Not like the others. You saw how wrong things were, both in the war and after. How unfair. It needs to change.'

'But not like this,' said Stark. 'Vote. Put the people who want to change things into power.'

'Vote!' scoffed Alf. 'If voting changed anything, they'd abolish it!' He brandished the pistol. 'This is the only way we're going to change things. When they see what we're doing, picking 'em off, they'll soon come round.'

Suddenly, Stark was aware that Alf had stopped, his boots were no longer heard ringing on the pavement.

'This'll do, Captain,' he said.

Is he going to shoot me after all? thought Stark. *He's told me too much.*

'Join us,' Alf said again.

'No,' said Stark.

There was a pause, then Alf said, 'A clever man would say yes to make sure I didn't shoot him.'

'I was never clever in that way, Alf,' said Stark.

'No,' said Alf. 'You was clever in the best way. The thing is, I wanted you to know why I done it. So you'd understand. But that's as far as it goes. If you come after me, I'm not gonna be taken. Not while things ain't right.'

'Do you really think shooting a few toffs and factory owners is going to make things right?' queried Stark. 'It won't change things. If anything, it'll only make things worse for the people at the bottom. Troops being sent in. Is that what your Hand of Justice people are after? Civil War on the streets of London?'

There was no answer.

'Alf?' called Stark.

His voice echoed eerily back at him from the thick fog.

Alf Rennick had gone.

THIRTY-SIX

Henry and Stephen were sitting at the kitchen table, working on the model aeroplane, when Stark arrived home.

Sarah came from the scullery at the back, wiping her hands on a towel. 'I thought you might be home earlier tonight, after having to go out so early this morning,' she complained.

'So did I,' said Stark. 'But I got held up.'

'By your fancy woman?' Henry grunted.

Stark ignored the comment. 'We know who carried out the killings,' he said. 'He's killed three so far, and he's likely to kill again.'

'Who is he?' asked his father.

'He's an ex-soldier,' said Stark. 'He used to be in my unit during the war.'

His father stared at him, dumbfounded.

'Are you going to catch him, Dad?' asked Stephen.

'I am,' nodded Stark. 'Which means I've got to go out again.'

'You're not going after him on your own?' asked Henry.

'No,' said Stark. 'I'm going to collect Sergeant Danvers. I think I'm going to be late back.'

'You were late back last night,' Henry pointed out.

'And I shall carry on being late back until we've caught this man,' said Stark firmly. 'There are people's lives at stake.'

'What about your dinner?' asked Sarah, her expression showing she was worried that he might fade away through lack of food. He thought of the meal he had eaten the night before, and the night before that, and thought ruefully, *If only you knew*. Aloud, he said, 'I'll grab something. If you need me for anything, you can call in at Camden Town police station and leave a message. They'll know where I am and can get hold of me.' He looked at

Stephen and apologized. 'I'm sorry about this morning, Stephen. I'll explain properly later.'

'That's all right, Dad,' said Stephen. As his father headed for the door, he called out, 'I hope you catch him!'

Stark made his way through the fog to Camden Town police station, a handkerchief held over his nose and mouth as he walked. He was glad to see that Charlie Watts was on duty; that would make things easier.

'Evening, Chief Inspector,' Watts greeted him. 'Bad night out.'

'A bad night indeed,' nodded Stark. 'I need to use your phone.'

'Local box not working?'

'This is police business.'

Watts handed Stark the phone, and he dialled the number of Danvers' flat. 'Sergeant,' he said crisply when Danvers answered, 'I've got definite confirmation that Alf Rennick is our man. But there are more people involved. We need to find out who, and we need to do it tonight. I'm sorry to do this to you when you've had a long day—'

'That's all right, sir,' said Danvers. 'It's the job.'

'In that case, I'll get Scotland Yard to send a car to pick you up. Bring it to Camden Town police station. We'll go on from here.'

Next, Stark telephoned Scotland Yard and arranged for the motor pool to send a car to Danvers' address. 'I think we're going to need him all night, so make sure you send a driver who isn't about to go off shift,' Stark instructed the motor pool sergeant.

As Stark hung up, Watts enquired, 'It sounds like things are moving?'

'They are,' confirmed Stark. 'We know who carried out the shootings. Now we've got to stop him before he carries out any more.'

It was another hour before the car with Sergeant Danvers arrived at Camden Town police station.

'Sorry it took so long, sir,' said Danvers. 'It's the fog.'

'You're here; that's all that matters,' said Stark. 'Driver, take us to Hazelton Street, Bethnal Green. Do you know where it is?'

'My aunt lives near there,' said the driver. 'But I don't know how long it's going to take us in this fog.'

'Just get us there,' said Stark.

As the car made its juddering stop-start way through the fog, Stark filled Danvers in on his encounter with Alf Rennick.

'So this Hand of Justice outfit is real,' said Danvers, astonished.

'If what Alf says is true, and there's no reason to think he's lying. So it's not just about stopping him killing anyone else, it's also about finding out who else is involved and stopping them. Alf said there are other ex-soldiers like him who are part of this organization, and they're going to be carrying out assassinations as well. The trouble is, we don't know how many of them there are – there could be just a couple, or there could be tens of them. And we don't know how this organization is structured, who gives the orders.

'Alf said he was brought into the organization by some bloke he met, but we don't know where and how he met him.'

'Is that why we're going to Bethnal Green?'

'That's right, Sergeant. I'm hoping we'll be able to get some answers there.'

When they got to Hazelton Street, Stark gave Danvers instructions to wait in the car. 'My gut feeling is that Alf will be gone. But just in case I'm wrong, keep an eye on the door of number five.'

'We should have armed ourselves,' said Danvers, concerned. 'Alf Rennick's got a gun.'

Stark shook his head. 'I know he warned me not to come after him, but I really believe he won't shoot me if he knows I'm unarmed.'

'How will he know that?' demanded Danvers.

'I'll tell him,' said Stark simply.

'And if you're wrong?' asked Danvers.

Stark didn't respond. He got out of the car and made for the Rennicks' door. This time, when Mrs Rennick opened the door to his knock, she didn't appear surprised. It was as if she'd been expecting this call. 'If you're after Alf, he's gone,' she said, looking at him with open hostility. 'He took a bag and left. He said he'd be in touch.'

That made sense. He knew that Stark would be coming after him, after his visit.

'He came to see me,' said Stark. 'To talk. He told me he shot those three men.'

She shook her head. 'I'm not sayin' nuffin'.'

'Mrs Rennick, I'm sympathetic to Alf. He knows that, and I think that's why he came to see me. I know why he shot them, that business of Alice and the twins—'

'They shoulda given 'er the money!' she burst out angrily.

'Yes, they should,' agreed Stark. 'But now it's moved on. Alf is going to kill more people, people who were nothing to do with what happened to Alice.'

'They'll still be guilty,' she said defensively.

'Guilty of what?' asked Stark. 'Some of them will be innocent. Some of them will have served in the war, same as me and Alf and Ted did.'

She shook her head. 'No, he won't do that. Alf won't kill people who don't deserve it.' She looked at Stark challengingly. 'He didn't kill you, and you're against him.'

'He didn't kill me because he wanted me to spread the word about why he's doing it,' said Stark. 'And I'm going to do that. The trouble isn't Alf, Mrs Rennick. It's the people telling him what to do and who to shoot.'

'Alf doesn't take orders!'

'Yes, he does,' said Stark gently. 'That's why he was such a good soldier. I know, I was his captain. They'll point him at someone and tell Alf to kill them, and he will. Because he believes what they've told him: that there's a war on.'

'There is a war!' burst out Mrs Rennick angrily. 'That's what Alf said last night before he went. A war between them and us. Between those who've got everything and us who've got nothing. That's why Alice died. That's why the twins died. That's why Ted died.'

'Ted died fighting in the war.'

'But it wasn't *our* war. It was *their* war. Only they put *our* men and boys in the front line to fight it.'

'It wasn't only our kind who died, Mrs Rennick. I was there. I saw men and boys from public schools dying there as well. Rich people's sons. Lord this, Lord that. Saw their sons mowed down by machine guns just the same way. Yes, more of us died, but that's because there were more of us.'

Mrs Rennick stood studying him for a moment, hesitating.

Then she said, 'You're a clever man with words, Captain. Ted always said that about you. You could make people do what you wanted. Charm birds out of trees, he said. That's why the men followed you, not because of that stuck-up toff of a general who was giving the orders.'

'Mrs Rennick, I know why Alf did what he had to do, shooting those three men. And there'll be plenty who'll believe he was right, regardless of what the law says. But from now on, when he starts killing people he doesn't know because those are who he's told are his targets, it all changes. He'll just be a murderer. A *mad* murderer. Is that how you want him remembered, instead of the hero he was, and still is? I need to find him and stop him before he kills again.'

'You'll hang him.'

Stark shook his head. 'That's for a judge and jury to decide. Right now I have to protect Alf's reputation, and that means stopping him before he kills again.'

She fell silent. Stark could tell his words had struck home and she was racked by indecision.

'What do you want me to do?' she asked at last.

'Tell me where he is.'

'I don't know,' she said. 'He said it was better for me not to know.'

Stark nodded. 'If he gets in touch with you, will you pass on my message? Tell him what I've told you, about maybe being able to get him off with prison. But he mustn't kill again.'

'I don't know if he is going to get in touch,' she said sadly. 'When he said goodbye, he hugged me and kissed me like it was the last time I was gonna see him. Like when he and Ted went off to war.'

I know that feeling, thought Stark bitterly. It had been the same for him. He had hugged Susan before he went so tightly that he was afraid she'd break. He'd wanted her to know how much she meant to him, just in case he didn't come back. But he had come back, and Susan was the one who had died.

'Is there anyone else it's worth me talking to?' asked Stark. 'Pals of his. People who would know where he might have gone to? Drinking mates.'

She shook her head. 'He used to go to the Blue Anchor, but these past few months he's been going somewhere else. A new crowd he'd got in with.'

Immediately, Stark was alert, although he did his best not to show it to her. 'Where?' he asked.

'Over Stepney way.' She frowned, trying to remember. 'It was a funny name for a pub.' Then she nodded and her face cleared. 'The Dragon Arms. Yes, that's it. That's where he used to go. He only told me in case I needed to get hold of him urgent. "You can always find me at the Dragon Arms, Mum," he said.'

The Dragon Arms, just around the corner from the offices of the Communist Party.

Stark hesitated before asking his next question. A lot hinged on this. 'Mrs Rennick, as I said, I need to find Alf before he shoots anyone else. Could I borrow that photo of him? The one with him and Ted? I'll need to put it out so my men know who they're looking for.'

Again, she hesitated. 'You won't kill him?' she asked.

Stark shook his head. 'If they find him, I'll go and talk to him myself. He knows I'll be unarmed. I'll try to persuade him to give himself up peacefully.'

She shook her head. 'He won't give himself up as simple as that,' she said. 'He knows he's gone too far.'

'I can try,' Stark promised her.

She nodded, then went into the house and came back shortly afterwards with the photo of Alf and Ted that Stark had seen on the mantelpiece.

'This is the only one I've got of them both, Captain,' she said.

'I'll take good care of it,' he promised her. 'I'll have it copied and get it back to you.'

THIRTY-SEVEN

Stark returned to the car.

'Everything all right, sir?' asked Danvers.

'Fine,' said Stark. He showed Danvers the photograph of Alf and Ted Rennick. 'She gave me this, and we're about to make use of it. That pub where you asked about Dan Harker, the Dragon Arms?'

'Yes, sir,' nodded Danvers.

'That's the place where Alf Rennick has been hanging about for the past few months.'

'So you think that Dan Harker and Alf Rennick . . .'

'I do indeed, Sergeant. You and I are going to pay a visit there right now.'

'But Dan Harker is working for Special Branch!'

'Never heard of double agents, Sergeant?' He leant forward and said to the driver, 'Stepney, please. The Dragon Arms pub in Eccles Lane.'

The car moved off and Stark told Danvers, 'You take the lead on this. You've been there before.' He passed the photograph to Danvers. 'But take good care of this. I've made someone a promise that it won't get damaged, and I want to keep that promise.'

The Dragon Arms was busy, all the tables weighed down with pints of beer and short whiskey glasses. Most of the crowd were men, although there were a few women, mostly older, clutching half-pints of stout. The landlord was clearing empty glasses from tables as Stark and Danvers came into the pub. He recognized the sergeant at once and hurried over to them.

'There's nothing going wrong in here,' he said. 'It's all legal.'

'So we won't say anything about a bit of illegal bookmaking,' said Stark drily.

'Who are you?' demanded the landlord indignantly, but Stark noted he shot a nervous glance at one of the tables where a large man in a checked coat was hastily stuffing slips of paper into his pockets.

'This is Chief Inspector Stark of Scotland Yard,' said Danvers. He held out the photograph that Stark had given him to the landlord. 'Do you recognize this man?'

The landlord hesitated. 'Which one?' he asked.

'Either of them,' said Danvers.

Stark purposefully gestured towards the man in the checked coat who was getting up from the table.

'We could always have a word with your friend in the checked coat,' he said. 'See what he's got in his pockets.'

'No need for that,' said the landlord. He nodded. 'Yes. The one on the left.' Alf Rennick. 'He's been in here.'

'With the man I asked about earlier? Dan the man with the gun?'

The barman nodded. 'Yeah. He was part of that crowd. And sometimes he'd be here with just that Dan bloke and some other bloke, and that woman from the commie office.'

'What woman?' asked Stark, and a feeling of dread hit him in the pit of his stomach. *Not Amelia!*

'The young one with the long black hair.'

'Naomi,' said Danvers.

The barman shook his head. 'I never caught her name,' he said. He pointed at the photograph of Alf Rennick. 'Nor his, neither. The only reason I knew the other one was called Dan was 'cos sometimes he used to sing it when he was drunk.'

'Sing it?'

'"I'm Dan Dan the military man". He thought it was funny.'

'You mentioned another man,' said Stark.

Again, the barman shook his head. 'I never caught his name, neither. He was the one who did most of the talking. Though you couldn't hear what he was saying 'cos he kept his voice low. The others had to lean in to hear him.'

'What did he look like?'

The barman frowned, thinking, trying to recall. 'Not very distinguishable, to be honest. Pretty ordinary-looking sort of bloke. Early thirties, at a guess. Bit of a moustache. Darkish hair kept neat and tidy. Average height. Average build.'

'Clothes?'

'Ordinary working clothes. Jacket. Trousers. Collarless shirt. Unusual, that, because most blokes wear a tie when they come in of an evening for a drink.' Suddenly, his face lit up as he remembered something, and he exclaimed, 'Yes, there was something odd about him!'

'What?'

'His eyes!'

'His eyes?'

The barman nodded. 'I only noticed it that time when he came to the bar to buy a round. His eyes were different colours. One was brown and one was blue. I've never seen that before!'

'I saw him!' exclaimed Danvers excitedly, then stopped as Stark trod on his foot to silence him.

'Thank you, landlord,' said Stark. 'Your assistance has been greatly appreciated.' He looked towards the table where the man in the checked coat had been sitting. 'I think you can tell your friend it's safe to return. I just hope he hasn't flushed the slips down the toilet.'

As Stark and Danvers left the pub, Danvers said, 'Sorry, sir. I didn't mean to . . .'

'That's all right, Sergeant,' said Stark. 'But it doesn't do to let the opposition see our whole hand.'

'You think the barman's the opposition?'

'He may not be, but someone else in that place may have been. Now, where did you see this man?'

'At the Communist Party offices the first time I went. He was talking to Naomi, and as I came in, he nipped off. He gave me a suspicious look and that was when I noticed his eyes. They were strange. I've never seen that before. Like the barman, said: one brown, one blue.'

They got back into the car and Stark ordered the driver, 'Stepney police station.'

'Yes, sir,' said the driver.

'How did you know that man in the pub was running bets?' asked Danvers.

'Local knowledge,' said Stark. 'My uncle used to run bets, and he also used to wear a jacket with a large checked pattern on it.' He grinned. 'I sometimes used to think it was like a uniform. Anyway, it was a hunch that I hoped might help persuade the landlord to help us. After all, he'd be facing a charge of allowing his premises to be used for illegal betting.'

Stepney police station was just a short distance away, and Stark was soon giving instructions for a team to go and bring in Dan Harker. 'If I'm not here when you return with him, put him in a cell and I'll talk to him when I get back.'

Stark then asked for the private use of a telephone and was taken to one in the inspector's office.

He dialled Lady Amelia's number and felt a tingle of pleasure as he heard her voice at the other end.

'It's Paul,' he said.

'Paul! I was hoping you'd telephone.'

'I'm afraid this is business.'

'Business?'

'Serious police business. Do you know where your office colleague, Naomi, lives?'

'Naomi? Why?'

'We need to talk to her urgently. We know who the murderer is, and it looks as if she might be involved.'

'That's impossible!'

'That's why we need to talk to her, to eliminate her from our enquiries.'

'I think she lives somewhere near Hackney. I'm not sure where.'

'Can you think of anyone might know her address?'

'It'll be in the files at the office.'

'Could we meet you there? Or I'll send a car for you, if you like.'

'Now? It's half past ten!'

'I'm serious, Amelia; this is really very urgent. I'm trying to stop more people being killed.'

'In that case, I'll come over. I'll get a taxi, but it might take a while in this fog.'

'We'll be parked outside your offices.'

'We?'

'Myself and Sergeant Danvers.'

There was a pause, then she said, 'I suppose if Bobby is there, I have to remain on my best behaviour. No throwing my arms around your neck.'

'Not at the moment, but soon,' promised Stark.

'I'll hold you to that,' she said. 'I'll be there as soon as I can.'

Stark hung up and returned to the main reception area.

'Lady Amelia Fairfax is going to meet us outside the offices of the Communist Party,' he told Danvers.

Danvers looked at him, surprised. 'At this hour?' he said. 'How did you persuade her to do that?'

'I told her people's lives are at stake,' said Stark.

THIRTY-EIGHT

Stark and Danvers sat in the back of the car parked outside the Communist Party offices and watched the fog swirl around.

'I'm sorry to subject you to this,' Stark told the driver. 'I expect you were hoping for a quiet evening.'

'That's all right, sir,' said the driver. 'My mother-in-law's staying with us at the moment, so, to be honest, I'm glad to get out of the house.'

'It might be a long night,' continued Stark.

'The longer the better, sir,' said the driver. 'My mother-in-law drinks, and when she drinks, she gets rowdy and noisy.' He looked at the clock on the dashboard. 'About now she'll be just getting started.'

'You have my sympathies,' said Stark.

'Someone's pulling up!' said Danvers.

Stark saw the yellow of the car headlights glimmering through the fog. 'She can't have made it this quickly,' he said, surprised.

'It's another police car,' said the driver.

Stark got out and saw the rear door of the police car open and a uniformed sergeant hurry towards him.

'Harker's gone, sir,' the sergeant said. 'Done a bunk, by the look of it. Neighbours say he was there this morning, but they reckon he took off this afternoon. He had a bag with him when he went.'

The same as Alf Rennick, thought Stark. *My visit to Mrs Rennick must have stirred them up. They believed I was on to them.*

'Thank you, Sergeant,' said Stark.

He returned to the car and clambered in the back to rejoin Danvers. 'Harker has gone,' he said. 'Just like Alf Rennick.'

'Perhaps this Naomi might be able to tell us where,' suggested Danvers hopefully.

Stark shook his head. 'I doubt it, Sergeant. My money is on her having done a disappearing act as well.'

It was another half an hour before a taxi pulled up in the street and Amelia got out. Stark and Danvers hurried over to her as she paid the driver.

'Thank you for coming, Lady Amelia,' said Stark.

Amelia turned, surprised at the formality of his address, and then spotted Danvers. 'I would have been here earlier but for this fog,' she said. 'The taxi had to crawl.'

She took a bunch of keys from her purse and opened the street door, then switched on the light and they followed her up the rickety stairs to the Communist Party offices. She switched on the lights and went to the desk where Naomi usually sat. She opened the top drawer, then another, and another, a puzzled frown appearing on her face.

She went to the two battered grey filings cabinets, unlocked them, and began to go through them, searching. Finding nothing, she went through to the inner office and began searching in there, while Stark followed and watched.

Finally, she turned to Stark, bewildered. 'The membership cards have gone,' she said, returning to the outer office, Stark following her.

'All of them?' asked Stark.

'So it appears.'

She saw Stark and Danvers exchange looks, and said, 'You think Naomi took them?'

'Does she have keys to the place?'

'Of course. She looks after everything. Opens the place up in the morning and locks it up at night.' She returned to the desk and began to rummage through the drawers again.

'What did the cards look like?' asked Stark.

'Like the one I showed you when you forced me to give you the address of that man, Dan Harker.'

'How many of them?'

'About two hundred. They were held together with a rubber band.' She stopped rummaging. 'They aren't here. You think she took them to stop you finding out her address?'

'If that was the case, she'd just take the one,' said Stark.

'But what use would they be to her?'

'To her, very little. But to the Hand of Justice . . .'

She looked at him, concerned. 'You're serious?'

'I'm afraid I am. It now looks as if the Communist Party has been infiltrated by this organization, which has its own, more violent, agenda. They've been making contact with your members, persuading some of them to join them.'

'Join them?'

'As assassins. Alf Rennick was one of them. The man who shot Lord Amersham, Tobias Smith and Walter Parrot.'

She stared at him, horrified, her face going suddenly deathly pale. 'You mean there are more?'

Stark nodded. 'At least, that's what Alf Rennick told me. We believe the ringleaders are Dan Harker, the man whose address you gave me, Naomi, and a man whose name we don't know, but he's got different-coloured eyes. One brown, one blue. Do you have any idea who he is?'

She stared at him, puzzled. 'One brown, one blue. How strange!'

'Strange, perhaps, but we need to talk to this man quite urgently.'

She shook her head. 'I'm sorry. With a description like that, I'm sure I'd remember if I'd seen him. No, I've never seen him.'

She looks as if she is going to be sick, thought Stark. 'It's not your fault,' he said. 'You weren't to know what was going on.'

'I was here almost every day with Naomi and I never saw what was happening!'

'You weren't here all the time. You said yourself that you were only filling in for Mrs Pankhurst.'

'But I should have seen what was going on right under my nose!' she burst out angrily.

'No,' said Stark. 'We never see what's right up close. None of us. Come, we'll take you home.'

She looked around the room, an expression of despair on her face. 'I thought we were doing so much good work,' she said. 'I admired Naomi for her dedication.'

'We don't know why Naomi got involved,' said Stark. 'I'm sure we'll find out when we catch up with her.'

They left the room.

'The stable door and the bolting horse leaps to mind,' she said bitterly as she locked the offices.

Downstairs in the street, she locked the front door, then climbed into the back of the police car with Stark and Danvers.

'Cadogan Square, driver,' instructed Stark.

THIRTY-NINE

The fog seemed to have eased slightly, although it was hard to be sure because it was now very late – almost midnight – and the yellow gaslight from the street lamps always seemed to have difficulty puncturing the darkness of the city streets, especially in these outer regions.

Stark and Danvers sat side by side on the back seat, with Amelia sitting opposite them, looking miserable and lost in her own thoughts. The sense of betrayal, thought Stark. He knew what that was like. The first time it happened, it was as if your whole world collapsed about you. People you had trusted were suddenly shown to be false, the whole thing a façade, a humiliating delusion.

He was glad she was sitting opposite him, because he knew if she had been next to him, he wouldn't have been able to resist reaching out and taking her hand to squeeze it and reassure her. In different circumstances, he would have put his arm around her, pulled her to him and hugged her close.

But this was a police vehicle, and Sergeant Danvers was there.

'It's not your fault,' Stark repeated gently. 'And I doubt if Naomi deliberately set out to dupe you. She had to protect the others. This man with the different-coloured eyes.' *I expect we shall find she was in love with him*, he decided. *Love makes fools of us all.*

They arrived in Cadogan Square, and Stark opened the rear door of the car. 'I'll see you to your door,' he offered, and walked with Amelia to her house.

'Do you think Bobby Danvers suspects?' she asked.

'About us? I don't know. He's a very good detective, very perceptive, but we've hardly been giving ourselves away tonight, I'd have thought.'

'I wanted to throw myself into your arms the whole time we were in the back of that damned car,' she said.

'I felt exactly the same,' he admitted.

They reached the door.

'I can't kiss you,' he said. 'I want to, but Danvers is watching us, and it will raise too many issues while this investigation is still ongoing.'

'The fog's thick,' she said.

'Not that thick,' he said.

She opened her purse and took out her key. 'If you want to come back tonight, I shall still be awake.'

'I do want to come back, but I'm afraid I won't be able to,' said Stark. 'This is going to be a very long night. Sergeant Danvers and I have a lot of work to do.'

'Tomorrow then?' she asked hopefully. 'It's not just the sex, it's . . . I want to feel your arms around me.'

He nodded. 'Tomorrow. I promise.'

He waited until the door had closed, then returned to the car.

'Scotland Yard,' he said to the driver.

'Do you think she's telling the truth?' asked Danvers. 'About never having seen this man, the one with the different-coloured eyes?'

'Yes, I do.'

'But he was at the offices. I saw him!'

'I know you did, Sergeant. But my guess is that he was making a rare visit to get information from his friend Naomi, and once he realized the police were hanging around the offices, he decided to keep his distance.'

Danvers fell silent, thinking. Then he said, 'You think the membership cards will have the names and addresses of the assassins?'

'I do,' nodded Stark.

'There are two hundred cards.'

'Then let's hope there aren't two hundred assassins.'

The first thing Stark did when they reached Scotland Yard was to phone the technical department.

'Higgins,' said a voice.

'This is DCI Stark. I need an artist,' said Stark.

'At this hour? It's nearly one o'clock in the morning! I'm only here manning the phone in case there's an emergency.'

'This is an emergency. I need an artist to draw some portraits for wanted posters.'

'Wanted posters? Can't it wait until the morning?'

'These people have murdered three high-profile men. If we don't catch them, they'll murder more. I want these portraits to be in the papers first thing tomorrow morning. So I need an artist *now*. In the next half hour.'

There was a pause, then Higgins said unhappily, 'I'll see what I can do. But I shall put in a report!'

'I would do exactly the same,' said Stark.

He hung up, then handed the photograph of Alf and Ted Rennick to Danvers.

'While we're waiting for this artist to arrive, I want you to get a copy of this photograph made, then copies made of just the man on the left, Alf Rennick. And, Sergeant . . .'

'Sir?'

'Take good care of that photograph. The photo people can do what they want with the copies, but I don't want them getting their inky fingerprints all over the original.'

'I'll take care of it, sir,' Danvers assured him.

As soon as Danvers had left, Stark lifted the phone again.

'Switchboard,' said the operator.

'Put me through to Chief Superintendent Benson at his home, please,' said Stark.

There was a long delay, during which Stark heard the ringing tone, before the phone was finally picked up.

'Benson,' muttered the chief superintendent's groggy voice.

'Chief Superintendent, I have DCI Stark on the line for you. You're through, DCI Stark.'

'Thank you,' said Stark. 'I'm sorry to trouble you at this hour, sir, but we now have the information we need. We know who committed the murders, and why.'

Briefly, Stark filled in Benson on what they had learned so far. 'The reason I'm phoning is that we need to put out wanted notices for these people and get them into the early editions of tomorrow's newspapers. I'd like to put a reward on them. That usually encourages people who might know them to come forward.'

'How much were you thinking? We have to watch the budget, you know, Stark.'

'I was going to suggest a hundred pounds for each of them.'

'Four hundred pounds?'

'That's right, sir.'

'That's a lot of money.'

'It might save the life of someone like the Home Secretary. Or even the Prime Minister.'

'You believe they are under threat?'

'If we are right, there is a secret army of assassins out there, ready to carry out more killings of important people. The people I want to put out the wanted notices for are the only people who know the assassins' identities. We need to get hold of them, and fast.'

'Very well,' agreed Benson. 'But it had better work, Stark.'

'I hope it will, sir,' said Stark.

He hung up, picked up a pen and began to draft out the wording for the wanted posters. The first one was straightforward.

Wanted for Murder
Alf Rennick
If you see this man, report him to your nearest police station.

This man is armed and dangerous. Do not approach him.
£100 Reward leading to his capture.

The second and third were less direct.

Wanted
In connection with a series of murders
Dan Harker
If you see this man or have any information about him,
report him to your nearest police station.
This man is armed and dangerous. Do not approach him.
£100 Reward leading to his capture.

and

Wanted
In connection with a series of murders
Naomi Pike
If you see this woman or have any information about her,
report her to your nearest police station.
£100 Reward leading to her capture.

The fourth was more involved:

Wanted
In connection with a series of murders
Description: A young man with eyes of two different
colours: one brown, one blue.
If you see this man or have any information about him,
report him to your nearest police station.
This man may be armed and dangerous. Do not approach him.
£100 Reward leading to his capture.

He then began composing a piece to accompany the wanted
posters, one that he could give to the newspapers.

The people suspected of being behind the recent tragic
murders of Lord Amersham, Tobias Smith MP and Mr
Walter Parrot, the owner of the *Daily Bugle* newspaper, have
now been identified as Alfred Rennick, a former soldier,

Daniel Harker, Naomi Pike and a man who is so far unnamed, but is distinctive in his appearance because he has eyes of two different colours: one blue, one brown. It is vitally important that these people are apprehended before more of these heinous crimes are carried out. A reward of £100 each has been offered for their capture.

If you see these people, or have any knowledge of their whereabouts, or information about their backgrounds, you are urged to contact Scotland Yard or your local police station.

He was just putting the finishing touches to the piece, when there was a knock at his door.

'Come in!' he called.

The door opened and a short, thin woman in her twenties appeared. She had long, dark hair that hung down, with a fringe almost covering her eyes, and a very sour expression on her thin face. Not unlike Naomi Pike, thought Stark. She was carrying a very large leather briefcase.

'I assume you're DCI Stark?' she said brusquely.

'Yes,' said Stark.

'Hester Pigeon,' she said. 'Your artist.' As she came into the room and put her briefcase down, she added, 'And if you're going to say "But you're a woman", I'd point out that you don't need physical strength to handle a stick of charcoal.'

'No, I wasn't going to say anything like that,' said Stark.

'Then you'll be the first,' grunted Pigeon. 'They don't want to use me. I make them feel uncomfortable. Just because my reproductive organs are on the inside and yours are on the outside.'

Stark returned her warning glare with one of his own, feeling affronted. 'Please don't lump me in with the rest of my gender,' he said stiffly. 'All I want is an artist, not a lecture on sexual politics. Are you any good?'

'Very good,' she said. 'But they don't give me a chance. The only reason I'm here is because no one else was willing to come out at this hour.'

'Right,' said Stark. 'We'll start with the description of one of the men.'

'How many are there?' she asked.

'Three. Two men and one woman.'

She began to unpack her briefcase, taking out a large sketch pad and sticks of charcoal, along with a bundle of pencils. 'I'm also cheaper than the men, which would make you think they'd employ me more, but they still don't.'

The door opened and Danvers returned, carrying the photograph, now safely back in its wooden frame, and some copies. 'All done, sir,' he said.

'Good,' said Stark, taking the photograph and putting it in his desk drawer. 'This is Hester Pigeon, our artist. This is my sergeant, DS Danvers. Miss Pigeon is going to be drawing the pictures for the wanted posters.'

'Sketches,' Pigeon corrected him. 'You wanted them done quickly, so they'll be sketches. Proper pictures would take longer.'

'As long as the faces can be recognized,' said Stark.

She set to work, charcoal moving swiftly and lightly over the blank pages in her pad, as Danvers and Stark described Dan Harker and Naomi Pike to her. Then Danvers gave his description, as far as he could remember it, of the man with the different-coloured eyes.

'I'm sorry, sir,' he apologized when he'd finished giving it. 'I only saw him for a few seconds.'

'Don't worry, Sergeant,' said Stark. 'The business of the different-coloured eyes is what will jog people's minds.'

They watched as Hester Pigeon brought the faces to life on the page, her fingers rubbing out some of the charcoal lines and redrawing as Stark and Danvers talked, honing the illustrations, until at last Stark and Danvers agreed, 'That's them!'

'Well done, Miss Pigeon,' Stark congratulated her. 'They are excellent. You have indeed brought them to life. In future, when I want something similar done, yours will be the first name I request.'

Pigeon looked suspiciously at Stark to see if he was being sarcastic, but when she realized he wasn't, she blushed slightly. 'Thank you,' she said formally, collecting her materials together.

'Right, just two more things to do, Sergeant,' said Stark. He indicated the photograph, the three charcoal portraits, the four drafts for the wanted posters, and the article he'd written to accompany them. 'Would you take these to the Yard press office. There should be someone there at this hour; they're always keen to find something to put into the early editions. Tell them we need this in all the papers first thing tomorrow morning. And on the front pages, not buried somewhere inside. Although I think the papers will be only too keen to splash it out as their lead story, especially the *Bugle*.

'The other is to get those wanted posters distributed to every station, every railway terminus, every port. Just in case they try to make a run for it.'

'Yes, sir,' said Danvers. He yawned. 'I'm sorry, sir. I'm more tired than I realized.'

'You've been on the go for close to twenty-four hours, and I'm not far behind you,' said Stark. 'Personally, I shall be in a little later tomorrow morning. I would advise you to do the same; otherwise you'll be in no fit state for the onslaught that will engulf us tomorrow, once these pictures hit the street.'

'Today, sir,' Danvers corrected him. He pointed at the clock, which showed a quarter to four.

Stark nodded, aware that a wave of tiredness was sweeping over him, and that he would succumb to falling asleep on his desk unless he departed for home.

'What do we do if people start getting in touch and we're not here, sir?' asked Danvers. 'I'm pretty sure the papers will be desperate for more information.'

'Put Chief Superintendent Benson's name at the bottom of the note for the papers,' said Stark.

'Yes, sir,' said Danvers, and he left, bearing the papers.

Stark got up from his chair and lifted his coat down from the coat rack. *So far so good*, he reflected. *For the first time, we've made progress. But now comes the big one: who are the assassins, and who are their targets?*

FORTY

I t was the noises from downstairs that woke Stark. The sounds of his mother and Stephen talking, the rattle of pots and pans, the sound of coal being shovelled and put on the range.

He looked at the clock beside his bed. Eight o'clock. He'd managed to get three and a half hours' sleep.

He considered turning over and going back to sleep, but he told himself, *You made a promise to Stephen. If you don't keep it this morning, it's likely you won't be able to keep it tomorrow, not once the story gets in the papers.*

Wearily, he dressed and went downstairs.

Stephen was having breakfast, and Sarah was cooking.

'I left you to sleep,' she said. 'I heard you come in and thought you needed it, but I was going to wake you for work at quarter past.'

'I'm not going at my usual time,' said Stark. 'I thought I'd walk Stephen to school.'

Stephen's face lit up at this, but his mother looked worried. 'Your dad was going to take Stephen this morning.'

Stark hesitated. He looked at his son, who looked hopefully back at him. 'Perhaps we could take him together,' he said. 'I'll see what he says. Is he out in the yard?'

'He's upstairs,' said Sarah.

Stark nodded and headed for the stairs.

'He might still be asleep!' she called after him appealingly.

Stark ignored her and walked up the stairs, then along the landing to his parents' bedroom, and knocked on the door.

'Who is it?' came Henry's voice.

Stark turned the door handle and went in. His father was sitting, fully dressed, in an armchair, looking at a carpentry magazine. He regarded his son disdainfully.

'I promised you I'd let you know if there was any progress with the killings before it got into the papers,' Stark told him. 'Well, we know who did it, who's behind it, and why.'

His father said nothing at first, just looked at him suspiciously. Then he asked, 'Who?'

'An ex-soldier called Alf Rennick, another ex-soldier called Dan Harker, a woman called Naomi Pike, and a man whose name we don't know, but he's got eyes of two different colours. We've put a notice about them in the papers, so you'll see it.'

His father frowned. 'Why did they do it?'

'Because they want to overthrow the society we've got and replace it with one they think would be fairer. They want to get rid of the aristocracy, and people who own factories, landlords, that sort of thing.'

'Bolsheviks!' sneered Henry. 'Like the Russian Revolution.'

'Possibly,' said Stark.

'And when did you find all this out?'

'Last night,' said Stark. 'That's what Sergeant Danvers and I were up to. That's why I didn't get in till half past four this morning.'

His father was silent, then he scowled and muttered angrily, 'I thought you were with your fancy piece again.'

'I was working,' stated Stark. 'And she is not my fancy piece.' He then added, 'I'm also walking Stephen to school this morning. I promised to take him a couple of days ago, but work kept getting in the way. Mum says you were taking him today. So I'm suggesting we could both go.'

Henry looked at him in surprise. 'You and me?'

Stark nodded. 'Why not? Three generations of Starks walking down the road together. It'll give the neighbours something to talk about.'

His father hesitated. Then, rather primly, he said, 'I hope you're going to wash yourself first.'

Stark, Henry and Stephen left the house, with a goodbye kiss for Stephen from Sarah.

'Take care crossing the road,' she warned them.

'We're only going to the school,' grumbled Henry crossly.

'Yes, but some of these drivers are mad the way they race along.'

They set off, Stephen in the middle, Stark holding his son's hand, Henry walking stiffly beside them.

We must look a fine trio, thought Stark, *all three of us washed and scrubbed, best clothes on*. Even Stephen seemed to have been dressed up for the occasion.

As they walked down Camden Street, Henry said, 'I used to walk with you to school.'

'I remember,' said Stark. 'Depending on your work.'

'Of course,' said his father. 'Work had to come first.'

They crossed the road, then continued on the pavement on the other side.

'Didn't people think it was strange?' asked Stark. 'A man taking his son to school? It was women who did that.'

Henry didn't answer at first, then he answered gruffly, 'You proud of Stephen? Does he mean a lot to you?'

'Yes, of course!' retorted Stark. 'You know he does!' And he squeezed his son's hand as Stephen looked up at him and smiled.

'Well, then,' said Henry.

They carried on in silence.

He's trying to tell me he loved me, Stark realized. *Loved me enough to face ridicule for a man walking his young son to school.*

They got to the gates of the school, and Stark remembered all those years ago when he'd come to these same gates, and waved to his mother or father before walking through into the playground.

They watched Stephen go in and join some friends, then they turned and walked back up Camden Street.

'I'm sorry, Dad,' said Stark. 'I didn't mean to hurt you.'

There was a pause, then Henry said gruffly, 'I suppose you want me to say sorry, too?'

'No,' said Stark.

'Well, don't think I'm letting you have the upper hand on this,' snorted Henry. 'I'm saying sorry whether you like it or not!' They walked on a bit further in silence, then he added with a grumble, 'I still think it's wrong.'

'What is?'

'You and her.'

Stark picked up a newspaper from the vendor outside Scotland Yard. The story was on the front pages of all of them, he was pleased to note.

Danvers was already in the office, and so was Inspector Rogers from Special Branch, who was sitting in a chair and leapt to his feet as Stark came in.

'Inspector Rogers of Special Branch has been waiting for you, sir,' said Danvers. 'And Chief Superintendent Benson would like to see you urgently.'

'Thank you, Sergeant,' said Stark. He nodded at the obviously furious Rogers. 'Good morning, Inspector. I trust you are well.'

Rogers didn't reply. He glared at Stark, obviously seething, barely containing his anger. 'Would you give us a moment, Sergeant?' he said to Danvers, but his angry gaze remained on Stark.

'Certainly, sir,' said Danvers.

As soon as Danvers had left the office, Rogers picked up a newspaper from the desk and brandished it angrily at Stark. 'What is this?' he demanded.

'It looks suspiciously to me like a newspaper,' said Stark calmly. 'Of course, I expect that's a result of my training as a detective.'

Rogers stared at him, bewildered. Then the anger came back into his face again. 'Are you trying to be insolent?' he shouted.

'You can only be insolent to someone considered superior,' said Stark, remaining calm as he took off his overcoat and hung it on the hook. 'You are only an inspector. I am a chief inspector.'

'Special Branch outranks the police!' snarled Rogers.

'Its personnel certainly act as if they believe it does.'

Once again, Rogers brandished the newspaper at Stark, the wanted posters displayed prominently on the front page. 'Why have you put this out about Dan Harker?' he demanded. 'You know he's one of our undercover agents!'

'He's also an agent for the Hand of Justice,' said Stark. 'While he's been pretending to work for you, he's been passing back to them as much information about Special Branch activities as he could worm out of you.'

Rogers gave a derisive snort. 'The Hand of Justice!' he repeated, mockingly. 'There's no such organization!'

'Yes, there is, and I talked to one of its members last night. The man whose photograph is on the front page. Alf Rennick. He shot Lord Amersham, Tobias Smith and Walter Parrot.'

'How can you be sure of that?'

'Because he told me so. And I know Alf Rennick well enough to know if he was lying. He served under me during the war.'

Rogers stared at Stark, aghast. 'And you let him go?'

'As he had a gun on me, and I was unarmed, I didn't have a lot of choice.'

'You could have thrown yourself at him!'

'And got myself shot, and so been unable to pass on to anyone what I'd found out? That wouldn't have been much help, would it? Out of curiosity, are those other two also yours: Naomi Pike and the mystery man with the different-coloured eyes?'

Rogers shook his head, still angry, and he held up the

newspaper again. 'This is all nonsense, Stark! We told you who was responsible for the murders! The Irish!'

Stark shook his head. 'No, Rogers, you told me who you wanted me to believe was responsible for the murders.'

Rogers glared at Stark. 'This is because of your grandmother, isn't it? Catholic from Cork. You're one of them!'

Stark looked at Rogers and then laughed. 'Because my grandmother came from Cork in the last century, you think I'm covering up for the Irish delegation?'

'Yes! You Irish go a long way back! You're always quoting history to justify your bloody actions!'

Stark shook his head. 'I investigated the Irish delegation, as you suggested, and it didn't add up.' He pointed at the newspaper that Rogers was still clutching. 'These people, however, are real. And guilty. Rennick certainly; Harker, Pike and the other man possibly so. We shall know for sure when we catch them.' His expression hardened as he added, 'However, you, Rogers, and your chief inspector, are guilty of perverting the course of justice by deliberately diverting attention away from the real culprits for your own political ends. Let me guess? The Unionist cause?'

Rogers was almost shaking with speechless fury as he glared at Stark. Finally, he burst out, 'I'll have you, you Fenian bastard!'

With that, he marched across the office to the door, wrenched it open and stormed out. Sergeant Danvers reappeared a moment later, came in and shut the door.

'Did you hear all that, Sergeant?' asked Stark.

'Well, the inspector did raise his voice a great deal,' said Danvers awkwardly.

'Yes, he did,' agreed Stark. 'I believe he was very upset about something.' He looked at the clock. 'Ten o'clock. I think I'd better go and see the chief superintendent. I assume he was as agitated as Inspector Rogers?'

'Yes, sir,' said Danvers warily.

Stark nodded. 'I always knew this was going to be an interesting day,' he said with a smile.

FORTY-ONE

Benson was on the telephone when Stark knocked at his door and looked in. Stark was about to leave and pull the door shut again, but Benson waved him in. Benson listened and nodded, every now and then opening his mouth to say something, but each time being cut off. Finally, he said, 'Yes, sir. I shall be seeing DCI Stark immediately.'

With that, he hung up and turned angrily to Stark. 'Where the hell have you been, Stark?'

'At home in bed, sir.'

'At home in bed?' The words came out as if they were an expletive.

'I didn't get home until four thirty this morning, sir, and I began at six o'clock the day before. Twenty-two hours' uninterrupted duty. I believed I was entitled to three hours' sleep before starting work again today.'

'Yes, yes,' snapped Benson, ignoring Stark's answer. He pointed at the telephone. 'That was the Commissioner of Police himself, Stark. He is furious, and justifiably so! All this stuff in the papers and he knew nothing about it.'

'With respect, sir, I didn't think I had high enough authority to contact the Commissioner direct, which is why I telephoned you.'

'In the early hours! When it's too late to do anything about it!'

'Unfortunately, the evidence was only finally gathered together in the early hours,' Stark pointed out.

'Yes, well . . . What are we going to do?' blustered Benson.

'I believe we are already doing it, sir. We've put out the wanted notices—'

'I mean about the questions that are being asked in Parliament?'

'That's hardly our area, sir—' began Stark.

'Of course it is, dammit!' raged Benson. 'They pay our wages, Stark! They need answers! How far has this thing spread? Who are the targets? When will they strike? Are they planning to blow up Parliament?'

The spectre of Guy Fawkes, thought Stark. 'We'll find out the answers to these questions once information starts coming in, sir.'

'It's already coming in, Stark! Every lunatic and money-grubber in the land has been pouring into their local police station, eager to get their hands on the hundred pounds you promised them! The switchboard here at Scotland Yard has been jammed!'

'Then perhaps, once we've sifted through the information, we'll have what we want.'

'How soon will that be? The Commissioner is waiting, and so is the Home Secretary.'

'I'll do my best to get some preliminary indication to you by noon, sir,' promised Stark.

'Noon! That's not good enough!'

'I'll do my best to let you have the information sooner, sir,' said Stark.

The telephone ringing made Benson jump. He picked up the receiver. 'Benson.' He frowned, put his hand over the mouthpiece and looked enquiringly at Stark. 'It's the switchboard. Chief Inspector Burns from Special Branch is on the line. Apparently, he's been trying to get hold of me for a while. What does he want, do you know?'

'I can guess,' said Stark. 'You can tell him I've already had a meeting with Inspector Rogers. Inspector Rogers will be able to fill him in.' He pointed at the clock. 'I think I'd better get on, sir, if you want that information as quickly as possible.'

'Yes, of course,' nodded Benson dismissively. Into the phone he said, 'Put him through.'

As Stark let himself out, he heard Benson say, 'Chief Inspector. Sorry you've had trouble getting through to me; the telephone lines here have been absolutely inundated with all manner of people eager to get an update: the Home Secretary, the Commissioner . . .'

Danvers was also on the phone as Stark came back into the office. He was nodding as he made notes on a pad.

'That was Buckinghamshire police,' he said as he replaced the receiver.

'Buckinghamshire?' repeated Stark, intrigued.

'It's another piece in the jigsaw puzzle that suggests that our friend with the different-coloured eyes is one Christopher Richards. Although the Buckinghamshire force referred to him as the Honourable Christopher Leyton-Richards, formerly of Chalfont St Giles.' He indicated the masses of small pieces of paper that were strewn across his desk, all with writing in different hands. 'This is just a sample of some of the notes that were handed in at different police stations. The tip of the iceberg. I understand there are more being sent by messengers even as we speak. And that's without the people phoning the Yard switchboard.'

'Tell me about this Christopher Richards,' said Stark. 'What makes you so sure he's our man?'

'Because his name keeps cropping up. There are other suggestions for who the man might be, but Christopher Richards gets more votes than most.' He lifted some of the sheets of paper, sorting through them. 'I'm in the middle of collating the different pieces of information, trying to build him into an overall picture.'

'Do we have an address for him?'

'Hackney,' said Danvers. 'Pierce Street. I've sent a patrol there, but if he's done the same as Alf Rennick and Dan Harker, he'll be gone.'

'What about Naomi Pike?'

Danvers turned his attention to another pile of papers, and Stark realized the sergeant had sorted all the pieces of paper into four piles, one for each of the suspects, with other piles for where one or more were mentioned in the same report.

'Hackney again, but a different address. Walters Place. But it's just around the corner from Pierce Street. I've asked the patrol to call there, too.' He looked at Stark. 'According to some of these reports, Christopher and Naomi are romantically linked.'

Why doesn't that surprise me? thought Stark. 'Good work. Anything on the other two?'

'No sightings, but lots of tales about them. More on Dan Harker, not so many on Alf Rennick.'

Because people genuinely liked Alf, thought Stark. *They're not going to sell him out, not even for a hundred pounds.*

'Get back to Christopher Richards. This business of him being . . . who did you say?'

Danvers checked his notes again. 'The Honourable Christopher

Leyton-Richards, third son of Lord Hinshelwood of Hinshelwood
Hall, Chalfont St Giles.'

'Age?'

'Twenty-five.'

'Did he serve in the war?'

'There's no mention of it.'

'No, I bet there isn't,' said Stark bitterly. 'Protected and kept
safe at home.'

'Actually, sir, I might know some people I was at school with
who know the family. Shall I do some asking around, see what
I can find out?'

'An excellent suggestion, Sergeant.'

The phone rang and Danvers picked it up. 'DS Danvers.' He
held out the receiver to Stark. 'It's Chief Superintendent Benson
for you, sir.'

Stark took the phone. 'Stark here, sir.'

'There's been a further meeting convened at Downing Street
for this morning, Stark. An emergency meeting. As you've stirred
this up, you'd better attend on Scotland Yard's behalf.'

'Yes, sir. Do you know who else will be attending?'

'I have no idea. I expect it will be the same as last time. But
tread carefully, Stark. These are important people, and our
reputation is on the line.'

'Yes, sir. I'll report back to you afterwards.'

Benson didn't reply; there was just a click to indicate he had
hung up.

'My presence is requested at Downing Street again,' Stark told
Danvers as he replaced the receiver.

'Will Special Branch be there?' asked Danvers warily.

'I'm glad you're becoming aware of the politics of police work,
Sergeant,' sighed Stark. He began to gather up papers from his
desk and put them into his case. *How will I be viewed today at
this meeting*? he wondered. *As the conquering hero, or the sacri-
ficial lamb?*

The committee room at Downing Street was busier than it had been
at the last meeting. More chairs had been found to go around the
long table. Stark was relieved to see that on this occasion he had
been placed separately from Burns and Rogers of Special Branch,
although whether that was by design or accident, he didn't know.

Burns and Rogers sat several places away from him, and as Stark took his seat, he saw Rogers glaring at him, a look of sheer hatred on his face.

He looked at the name card placed on the table in front of the empty chair next to him. W.S. Churchill. On cue, the tall, bulky figure of Churchill entered the room and marched along the length of the table to crunch down heavily into his chair next to Stark.

'Good work, Stark,' he muttered. 'I always said it was Bolsheviks, and now you've nailed them. Well done.'

'We haven't nailed them yet, sir,' Stark whispered back. 'They're still out there. Still on the loose.'

'But you've identified them and their cause,' said Churchill. 'You've put an end to all this nonsense about *other* political issues being behind these murders.' As he spat out the word 'other', he glared along the table towards Burns and Rogers, who both pointedly turned away from his gaze.

At least I have one ally on my side, thought Stark. *And this is how political alliances are formed: my enemy's enemy is my friend.*

The Home Secretary, Edward Shortt, entered, accompanied by two civil servants, and the three men took their seats.

'Good morning, gentlemen,' Shortt greeted the gathering. 'I will begin by asking Detective Chief Inspector Stark of Scotland Yard for an update on the identities and possible whereabouts of the suspects named in the newspapers this morning.'

Thank heavens for those calls coming in, thought Stark as he took his papers from his briefcase.

'Thank you, Home Secretary,' he said. 'It is now our belief, from information received, that the unnamed member of this conspiracy, the man known as "the mystery man with the different-coloured eyes", is the Honourable Christopher Leyton-Richards, third son of Lord Hinshelwood of Hinshelwood Hall, Chalfont St Giles.'

There was some muttering around the table at this, and unhappy looks. *They don't like the fact that one of their own turns out to be a murderous Bolshevik*, thought Stark.

'Led astray, would you say, Stark?' asked one of the field marshals at the other end of the table.

A friend of the family protecting the good name of the

Hinshelwood family, reflected Stark. 'We are still gathering information, but it would appear that the contrary is true: that Christopher Leyton-Richards, who also calls himself Christopher Richards, is the ringleader of this conspiracy. Of the others, Alfred Rennick is a former soldier I am familiar with; he served in my unit during the war.'

'DCI Stark was promoted in the field,' interrupted Churchill aggressively. 'Captain. Won the DSM. Fought the whole war. A leader of his men.'

'Thank you for that, Winston,' said Shortt calmly. 'Please continue, Chief Inspector.'

Churchill's protecting me, realized Stark. *He knows that there are some here – friends of Lord Hinshelwood – who will be unhappy at what I'm saying and will want to cut me down.* 'Daniel Harker also claims to be a former soldier, although we are currently investigating his background.' And he shot a glance at Burns and Rogers, who shifted uncomfortably in their seats. 'In my opinion, neither of these men is a leader. Rennick was a good soldier who obeyed orders. Harker, I believe to be duplicitous, and someone who keeps a deliberately low profile, but not someone who leads. Naomi Pike used to work until recently in the offices of the British Communist Party. We believe her role there was to gather information that could be used by this Hand of Justice, in particular the names of former servicemen disaffected after the war, who might be pliable to using their skills with weapons to carry out assassinations, as happened with Lord Amersham, Tobias Smith and Walter Parrot.'

'I don't see that this puts Hinshelwood into the frame as the brains behind this,' blustered another of the uniformed men, a brigadier. 'I know Lord Hinshelwood. The family have always been patriots. His eldest son, Gerald, was a war hero. Died at the Somme. The younger son, Eric, badly wounded, came home an invalid.'

'Then if you know the family, sir, do you have an opinion on Christopher?' asked Stark calmly.

The brigadier opened his mouth to reply, then seemed to think better of it. 'There's always the chance of one rotten apple,' he growled.

'Thank you, Brigadier,' Shortt acknowledged. He turned to

Stark. 'Do you have more for us, Chief Inspector? The suspected whereabouts of these people?'

'The police are still conducting enquiries to that, sir,' said Stark. 'But the main cause for concern is the assassins they may have unleashed. Information we have received indicates there may be a substantial number of ex-servicemen who have been primed to continue with the kind of murders we have seen. The problem is, we don't know who they are, or how many of them there are, and we don't know who their actual targets are. That's one of the reasons our search to locate Christopher Richards and Naomi Pike is so urgent: we believe they are the ones who know the targets, and the assassins.'

'How many assassins do you believe are out there, Chief Inspector?' asked Shortt.

'It could be just a handful, or it could be a hundred, sir.'

There was a sharp intake of breath around the table.

Shortt addressed Burns. 'Chief Inspector Burns, do you at Special Branch have anything further to add on these people?'

'We are conducting our own enquiries, but at this moment we have little to add to what DCI Stark has reported,' said Burns.

Next to him, Stark heard Churchill give a low throaty chuckle at this.

'Very well,' nodded Shortt. 'Is that all, Chief Inspector Stark?'

'Not exactly, sir,' said Stark, and, beneath the calmness of his exterior, he felt a knot in his stomach. *This is where I put my career on the line and get shot down in flames.* 'But this is a suggestion, rather than information. It could take time before these people are apprehended. There is a serious danger of more assassinations being carried out by this secret army before that happens.

'These men have been duped by dangerous propaganda spouted by Richards – radicalized, if you will, to fight for this cause. However, it is my view that most ex-servicemen are patriotic. We need to get a message out to these men and appeal to the same patriotism that persuaded them to serve during the war, that this is not the way forward.'

'And how do you propose we send these men this message?' asked a field marshal sarcastically.

'Through the medium of the wireless,' said Stark. 'A voice of the nation's authority speaking directly, urging them to stop. A live broadcast from the Marconi factory at Chelmsford.'

Stark looked around the table and saw that his suggestion had gone down badly: some of them, especially the military ones, wore expressions of blatant disapproval, while most of the others looked puzzled or shook their heads dismissively.

'There is no audience for wireless broadcasts,' said one of the civil servants. 'No one will hear it.'

'With respect, sir, there was a great deal of interest in the first broadcast last year, the recording of Dame Nellie Melba. As I understand it, the audience for that was in the thousands.'

'Yes, but there have been hardly any broadcasts since.'

'That is because they have been discontinued,' Stark pointed out.

'And rightly so,' grunted a field marshal. 'They are dangerous. These transmissions interfere with military communications.'

The civil servant who'd dismissed the idea earlier shook his head. 'I repeat, there is no audience for wireless broadcasts,' he said.

'Actually, I disagree.'

All eyes turned to the person who'd spoken, who was sitting next to Edward Shortt – one of his secretaries, Stark presumed.

'There are many hundreds of wireless clubs across the nation. I know because I am a member of one, and we have a very active and keen membership. I believe this proposal has merit.'

There was an uncomfortable pause after this. Whoever this man was, he clearly had authority.

'That may be true, Sir Jocelyn,' said a brigadier, 'but how would these – er – wireless enthusiasts know that the transmission was happening.'

'The same as with the Melba broadcast,' said Sir Jocelyn. 'An announcement in the newspapers telling the people it was occurring, with details of the frequency they need to tune their receivers to.'

Whoever Sir Jocelyn is, thank God he's a wireless enthusiast and thank God he's here, thought Stark.

Edward Shortt looked at Stark and asked, 'Are you proposing that I, in my position as Home Secretary, make a wireless broadcast to these men, urging them to stop?'

Now we come to the contentious part, thought Stark. Aloud, he said, 'With respect, sir, I was thinking someone . . . shall we say . . . at a higher level.'

'The Prime Minister?' scoffed Burns.

'Actually, I was going to suggest someone who is not a politician, as much of the anger of these men is directed at politicians.'

'Who?'

'The King.'

A hubbub of outrage burst out around the table at this proposal.

'Unthinkable!' said one voice.

'Palpable nonsense!'

'The man's mad!'

Keep a cool head, Stark told himself. *Don't lose your temper, or get deflected.*

'You'd put the King at risk!' snapped Rogers accusingly.

Stark shook his head. 'Despite the rumours about Bolsheviks trying to do the same to our royal family as the Russians did to theirs – and that may be true of Christopher Richards and Naomi Pike – it is my opinion that the majority of these men have respect for the royal family, sir. They fought for king and country. I believe they will listen to him. At least, enough to prevent a wholesale massacre. And that is the alternative if we don't do this.'

'No. Absolutely not!' snapped Burns. 'It would be impossible to afford the King proper protection at somewhere as public as the Marconi factory.'

'It could be if done by the proper people,' said Churchill. 'I would propose DC Stark lead a team of police bodyguards. He's an experienced soldier, used to action, and he also knows the people we're looking for.'

That was not what I was expecting, or proposing, thought Stark.

'Out of the question!' snapped Burns. 'The protection of the royal family is the responsibility of Special Branch!'

'Then I would suggest a joint enterprise,' said Sir Jocelyn. 'Special Branch to ensure security at the Marconi factory, while Chief Inspector Stark and his team protect the King on his journey to the factory, and offer additional protection during his visit. After all,' he added, his voice adopting a very serious tone, 'if Chief Inspector Stark is right, there is the serious possibility of attacks by these assassins, and they could happen very soon. The whole Cabinet could be killed. Who is to say these men would stop at using firearms. There are many men who returned from the war who are experts in explosives.'

A silence descended on those around the table as the implication sank in. Bombs and guns used by experts. The destruction of the Cabinet, of leading military figures, top industrialists. The destruction of the structure of British society.

'But why wireless?' burst out a brigadier plaintively, obviously still unhappy at the idea of this technology being used for anything other than military purposes. 'If we're going to put something in the newspapers about it, why not leave it at that! More people read the newspapers than will ever listen to the wireless! There aren't enough domestic receivers in this country for lots of people to be able to hear to it!'

'Because I believe actually hearing the King's voice saying the words would have much more impact,' said Stark. 'It's real; they would be hearing it.'

'And if the brigadier would permit me to take issue with his view on the numbers who will listen, at the time of the Melba broadcast, people went to houses of their friends and neighbours to hear it,' said Sir Jocelyn. 'I believe the same will happen here.'

'Thank you, Sir Jocelyn,' said Shortt. 'I propose we vote on the issue. If we could have a show of hands on the proposal. Those in favour?'

Churchill's and Sir Jocelyn's hands went up first, followed by Stark's. A brief hesitation, then more hands rose to signal assent. Stark did a quick calculation: more than half of those around the table had voted in favour.

'Those against?' asked Shortt.

Burns, Rogers, a field marshal, a brigadier and two of the civil servants raised their hands.

'Abstentions?'

Two.

'The motion is carried,' said Shortt. 'I will contact the King to ask him if he agrees with the proposal. And, in view of the urgency expressed, I will do that immediately this meeting finishes and try to arrange the broadcast for tomorrow.'

FORTY-TWO

As the meeting finished and people began to drift away, Stark made a point of seeking out the civil servant who'd supported the use of wireless.

'Sir Jocelyn,' he said, 'I just wish to thank you for speaking up the way you did. I have no doubt that, without your intervention, my proposal would have been dismissed.'

Sir Jocelyn nodded. 'And I, in turn, wish to thank you, Chief Inspector, for making the proposal. This country spends too much time looking backwards instead of forward. Wireless is the future. I see the day when a wireless broadcast in one country will be heard across the world.' His eyes glinted. 'Think of the power! Propaganda! Wars will be won without a shot being fired, just by the power of a wireless broadcast!' He gave a slight bow, and left to hurry after the departing Home Secretary.

'Good work, Stark,' Churchill muttered in a low growl, coming to stand beside him. 'The King will agree, I'm sure of it. And it'll be up to you to keep him safe. If I were you, I'd start to put together your team of bodyguards in readiness. Men you can trust. The country is depending on you.'

Stark walked into the office and saw that the piles of paper on the desk had increased enormously. 'More information?' he asked.

'Tons of it, sir,' said Danvers. 'Some useless, some good. Every piece with a name and address attached. Everyone's hoping to lay their hands on the rewards. How did the conference go?'

'If my proposal is accepted by the King, we have an important task ahead of us.'

Danvers looked at him, a bewildered expression on his face. 'The King, sir? King George V?'

'How many other kings do you know, Sergeant?'

'Yes, sir, but . . .' He looked nonplussed. 'If he accepts what, sir? What proposal?'

Stark briefed him on the events at the conference and the

proposal for the wireless broadcast. 'The meeting approved it, but we have to see if the King agrees.'

'It's asking a bit much, sir,' said Danvers doubtfully. 'I mean . . . the King! And wireless is not exactly . . . well, I heard that Melba broadcast last year, and it was a bit scratchy. Difficult to listen to.'

'I'm sure the technology will have improved since last year. And, if the King agrees, people will tune in because it's not been done before,' said Stark. 'We have to make preparations on the basis that the King will agree. You and I have been authorized to act as the King's bodyguards for his visit to the Marconi factory at Chelmsford.'

'Us, sir!' Danvers' expression showed that he was obviously delighted, but then his face clouded. 'What about Special Branch? Won't that put their nose out of joint?'

'Very much, but a compromise was suggested, which they will be forced to accept, however reluctantly. We look after the King on the journey to Chelmsford; Special Branch are responsible for security at the factory.'

'They'll need to be on top of it, sir,' said Danvers.

The note of serious concern in the sergeant's voice made Stark frown. 'In what way? Why?'

Danvers sifted through the pieces of paper in one of the piles, then found the one he was looking for.

'Daniel Harker. Served in the Royal Engineers during the war. Part of the team that blew up the mines of Messines.' He looked at Stark. 'He was a demolition expert, sir. The mines of Messines . . .'

'Six hundred tons of explosives,' nodded Stark. 'Ten thousand Germans killed in that one blast.' He winced as if in pain. 'My God! And I've told them to put out advance notice of the broadcast in the newspapers!' He grabbed the telephone. 'I have to stop them talking to the King.'

'Switchboard,' said the voice of the operator.

'DCI Stark,' said Stark. 'Can you find the number for the Home Secretary's office. Edward Shortt. I need to speak to his personal private secretary. Urgently.'

'I'll call you back,' said the operator crisply.

Stark hung up. 'Why didn't Special Branch say anything at the meeting!' he exploded angrily. 'They must have known his background! An explosives expert! In a factory like Marconi's, with all that wiring everywhere and all those machines, it'll be easy for him to plant a bomb!' He looked at the telephone, willing it to ring.

'By the way, sir, I called a few people about this Christopher Richards, and spoke to someone who knows the family quite well. His older brother, Gerald—'

'A war hero. Died at the Somme. Younger son, Eric, came home from the war an invalid,' interrupted Stark. 'I was told so at the meeting by someone who was keen to protect the good name of the Hinshelwood family.'

'Did they tell you that Christopher was expelled from Eton?'

Stark shook his head. 'No,' he said.

'Nor that he was suspected of poisoning the family's dogs when he was a teenager?'

Again, Stark said, 'No.'

Danvers looked at his notes. 'There's an awful lot about him. Manipulative. A cheat. A liar. And a bit of a heartbreaker. At least two young women are said to have had illegitimate children by him and then just been abandoned. He's also described as charming, persuasive . . . all that sort of thing.'

'I get the picture, Sergeant. Have we got anything on Naomi Pike?'

Once more, Danvers sorted through the pieces of paper on his desk. 'Twenty-one years old. It seems she was originally from Derbyshire, one of a family of six, with four brothers and a sister. Her father was a coal miner who was also active in the trade union. He was killed in an explosion at the pit two years ago when she was nineteen. Ten other miners also died in the accident. She got into trouble for writing letters to the owners of the mine accusing them of being responsible for her father's death. The owners of the mine threatened to have her jailed.'

'On what charge?'

'Threatening behaviour, according to this report. The mine owners had the backing of the local police and the magistrates.'

'There's a surprise,' murmured Stark sarcastically.

'It seems that made her decide to come to London. She joined the Communist Party and started work there, and has been working for them ever since.'

'And at some time she met Christopher Leyton-Richards, and he must have persuaded her that the only way to get social change is by violent revolution,' said Stark bitterly. The phone rang, and Stark snatched up the receiver. 'DCI Stark.'

'I have your call for you, Chief Inspector. Sir Jocelyn Stevens is on the line.'

There was a click, then the voice of Sir Jocelyn said, 'Stark. I was about to call you. The Home Secretary has received confirmation from the Palace that His Majesty will undertake the broadcast tomorrow.'

'That's just it, Sir Jocelyn!' said Stark agitatedly. 'We have to cancel it.'

'Cancel it?'

'We've just discovered that one of the suspects, Daniel Harker, is an explosives expert. He was part of the team that carried out the explosion of the mines at Messines. I have no doubt that the Hand of Justice will try to blow up the King at Chelmsford.'

There was a pause, then Sir Jocelyn said curtly, 'Then you'd better make sure that doesn't happen.'

'But, sir—' began Stark desperately.

'It is too late to change it now, Stark!' snapped Sir Jocelyn. 'Everyone around that table was aware that an attack on the King was a possibility, as, I am sure, is His Majesty himself. It is your responsibility to ensure that doesn't happen. Remember, you were the one who said that ordinary soldiers would not take action against the King.'

'But Harker isn't an ordinary soldier! I also said that he was duplicitous—'

'That's enough! Arrangements have been made for you and your team to be stationed overnight at Buckingham Palace so you'll be ready for the journey to Chelmsford. Accommodation has been provided for you in the stable block. You will have breakfast in the servants' quarters, and then you will proceed in convoy with His Majesty at nine o'clock tomorrow morning. It is expected you will arrive at the Marconi factory at eleven. Firearms will, of course, be issued to all of you. The country is depending on you to keep the King safe.'

There was a click. Stark replaced the receiver, a sinking feeling in his heart.

FORTY-THREE

Danvers looked questioningly at Stark. 'I take it he said no?'

Stark nodded. 'Special Branch could have said something about that at the meeting, and they didn't!' he fumed angrily. 'Harker is their man! They must have known!'

He picked up the receiver and asked to be connected to Inspector Rogers at Special Branch. When Rogers answered, Stark dispensed with false social niceties and barked, 'Why didn't you tell me that Harker is an explosives expert?'

'You're the detective,' retorted Rogers icily. 'I assumed you'd find that out. Or do you want us to do your work for you?'

'Look, Rogers, we're supposed to be on the same side—'

'Except when it suits you,' snapped Rogers.

'Can we concentrate on tomorrow?' said Stark. 'I think that the Hand of Justice will try something at Chelmsford.'

'So do we,' said Rogers. 'Which is why, as you may have noticed, we voted against this stupid and reckless proposal.'

'Harker's going to set off a bomb.'

'If he has time to prepare it.'

'He's an expert, for God's sake! He'll prepare it ahead of time, then put it in place. The early editions of the papers hit the streets at six. This outfit will make sure they get hold of them as soon as they do to see what the news says about them. They'll have five hours to get the bomb to Chelmsford and put it in place.'

'We're taking care of it,' said Rogers.

'What does that mean?'

'That we're doing our job!' shouted Rogers angrily.

'You need to stop all people from going in and out of the factory who aren't known to the company. In fact, *everyone* needs to be checked. For all we know, some of these secret assassins may be workers at Marconi!'

'Don't tell me how to do my job!' stormed Rogers. 'Yours is to deliver the King to the factory.'

'And stay with him while he's there,' said Stark. 'We're his protection.'

'Then God help the King!' snapped Rogers, and slammed the phone down.

Stark replaced the receiver and shook his head. 'I'm not sure if their job is protecting the country or protecting themselves,' he said angrily.

'I'm sure that we'll be all right working together tomorrow,' said Danvers.

'That's just it. This . . . division between us means we're not working together! They seem to think we're in competition!' He sighed. 'I'm sorry, Sergeant.'

'For what, sir?'

'For landing you in this. You heard my conversations with Sir Jocelyn Stevens and Rogers. This could go drastically wrong, if Harker gets a bomb inside there.'

'The King could be killed,' said Danvers sombrely.

'And us as well. We'll be with him.'

There was a thoughtful pause at this from Danvers, then he asked, 'Who are you thinking of for the rest of the protection team, sir?'

'I *was* thinking of getting in touch with Sergeant Alder of Maida Vale station.'

'A good choice, sir,' nodded Danvers approvingly. 'He's a very good man.'

'That was before you found out that Harker is a bomb expert.' He sighed.

'You should at least give him the chance. Sergeant Alder, that is. We're going to need reliable people on the job tomorrow, and he's one of the best I've seen since I've been on the force.'

Stark nodded. 'Yes,' he said. 'I'll get in touch with him.'

'What do you want me to do, sir?'

'I want you to go and see your family.'

Danvers frowned, puzzled. 'Sir?'

'If things go wrong tomorrow, and if Harker is able to get his bomb into the factory, and it goes off, that'll be it for us, as well as the King. You need to see your family. Just in case.'

Danvers sat silent for a moment, then he said, 'My father and I don't get on, sir.'

'I know,' said Stark. 'My father and I don't get on either.

Which is why I shall be going to see him after I've spoken to Sergeant Alder and organized the rest of our protection team.'

Danvers sat, doubtful. 'I'm not sure if my father would welcome me, sir.'

'There's only one way to find out. And I'm pretty sure your mother and sister will be pleased to see you. As will Mr Bridges.' He paused, then added, 'It's only being fair to them, if anything should happen. People need to know they had the chance to say goodbye.'

Danvers continued sitting there, thinking, weighing it up. Finally, he nodded. 'Yes, sir. You may be right.' He got up. 'I'll go along there now, if I may, sir.'

'You may. In fact, I insist upon it.'

'What time do you want me at the Palace?'

Stark looked at the clock. Three o'clock. 'Report back here at the Yard at six. And bring an overnight bag.' As Danvers headed for the door, he asked, 'Do you have a favoured weapon among your father's collection of guns?'

'No, sir. My father was very precious about his firearms.'

'Then we'll get you fitted out at the armoury when you return.'

Danvers left, and Stark reached for the telephone again. 'Maida Vale police station,' he said.

There were the usual series of clicks as plugs were pushed in and numbers dialled, and then a voice said, 'Maida Vale police station. Sergeant Thomas speaking.'

'Good afternoon, Sergeant. This is DCI Stark from Scotland Yard. Is Sergeant Alder there?'

'Actually, he is, sir. He's just come on duty. If you'll hold on a moment, I'll get him for you.'

There was a long pause, during which Stark could hear the background noises of the station reception area – chattering, clattering, some raised voices – and finally the receiver was picked up.

'Sergeant Alder speaking, sir.'

'DCI Stark, Sergeant. Tomorrow His Majesty the King will be travelling to the Marconi factory at Chelmsford to make a wireless broadcast to the nation. I've been given the task of arranging police protection for him. I and my Sergeant, DS Danvers, will be heading the team. I would appreciate it if you would consider being part of that team.'

There was a pause, and then Alder said in a tone of astonishment, 'His Majesty the King, sir?'

'This is not an order, Sergeant. I can only ask if you'd volunteer.'

'Yes, sir!' said Alder. 'I'd be proud to. And thank you for asking.'

'Wait one moment, Sergeant, before you say yes. I have information that there may be an attempt on the King's life during his visit to the Marconi factory.' He hesitated, then said, 'It may well take the form of a bomb secreted somewhere in the factory. It could be very dangerous.'

'That goes with the territory, sir,' said Alder. 'I was aware of that as soon as you said the task was police protection.'

'And you are still willing to take part?'

'Yes, sir. As I said, I would be proud to serve the King at such close quarters.'

'Thank you, Sergeant. One more thing: I need a team – eight of us altogether. There'll be you, me and Sergeant Danvers; I need five more men I can trust. As it's short notice, do you know five of your men whom you would be able to trust for this operation? Men you would trust with your life?'

'I do, sir. I have the five men who would be ideal for it. I know them well, and trust them implicitly.'

'They need to know what is in store for them. The danger.'

'They're all good police officers who've been tried and tested on the street. And four of them are veterans of the war. They all know what danger is.'

'Thank you, Sergeant. I look forward to seeing you and your team here at Scotland Yard. Ask for me.'

'Yes, sir. What time?'

'Six o'clock this evening. We'll be spending the night at Buckingham Palace.'

There was a pause, then Alder's voice said, 'Did you say Buckingham Palace, sir?'

'I did, Sergeant.'

There was another pause, then he queried, '*The* Buckingham Palace, sir? The one at the end of the Mall?'

'It's the only one I know of, Sergeant. So, yes. That one.'

There was another pause, then a chuckle. 'My old woman won't never believe this, sir! Me at Buckingham Palace!'

'We'll be in the stable block, Sergeant. Not the main building.'

'That doesn't matter, sir!' He chuckled again. 'Me, spending the night at Buckingham Palace! My old woman will dine out on this for years!'

After he'd hung up, Stark thought to himself apprehensively, *Let's hope that after tomorrow you're around to enjoy the memories with her, Sergeant.*

He picked up the receiver again and asked for an outside line. *I've never used a telephone so often in such a short space of time*, he reflected. *I could get used to this. Maybe I do need one of these at home.*

He dialled Amelia's number, and when she answered, he took a deep breath, then said bluntly, 'It's Paul. I'm afraid I won't be able to come tonight.'

'Your son?' she asked.

'No, I have to spend the night at Buckingham Palace.'

There was a pause, then she said, 'That's the most feeble excuse I've ever heard.'

'It's actually true. I've been asked to guard the King when he travels to make a live wireless broadcast tomorrow. It'll be in all the newspapers in the morning, so you'll be able to read about it.'

'But . . . why you? Surely that's a job for Special Branch. Aren't they the people who are supposed to handle royal protection?'

'Normally, yes. But these aren't normal times.'

'The Hand of Justice?'

'Yes.' He paused, then said, 'The thing is, if things should go wrong, and anything happens to me tomorrow . . .'

'Why should anything go wrong?'

'These are dangerous people we are dealing with. And they may not like the idea of the King making the broadcast.'

'Paul, if you die, I shall never forgive you.'

'I have a duty, and the broadcast was my idea.'

'Then you're a fool!'

'I won't die.'

'Is that a promise?'

'Yes.'

'The same sort of promise you made when you said you'd come to me tonight?'

'I'm sorry,' he said. 'It goes with the job.'

'Yes,' she said, her voice suddenly sad. 'I suppose it does.'

She was silent at her end of the phone, and he said, 'I shall come to see you after this is over. Tomorrow.'

There was a note of bitterness in her voice as she asked, 'Is that a promise?'

'Yes,' he said. Then added, 'In as far as I can.'

He waited for her to speak. Finally, she said, 'Yes, I understand. I'm sorry I was harsh.'

'You weren't harsh,' he assured her.

'In that case, I didn't express myself properly. I feel harsh.' She paused. 'Please come back safely.'

It suddenly hit him that those were the self-same words that Susan had said to him when he set off for the war, and – before he could stop them – tears began to come from his eyes and roll down his cheeks.

'Paul?' she asked, suddenly concerned.

'I have to go,' he said. 'I'll see you tomorrow, when I return.'

FORTY-FOUR

D anvers rang the bell of his parents' house. He still had a key to the front door, but he felt unsure of his ground. How long had it been since he'd left? Since he'd last spoken with his father? Nine months, surely. Perhaps more.

The door opened, and Bridges looked out at him. 'Master Robert!' he gasped, and his face lit up with momentary pleasure before returning to his usual formal expression of welcome.

'Is my father in?' asked Danvers.

'Yes, sir. He's in the drawing room with your mother and Miss Letitia.'

'Would you announce me, Bridges?' Then he changed his mind. 'No, on second thoughts, I'll announce myself.'

Bridges looked doubtful. 'If you're sure, Master Robert,' he said uncertainly.

'Yes, I think I am,' said Danvers. *I'd rather he ordered me out than slammed the door in my face and refused to see me*, he decided.

Danvers followed Bridges to the drawing room.

'Excuse me, sir . . .' began Bridges, but he was interrupted by Lettie getting to her feet and uttering a cry of delight. 'Bobby!'

Colonel Danvers turned and stared at his son, a look of indignation on his face as if he couldn't believe it. 'What the devil do you mean by barging in like this, without prior notice?' he demanded.

'Deverill . . .' began Victoria Danvers to her husband unhappily.

'I apologize for the unscheduled arrival,' said Danvers, 'but I have to go to Buckingham Palace this afternoon on an assignment, and . . .' He hesitated, then finished, 'We are uncertain about the outcome.'

'The outcome?' repeated his father, bewildered.

'Buckingham Palace?' echoed his mother.

'The King?' asked his sister.

'Robert, sit,' ordered his mother. 'Bridges, bring tea.'

'Yes, m'lady,' said Bridges, and he withdrew to the kitchen.

Danvers looked at his father. 'May I sit, Father?' he asked.

'If your mother says so, of course,' grunted Colonel Danvers.

Danvers took a seat on one of the settees, and immediately Lettie left her own chair and sat down next to him, taking his hand in hers. 'Oh Bobby, it's so good to see you here!' she said.

'Enough of that!' said the colonel sternly. 'Let's hear about this business of Buckingham Palace. What do you mean?'

'You may have heard about an organization called the Hand of Justice,' said Danvers. 'They were behind the murders of Lord Amersham, the MP Tobias Smith and Water Parrot, the newspaper owner.'

'Your CO, Stark, came round here and accused me of killing Amersham!' growled the colonel. 'I suppose that was your idea!'

'No, Father. It was me,' said Lettie. 'I heard you threaten him.'

Colonel Danvers scowled and shook his head. 'My own daughter, betraying me!'

'She didn't, Father,' said Danvers. 'She came to me because she was worried. It was I who told Chief Inspector Stark.'

The colonel turned his angry glare on his son. 'I knew it!' he snarled. 'Well, let me tell you—'

'Deverill, desist!' his wife ordered, her voice suddenly sharp.

The colonel turned to her, surprised. 'Now look—' he began.

'I have been hoping for almost a year that Robert would walk through that door again, and now he has, you continue to abuse him as you always did!'

'I never abused him!' protested the colonel.

'Not physically, perhaps, but you verbally chastised him and humiliated him, just because his views may have been different to yours. Now that he has come back, I for one want to hear what he has to say.' She turned back to Danvers. 'Let's start with why you are here.'

'Buckingham Palace!' burst out Lettie.

Danvers told them: the threats from the Hand of Justice, the planned wireless broadcast that was to take place the next day, and his role as police protection for the King.

'The King chose you?!' asked Lettie, delightedly.

'I don't think he knows I exist,' admitted Danvers. 'But they chose my boss, DCI Stark, and he asked me.'

'They must think very highly of this chief inspector if they've asked him to protect the King,' commented Danvers' mother.

'They do,' said Danvers. 'It was he who solved the murders.'

'They need a soldier for that sort of protection work, not a policeman!' snorted Colonel Danvers.

'He was a soldier during the war,' said Danvers. 'Rose through the ranks to become a captain. Won the DSM for bravery. He's very highly regarded.'

Colonel Danvers fell silent.

'And he's chosen you!' said Lettie brightly.

'Luckily,' nodded Danvers. 'The thing is, we're not sure how successful we're going to be tomorrow, with catching these villains.' He hesitated. 'The DCI suggested I call to see you, just in case things don't turn out well.'

Danvers' mother and sister exchanged puzzled looks, then Victoria Danvers half-closed her eyes with a shudder, while Lettie looked at her brother, puzzled.

'Don't turn out well?' asked Lettie. 'They might get away, you mean?'

Danvers hesitated, then nodded. 'Yes.'

Colonel Danvers suddenly stood up. 'Robert,' he said, 'I'd like to talk to you in the library. Then perhaps you could stay for

some sandwiches.' He looked at his wife. 'That will be all right
with Mrs Henderson, don't you think?'

'Yes, I'm sure it will,' said Victoria Danvers.

'I have to be back at Scotland Yard by six o'clock,' said
Danvers.

'We'll make sure you're back in time,' his mother said.

Colonel Danvers headed for the door of the drawing room.
Danvers got up and followed him. They passed Bridges, who
was entering with a tray with teapots, cups and biscuits.

'Tea, sir,' said Bridges.

'Serve it to the ladies, Bridges. Master Robert and I will be
back shortly.'

Danvers followed his father along the short corridor to the
library. They went in and the colonel closed the door.

'This business tomorrow,' he said. 'Could be trouble?'

'It could be, sir. These are dangerous people.'

'More than just guns, I assume?'

'That's what DCI Stark thinks.'

The colonel nodded. 'He's an intelligent man. Too much of a
Bolshie for my liking, but a good grasp of the situation.
Explosives? Bomb to kill the King?'

'We hope not, sir, but there is that possibility.'

The colonel nodded thoughtfully. 'You'll take care of yourself?' he asked, and for the first time since Danvers could
remember, his father's voice was tentative, unsure.

'I'll do my best, Father,' he said.

The colonel nodded again. 'Make sure you do,' he said. He
headed for the door. 'We'd better rejoin your mother and sister;
otherwise they'll think we're having words, or some such
nonsense.' He opened the door, then turned to his son and said,
'By the way, say thank you to that inspector of yours, will you,
for suggesting you call.'

As Stark entered the reception area of the small hotel in Cadogan
Square, he saw Collins and Broy in low and animated conversation with two other men, who nodded as they listened. Broy
seemed to be doing most of the talking, but he stopped when he
saw Stark and strode towards the chief inspector, a scowl writ
large on his face.

'You're not welcome here!' he snapped.

'Jaysus, Ned, will you let the man say what he's come for before you jump down his throat!' sighed Collins, joining them. 'For all we know, he's just popped in for a quiet pint and nothing to do with us at all!'

But he smiled as he said it, and Stark nodded to acknowledge the quip. 'Indeed,' he said quietly. 'But, as it happens, I would appreciate a few moments of your time, Mr Collins.'

'There'll be no questions asked of us by the police without a warrant!' barked Broy.

'In a non-official capacity,' added Stark, his eyes remaining on Collins. 'Nothing to do with police business.'

Broy studied Stark, the scowl still on his face, but now his brow creased in suspicion. 'It's a trick, Michael,' he announced.

'No, I think not,' said Collins casually. 'The chief inspector and I understand one another. You fellas talk among yourself while I have a word with Mr Stark.'

'Be careful!' hissed Broy.

'I'm always careful, Ned,' smiled Collins. 'Jaysus, I wouldn't have survived as long as I have if I wasn't. Shall we repair to the bar, Mr Stark?'

Collins led the way through to the small bar. Although it was busy, the crowd parted for Collins as he strolled to where two men were sitting in armchairs. As they saw Collins approach, they stood up and let Collins and Stark settle themselves down.

'Thank you, fellas,' nodded Collins.

The two men stood, scrutinizing Stark warily. Part of the delegation, thought Stark. Foot soldiers, possibly bodyguards.

'Would you fetch us a couple of whiskies, Sean?' asked Collins. He turned to Stark. 'They do a lovely Irish here. And I believe you're off duty, if this isn't police business.'

'Thank you, Mr Collins,' nodded Stark. 'I am indeed.'

Sean headed to the bar, and a nod from Collins to the other man resulted in the space around them suddenly getting larger as, with discreet nudges, the others in the bar moved to give them privacy. The commander of his troops, reflected Stark.

Sean reappeared with two tumblers filled with the glowing amber liquid, which he placed on the small table between the two armchairs, before moving back to join his compatriots, and Stark realized that the whole bar was the territory of the delegation.

Stark and Collins raised the glasses.

'Slainte!' toasted Collins.

'Cheers,' returned Stark.

Collins smiled. 'We'll have to get you making a proper toast before we leave, Mr Stark.' He savoured the whiskey approvingly. 'You know the word "whiskey" comes from the Gaelic? From the early monks. It means water of life.'

'Smoother than Scotch,' commented Stark, letting the liquid roll around his tongue. It was indeed less harsh than Scotch, with a beautiful flavour.

'So, Mr Stark?' enquired Collins. 'What brings you here, upsetting poor Ned?'

'A short while ago you came to me with some advice which was very helpful.'

'Your attackers,' nodded Collins.

'Indeed,' said Stark. 'You were right, of course.'

'I still didn't expect a personal thank-you visit,' said Collins, his voice wary.

'Let's just say I hope I'm returning the favour.'

'Officially?'

Stark shook his head, then looked at the men in the bar.

'You've no need to worry about them, Mr Stark,' said Collins. 'I know every man here.'

'That's not necessarily a guarantee of your security,' said Stark.

Collins bridled. 'If you're suggesting . . .' he growled, stung.

'I've just been put in a difficult position,' said Stark. 'By my own people: the police authorities and the government. Nothing to do with the Irish talks – a purely domestic matter, but a sensitive one. The problem is that if things go wrong, they will need someone to blame.'

'A scapegoat.' Collins drank more whiskey, then said, 'I'm guessing you're here to talk parallels, Mr Stark.'

'I've been talking recently to a very experienced British diplomat.'

'I trust Sir Edwin Drake was well,' said Collins, and smiled as he saw Stark react. 'I like to be kept informed.'

'He's worried,' said Stark. 'He thinks that if the talks reach an agreement that . . . a different faction is not comfortable with . . . it could lead to a bloody civil war.' He looked Collins squarely in the face and said, 'Ireland needs a good leader if it is to go forward. I would hate the man who should be that leader to die for all the wrong reasons before good things can be achieved.'

'And who might you be referring to?' Collins asked with a hint of gentle mockery. Then he looked serious. 'Mr Stark, what matters to me is Ireland's freedom.'

'At what cost?'

'It's already cost thousands of lives. But the end is in sight. Yes, there are different views on how to achieve it. Some of us feel that one step at a time may be the only way. Others differ. But we are united in our aim.'

'I *should* trust my colleagues in the police and my masters in the government, because we are also after one thing: the security of the state,' said Stark. 'But if it doesn't go to plan . . .'

Collins smiled. 'You've got a good and decent heart, Mr Stark, and I thank you for your concern,' he said quietly. 'But those of us who get involved with politics . . .' And he raised his almost empty glass to Stark, who held his own out to Collins.

'Slainte!' said Stark, and drained the rest of his drink.

FORTY-FIVE

S tark let himself in and walked through to the kitchen. Sarah was darning, and Henry and Stephen were once more at work on their model aeroplane.

'You're home earlier than usual,' said Sarah. 'I'll put the kettle on.'

'I've come to tell you that I'm going to be out all night tonight,' he said.

Henry looked at him, scowled, then pursed his lips in silent disapproval.

'I shall be at Buckingham Palace,' Stark added, before his father could mention Amelia.

His parents and Stephen stared at him, their eyes wide in shock.

'Buckingham Palace?' repeated Stephen. 'With the King and Queen?'

'Near to them,' nodded Stark. 'Sergeant Danvers and I and

the rest of our team will be staying in the stable block at the Palace.'

Henry and Sarah continued to stare at him, bewildered, as if he was talking to them in a foreign language.

'Why?' his father managed to babble out.

Once again, Stark related the story of the King's wireless broadcast from the Marconi factory, and the fact that he would need protection.

'We'll have to find someone with a wireless receiver!' burst out Sarah excitedly.

'Billy Wills!' exclaimed Henry. 'He's got one!' He turned to Stark. 'What time's this broadcast?'

'Eleven o'clock tomorrow morning,' said Stark. 'The details about it will be in the newspapers tomorrow.'

His father got up and took his jacket from the coat stand. 'I'd better go round to Billy's and make sure his wireless is working!' he said. He was about to hurry to the door when he stopped and turned to Stark, his hand held out. 'I'm sorry, son,' he said. 'Shake my hand.'

Stark took Henry's hand in his, a good firm grasp. 'It doesn't change the way I feel about . . . someone,' Stark told him.

Henry hesitated, and for a moment Stark thought his father was going to take his hand away. Instead, he gave Stark's hand a further firm squeeze. 'We'll talk about that when you come back,' he said. 'Right now, take good care of the King. And of yourself. I'm proud of you, son.'

They heard the door shut as he went out.

Stephen looked up at his father, his eyes filled with admiration. 'You're going to protect the King!' he said excitedly.

'I am,' nodded Stark. He looked at the pieces of the model aeroplane and the pot of glue on the spread-out newspaper. 'This is looking good,' he commented. 'Do you mind if I have a go with you, while Grandad's out on his errand?'

Stephen looked doubtful. 'We're at a difficult bit,' he said.

'I promise I won't mess it up,' said Stark. 'I'll check with you before I do anything.' He reached out and put his arms gently around his son. 'Stephen,' he said, 'you know I love you, don't you?'

'Yes, Dad,' said Stephen.

'And I'm sorry I'm hardly ever here.'

'It's work,' said Stephen. 'You have to go to work.'

'Yes, I do,' said Stark. 'But I know I should have been here more. With you. But you were always in my heart, wherever I was.'

'I know, Dad.'

There was a pause, then Stark released Stephen and sat down at the table. He gave his son a smile. 'Right,' he said. 'So, what can I do?'

Stephen smiled back and handed him the small knife. 'You can cut out the wheels. But be careful. The wood breaks easily.'

Stark found it difficult to sleep that night. The discomfort of the hard bedding arranged for them in the stable block at Buckingham Palace didn't bother him, nor did the strong smell of horse manure that drifted up from the stables below. Nor did the fact that he was sharing this one room with nine others: sergeants Danvers and Alder, constables Forsythe, Smith, Adams, Rushmore and Whittaker, and their two police drivers. Stark was glad to see that the two drivers assigned to them by the motor pool were both men he was familiar with and had confidence in: Ted Post and Jimmy Webb. All of this was nothing he hadn't experienced in Flanders – and far worse – during the war. No, he was fearful because he was responsible for the life of the King.

He'd confidently said to the meeting that none of the old soldiers would threaten the life of the King. But what if he was wrong? He'd based that on Alf Rennick, and the other soldiers he'd served with in the trenches. Many of them had been open about expressing their dislike of the field marshals and brigadiers safe back at HQ, and the politicians who took life-and-death decisions but were never at risk themselves – although, he had to admit, Churchill was the exception. Churchill had served in the trenches, wearing that distinctive French helmet, almost to taunt the Germans to try to kill him. But when it came to the issue of the King, he had never heard one soldier express disapproval of George V or the royal family. Some even considered the King as 'one of our own' because he'd served in the Royal Navy, even being put in command of two naval vessels and a torpedo boat before becoming next in line to the throne on the death of his older brother, Prince Albert Victor. Once that happened, his active naval career was at an end. He retained the rank of naval commander, but in an honorary capacity only. It was too dangerous for him to serve in the field. *And now here he is as King, being put in extreme danger because of me*, thought Stark. Because, as well as Alf Rennick and the like, there are Dan Harkers out there. Ex-soldiers who feel only anger.

A secret army of ex-soldiers, Alf had said. Resentful and trained to kill.

How many of them would be following them to Chelmsford tomorrow?

Next morning, they were up early. Before they went to breakfast, Stark insisted the team checked that the weapons they'd been issued with by the police armourer were in good working order and loaded, but with the safety catches on.

'I don't want anyone accidentally shooting themselves,' he warned them. 'Or, worse, shooting one of us, or the King.'

After breakfast, they left the servants' kitchen at the rear of the Palace and walked round the corner to the courtyard, their departure point, and stopped. The royal car was parked there, its paint gleaming black and chrome, the royal standard fluttering above the bonnet in the light breeze, the driver standing to attention beside it. Two police cars were also there, waiting, but in addition there was another vehicle, beside which stood Inspector Rogers and three other officers.

'Special Branch!' snorted Stark, annoyed. He strode across the courtyard to Rogers, the rest of his team following him. 'I thought your area of responsibility was the Marconi factory,' he said.

'It is,' said Rogers. 'But our prime responsibility is the safety of the royal family. You said we should work together. Well, we are. Our car will lead the convoy. The King's car will be next in the convoy, then your two cars bringing up the rear.'

'You don't trust us to do our job properly,' said Stark accusingly.

'No, to be frank, we don't,' said Rogers. 'Officially, this part of the assignment may be your shout, but I shall be watching you. And the King.'

'I'm glad to hear it,' said Stark. 'What's the situation at Chelmsford?'

'Our men are checking the place,' said Rogers.

Suddenly, Rogers saw a movement somewhere behind Stark, and hissed, 'The King!'

Stark turned, and saw the figure of King George V walking towards the waiting cars. Next to him walked Edward Shortt, the Home Secretary, with Sir Jocelyn Stevens just behind them.

'Attention!' Stark ordered.

Immediately, Danvers, Alder and the rest of the team formed themselves into a neat straight line beside Stark and stood rigidly to attention. *It's like being back in the army again*, thought Stark. Rogers had departed hastily to stand to attention by the first car in the convoy, along with his three Special Branch operatives.

The Home Secretary stopped in front of Stark. 'Your Majesty, allow me to introduce the leader of your protection detail today, Detective Chief Inspector Stark.'

King George was dressed in an official naval commander's uniform, adorned with medals and a broad sash. His hair was parted neatly in the middle, his beard and moustache neatly trimmed. Inwardly, Stark groaned: there was no chance of hiding the King from a potential assassin: the uniform, the medals, the epaulettes, the sash were so garish as to single out the King as a target.

'I understand you served in the war,' said the King.

'Yes, Your Majesty.'

'Promoted in the field to captain. DSM.'

So, Churchill again. Or was it Shortt or Sir Jocelyn who'd passed on this information? 'Yes, Your Majesty. I was very fortunate.'

'On the contrary, we were fortunate to have you. My son, Prince Albert, served, you know. He was at Jutland. A sublieutenant on the *Collingwood*.'

'I wasn't aware of that, Your Majesty.'

'No reason you should be. Many men at Jutland. Too many lost.' He looked at Shortt. 'I suppose we'd better get on our way. I see Special Branch are here.'

'Yes, Your Majesty. They'll be in the lead car.'

'Good. Then let's get going. And let's hope this wireless stuff works. It always gave us problems when I was in the navy.' He walked to his car, escorted by Sir Jocelyn.

'Amazing!' said Alder, looking after the figure of the King, awed. 'Me and the King!'

'Time to get on board, lads,' said Stark.

The drive to Chelmsford was long, not so much because of the distance – Chelmsford wasn't that far from London – but because of the slow speed of the procession. And it was a procession rather than a convoy. Because of the announcement about the planned broadcast in the morning's newspapers, crowds lined the streets of every borough and town they passed through, just to take the opportunity to wave at the royal car as it passed.

'If this bloke Harker has put a bomb in place, how do you think he'll detonate it, sir?' asked Alder.

'At Messines they used copper wires,' said Stark. 'The difficulty is going to be spotting wires that shouldn't be there. At a place like Marconi, the whole place is a maze of copper wires.'

'Telegraph wires,' nodded Whittaker. 'We saw a lot of them in France.'

'If Harker is going to be inside the building, my guess it will only be a medium-sized charge centred near the microphone,' said Danvers thoughtfully. 'He won't risk bringing the building down on himself. Nothing on the scale of the mines of Messines.'

'Unless the Hand of Justice lot have persuaded someone inside the factory to actually detonate the explosives,' said Stark. 'Letting them think that it's only going to be a small explosion.'

'Kill one of their own?' asked Alder.

'Trust me, these people are capable of it,' said Stark.

It took nearly two hours' travelling, but finally they came to the outskirts of Chelmsford.

'I'm so looking forward to this!' announced Constable Adams suddenly.

'Which aspect of it?' asked Stark.

'The factory!' said Adams. He leaned forward and said excitedly, 'I'm a member of a wireless club. This Marconi factory is the home of wireless. Do you know that when they did the Melba broadcast from here, it was heard as far away as Canada! It was heard right across Europe!'

Oh God, thought Stark, *I'm trapped with an enthusiast. Perhaps I should introduce him to Sir Jocelyn Stevens; they can wax lyrical about the future of wireless together, the potential for world domination.*

'The two aerial masts they've got here are four hundred and fifty feet high!' continued Adams enthusiastically. 'Imagine that!'

The convoy reached the gateway that led into the factory complex. Above the gateway was a huge engraved sign that read *Marconi's Wireless Telegraph Company*. Inside, in the courtyard, some of the workforce had been assembled in neat lines to welcome the arrival of the King.

When he saw this, Stark's heart sank. 'Look at them all! Any one of them could be an assassin! What on earth are Special Branch doing letting this happen?'

'I'm sure they know what they're doing, sir,' said Alder.

'I doubt it,' said Stark sourly.

'I expect it's because it's a big day for the factory,' said Forsythe. 'It's not every day you get the King calling.'

'Who's written his speech, sir?' asked Whittaker. 'Was that you?'

Stark shook his head. 'That's far above my pay grade,' he said. 'That's government level. Our job is to see the King is alive to read it, and that's what I intend to do.'

The convoy pulled to a halt, and Stark was the first one out. He hurried to the royal car and tapped gently on the rear door, as if he was knocking at a street door.

The King's private secretary, travelling with the King, wound down the car window and looked out at Stark questioningly.

'I wonder if you'd mind waiting in the car just a moment, Your Majesty, while we go ahead to check that everything is in order.'

The King nodded, and the private secretary wound the window up again.

As Stark headed towards the main entrance, Rogers came hurrying towards him. 'What are you up to, Stark?' he demanded.

'Just checking that everything's safe before His Majesty goes into the building.'

'We've already had our people do that! We've checked the inside thoroughly, especially the room where the microphone has been set up.'

Stark stopped as something on the building caught his eye. 'And the outside?' he asked.

'What about the outside?' demanded Rogers.

'Look above the main entrance,' said Stark. He pointed to a patch just above the lintel of the doorway to the main reception area on the white building. 'That's fresh paint.'

'How can you tell?' asked Rogers.

'By the way the light hits it. And look there, running down by the side of the left-hand column.'

Rogers looked. 'Cables,' he said doubtfully, adding hopefully, 'They could be for the lighting.'

'They're new,' said Stark. 'Trust me, I know what new cables look like. I saw enough of them in the trenches during the war.'

He turned to the driver of the royal car and shouted, 'Get the car away from here!'

He was too late. Suddenly, there was an explosion from the above the doorway. Stark threw himself to the ground, covering his head with his arms, as shattered bricks and small pieces of concrete rained down on them. Rogers had taken similar evasive action. A cloud of thick orange dust billowed around them, choking them.

Stark staggered to his feet, covered in dust and coughing. He looked towards the royal car, which seemed to be undamaged, except for a layer of brickdust.

Rogers staggered to his feet. 'The King!' he shouted in alarm.

'I think he's safe,' said Stark.

As the smoke began to clear, they both looked at the entrance. Or, rather, where the entrance had been. Now there was just a huge pile of rubble. The whole of the first floor of the building had collapsed.

Suddenly, Stark heard the sound of a gun being fired, and a bullet ricocheted off the roof of the royal car. He spun round and saw a puff of smoke from the hedge that bordered the lawn area at the side of the building as another shot was fired. This time, the bullet hit the side of the royal car.

'There!' yelled Stark, pulling his revolver from its holster and running towards the hedge. He was aware of Rogers running along beside him, pulling out his own pistol. Stark fired at the hedge, and saw a man and a woman get up from behind it.

There was another shot, and Stark saw Rogers stumble, then fall.

Stark fired again, and the man and woman turned and began to run. He chased after them. 'Stop! Police!' he called.

The man stopped, but instead of putting his hands up in surrender, he aimed the gun at Stark. Stark jerked to one side to dodge the bullet and fired back.

The man staggered a few steps. Stark saw him raising his gun, and fired again. This time the man went down.

Stark ran on, through the hedge. The man was lying on the ground, the woman kneeling beside him, making a dreadful sound, a heart-breaking howl of anguish. As Stark drew nearer, she turned to look at him, a look of sheer hatred on her face. Naomi Pike. Suddenly, she snatched up the man's fallen revolver and pointed it at Stark.

The gun going off beside him echoed in Stark's head. He turned and saw Rogers pointing his pistol. He looked back towards Naomi Pike and saw that she had fallen to the ground.

There was a thud beside him, and Stark saw that Rogers had collapsed, his left sleeve soaked in blood.

He heard running footsteps behind him, and he turned and saw two Special Branch men heading towards them. 'Rogers has been shot!' he said. 'Take care of him! I'll look after these two!'

He ran to where Naomi Pike had fallen. She was dead, her eyes and mouth wide open. Stark looked down at the man. His eyes were also open: one brown, one blue. Christopher Richards.

He was aware that Constable Adams had joined him, gun in hand.

'Everything all right, sir?' the constable asked, taking in the two dead bodies.

'That depends,' said Stark. 'How is the King?'

'He seems all right, sir,' said Adams. 'I saw him walking into the building!'

'What?' yelled Stark in alarm.

'He insisted, sir,' said Adams. 'Sergeant Danvers and Sergeant Alder went with him!'

'The damn fools!' shouted Stark. He pointed at the two bodies. 'Stay here and watch over them, Adams. Don't let anyone touch the bodies!'

With that, he ran back towards the building.

'Sir!'

The shout made him stop. He saw that two of the constables,

Rushmore and Whittaker, were hurrying towards him. They had firm grips on the arms of Dan Harker, who was struggling to get free of them.

'I'm innocent!' he was shouting, but when he saw Stark, his struggles stopped.

'We caught him hiding,' said Rushmore. 'When we challenged him, he tried to make a run for it.'

Stark reached a quick decision. 'Put him in one of our cars and take him back to London. Do it now. And keep a tight watch on him.'

'To Scotland Yard, sir?'

'No, to your own station at Maida Vale. Don't let anyone else know you've got him. Keep him under wraps.'

As the two constables led Harker away, Stark ran towards the royal car. The rear was, indeed, empty. 'Where's His Majesty?' he snapped at the driver, who was still sitting behind the steering wheel.

'He went inside to make the broadcast. Two of your officers, and some from Special Branch, were with him.'

'How did they get in?'

'They used a side entrance.'

'Damn, damn, damn!' cursed Stark.

Danvers stood next to Sergeant Alder in the large room, along with the Special Branch officers, various dignitaries from the Marconi company and, standing by the microphone, resplendent in the uniform of a naval commander, the King.

At the microphone was a bespectacled man in a neat dark suit, holding a single sheet of paper. He was standing on a red 'X' which had been painted on the floor next to the microphone.

Danvers and Alder moved their glances around the room, looking for any signs of new wiring similar to that spotted by Stark outside the building, but everything seemed to be in order.

The man at the microphone looked at the large clock on the wall. As the second hand touched the hour, he pointed at a technician in a long white coat, standing by a machine with a large flared horn coming out of it, with a rotating wax cylinder beneath the horn. The technician moved a switch, and immediately the strains of the national anthem, played by a military band, filled the room.

Automatically, everyone in the room stood to attention, with the exception of the King, who was concentrating on the single sheet of paper he held in his hand.

The music died away, and the man at the microphone announced, 'The Marconi Wireless Telegraph Company is proud to present this wireless broadcast by His Majesty, King George the Fifth.'

The man stepped away from the red X on the floor, and his place was taken by the King.

'People of Britain,' began the King. 'This is your King, George the Fifth, speaking to you through the medium of wireless.

'Not very long ago our country, along with the other countries of the Empire and our allies elsewhere, were engaged in a terrible conflict, which was described as the war to end wars. Unfortunately, we are still suffering the consequences of that dreadful war.

'Many returned from the battlefront to find that things were more difficult for them than they had been before 1914. I have been told that many, who had made great sacrifices, feel let down by the authorities since the end of the war. I understand their grievances.

'I have also been told that very recently a movement has sprung up formed of former servicemen, who have been led to believe that, by committing acts of violence and murder, their situation will change for the better. I regret to inform those former servicemen that they have been duped by persons with an ulterior political motive.

'As someone who served in the armed forces myself, it saddens me to learn of this. Before I became King, I spent many years in the Royal Navy. My son, Prince Albert, served during the recent war as a sub-lieutenant on HMS *Collingwood* at the Battle of Jutland. From my personal experiences, I know the British serving man to be the finest in the world.

'I therefore appeal to these men to stand aside from this course of action. Committing acts of violence and murder on the streets of our country for political reasons is not the British way.

'I have asked my government to look into the social issues that lie at the heart of this discontent and see if answers cannot be found, so that any social injustices are rectified.

'After the dreadful years of the war, it is my belief that better times lie ahead for this great country of ours. But those better times will not happen if we allow our society to be torn apart by violent revolution, as we have seen happen elsewhere.

'I thank you for listening, and wish you all well for the future.'

With that, he stepped back from the microphone, his place taken once more by the bespectacled man.

'You have been listening to a wireless broadcast by His Majesty, King George the Fifth.'

Once again, he pointed at the man in the white coat, and from the large horn above the rotating wax cylinder came the strains of the national anthem.

Stark ran to where Adams was standing guard over the bodies. 'Anyone been nosing around?' he asked.

'No, sir,' replied the constable. 'One Special Branch officer came over to make sure they were dead, then he went back to where the others were taking care of the one who'd been shot. Inspector Rogers.'

Stark looked down at the two dead bodies. They'd been on the run, staying away from places where they were known. So where would they stash something as important as the membership cards? Nowhere. Those cards were far too precious. They were the key to their revolution.

He knelt down and began to go through their pockets, first Richards', then Pike's. He found what he was looking for in the large inside pocket of Naomi Pike's coat. A bundle of index cards, held together with a rubber band. The missing membership cards.

FORTY-SIX

The journey back to London was made in a mood of elation and self-congratulation, although the police car was uncomfortable with six officers cramped in the back instead of four.

'Where are Rushmore and Whittaker?' demanded Alder when he saw that one of their cars had gone.

'They've gone back to London on my instructions,' said Stark.

Alder caught the tone in Stark's voice, and nodded. 'Very good, sir,' he said.

'You had one over on Special Branch, sir,' said Danvers. 'If the King had listened to them, he'd have been killed as he walked through that main entrance.'

'It was just a case of thinking like them,' said Stark. 'They had to be able to see their target to make sure that he was hit when the charge went off. They couldn't do that inside the building without putting themselves at risk. Harker isn't the sort of man who'd take a chance on being killed himself. So the main entrance seemed the most likely. Luckily, it was just a small charge, enough to bring down the lintel and collapse the wall above; otherwise we'd have been blown to smithereens.' He gave Danvers and Alder a look of disapproval. 'I'm not happy about you letting the King go into that building. There was still the risk of a marksman inside.'

'We couldn't stop him, sir,' said Alder. 'He sat in the car for a bit, then he suddenly said, "The people are expecting me to give a broadcast."'

'We tried to persuade him not to go,' added Danvers, 'but he looked at us and said, "I haven't come all the way here just to turn round and go away again."' He looked at Stark with helpless appeal. 'What could we do? He's the King!'

'And very brave, sir,' said Alder. 'Not many people would have carried on with it the way he did.'

'What was the broadcast like?' asked Stark.

'Astounding!' said Danvers enthusiastically. 'His voice was as steady as anything. You'd never have known that someone had tried to blow him up, and shoot him, just a couple of minutes before!'

The rest of the journey back to London was a hubbub of chatter about the day, reliving the explosion, the shootings, the broadcast. They arrived back at Buckingham Palace in convoy. When the rear door of the royal car opened, and Stark realized that the King was heading towards their car, Stark ushered his men out of the car and lined them up.

'Good work,' nodded the King.

To Stark's surprise, George V saluted. Immediately, Stark and the rest of his team returned it with their own smart salutes.

As the King disappeared into the Palace, surrounded by a bevy of Special Branch officers, Adams gave a sigh and said, 'Best day of my life!'

'I wouldn't let your old woman hear you say that,' commented Alder.

'Stark!'

The shout made them all turn, and they saw the bulky figure of Winston Churchill heading towards them, a broad smile on his face.

'Excellent work, Chief Inspector!' he boomed as he reached them. He grabbed Stark's hand and pumped it energetically. 'A telephone call alerted me to the explosion.' He looked at the rest of the team and gave them his confident smile. 'Excellent work by all of you! Bravery above the call of duty! The country's proud of you!' He looked at Stark again. 'What did you think of the speech?'

'I'm afraid I didn't hear it, sir,' said Stark. 'I was . . . otherwise engaged at the time.'

'Sergeant Alder and I were with the King during the broadcast, sir,' said Danvers. 'We both thought it was excellent.'

'Good, good,' grinned Churchill. He winked at them. 'Far be it for me to boast, but I had quite a bit of a hand in that. I know what makes the troops sit up!' He looked towards the Palace. 'I'm here to update the King on the Irish talks. Better go! Well done, again!'

With that, he bustled away.

'Now if there were more politicians like him, we wouldn't have half the trouble we've got,' said Forsythe approvingly as they watched him go.

The power of the chancer, thought Stark. *That man could sell snow to Eskimos.*

Sergeant Alder looked at Stark. 'To Scotland Yard, sir?'

'No, Maida Vale,' said Stark. He motioned them away from the vehicle so they would be out of earshot of anyone else, then told them in a low voice, 'That's where Rushmore and Whittaker went. They took Dan Harker with them.'

'Harker!' exclaimed Danvers.

Stark nodded. 'Officially, it's better if none of you know, just in case there are repercussions. Special Branch won't be happy once they find out about it.' He looked at Danvers. 'So, Sergeant. Once the rest of us have been dropped off at Maida Vale, you take the car back to Scotland Yard and start preparing a report for the chief superintendent. Put in everything, except the bit about Harker, although we'll have to add that at some point. I'll join you at the Yard later.'

Stark sat across the table from Harker. They were in one of the interview rooms at Maida Vale police station. Constable Forsythe stood immediately behind the prisoner.

'So, you tried to blow up the King,' said Stark.

Harker shook his head. 'It was Richards who set off the charge. I tried to stop him!'

'You were the one who laid the explosives.'

'He made me do it. At gunpoint. After what happened to Alf, I had no choice.'

'What happened to Alf?'

'Richards shot him. Richards wanted Alf to shoot the King. Alf said no. He said no old soldier would do it, either. Not kill the King. So Richards pulled out a gun and shot him. Said he was a traitor and he couldn't be trusted.'

'Why didn't you go to Special Branch? They'd have protected you. You could have told them what was being planned.'

'Because, after what happened with Alf, Richards was keeping a close eye on me. Wouldn't let me out of his sight.'

'He must've done to give you time to make the bomb.'

'He was with me the whole time. Said he wanted to watch me. He wanted to learn how to do it.'

'How were you able to put the charge in place?'

'Simple. Told them at the factory I was maintenance and needed to replace a wire to a light.'

'What happened to Alf's body?'

'We dumped it in one of the pits in Stepney gasworks.'

The door opening made Stark turn. Chief Superintendent Benson was standing in the doorway, a grim expression on his face. 'Stark,' he said, 'I need you outside.'

'Keep an eye on him,' Stark said to Forsythe.

He stepped out into the corridor, and came face to face with Chief Inspector Burns and Rogers, who had his arm in a sling. The inspector looked pale. He also looked very angry.

'Thought you'd hide him, did you, Stark?' snarled Rogers. 'Well, we checked with the motor pool! Once we realized that one of the cars had left early, we knew something was up.'

'You didn't report that you had Harker!' Burns growled at Stark.

'The report on today's events is still being compiled,' said Stark. 'Harker's transfer here will be included.'

'Hand him over to them, Stark,' said Benson. 'He's their man.'

'He's not theirs,' snorted Stark. 'He's anybody's who'd pay him. He knew about the plot to kill the King, but he didn't go to Special Branch with it.'

'He's still our man,' repeated Burns.

'Hand him over, Stark,' said Benson. 'They have priority.'

'Not yet,' said Stark.

'Your questioning of him is over!' snarled Rogers. 'We're taking him now.'

'First, he's going to show me where they dumped Alf Rennick's body.'

'Why are you so concerned about a common criminal?' demanded Burns.

'He wasn't a common criminal. He was a patriot. He died because he refused to take part in the plot to kill the King, unlike friend Harker. And I owe it to his family to see they get his body back.'

'Save your sympathy, Stark!' snapped Burns. He turned to Benson. 'Chief Superintendent, bring our man out. We're taking him.'

'If you do that before he's shown us where they dumped Alf Rennick's body, I shall resign,' snapped Stark.

'Resign, then!' snapped Burns.

'And I shall tell the newspapers why,' continued Stark. 'It might make interesting reading for the Prime Minister and the Home Secretary, not to mention the King and his family.'

The three men stared at him, incredulous and uncomprehending.

'You're bluffing!' scoffed Rogers.

'No, I'm deadly serious,' said Stark.

There was a pause, then Burns warned him, 'You're on very thin ice, Stark. It could be you in that room, as a threat to national security.'

'Which would make the story even more interesting reading,' said Stark doggedly.

Burns and Rogers exchanged querying looks, then Rogers burst out, 'Oh, for God's sake, let him have Rennick's body if it's so important to him!'

'Thank you,' said Stark.

'Don't thank me!' glowered Rogers. 'I shall have you for this,

Stark. At the earliest opportunity. Your days in the force are numbered.'

Stark looked at Benson, who averted his eyes, embarrassed.

'You can take Harker,' Benson muttered.

Stepney gasworks looked like a wasteland, with four huge gasometers sprouting up from the cinder and gravel and towering over it. Harker clambered out of the car, handcuffed to Stark. Burns had suggested that Harker travelled in the Special Branch car, with Stark following in a police car, but Stark knew that there was a good chance of them simply driving off with him if that was the case.

Harker walked to where there was a series of large pits sunk into the ground, each filled with dark, thick, stagnant water.

'That one,' he said, pointing to the second pit from the end.

Stark nodded to the uniformed officers who'd accompanied them and had taken grappling hooks from the police car. They dropped the hooks into the water and began to drag them from side to side. It was at the third pass they stopped as the hooks snagged on something.

'We've got something, sir,' said one.

They hauled on the ropes, and gradually a bicycle emerged from the swampy depths. They hauled the bicycle out and laid it on the ground.

'This was the one!' insisted Harker. 'He couldn't have got out and walked away!'

Stark nodded at the police officers again, and once more they dropped the hooks in and dragged them across the pit. This time, when they snagged on something hidden, it needed more effort to haul the ropes in and up. Stark stepped forward and took one of the ropes in his hands, lending his strength to their efforts, pulling along with them. Gradually, something began to emerge, breaking the surface of the dank water. It looked like a bundle of rags, but as it came out Stark saw an arm, then a leg. They pulled even harder, and soon the body of a small, thin man was laid out on his back beside the pit, dark water pouring away from him.

'Rennick?' asked Burns.

Stark nodded, his eyes on Alf's face. His eyes were still open, staring. 'Turn him over,' he ordered.

The police constables did so, and Stark saw the bullet hole in the back of Alf's skull.

'I didn't do it!' babbled Harker. 'It was Richards!'

'You've got what you wanted, Stark,' said Burns. 'We'll take our man now.'

Stark unlocked the handcuffs and Harker moved to join Burns and Rogers, rubbing his wrists. The two Special Branch men put Harker in their car and pulled the doors shut, and the car moved off.

'What do you want done with him, sir?' asked one of the constables, gesturing at Alf's body.

'Take him to the mortuary at Scotland Yard,' said Stark. 'I'll advise the family.'

Danvers was hard at work writing his report when Stark walked into the office. 'The chief superintendent came in looking for you soon after I got back, sir,' he said apologetically. 'I couldn't phone you at Maida Vale and tip you off, because officially I didn't know anything. And I thought if I left a message, it might make things worse.'

'You did the right thing, Sergeant,' said Stark. He took the bundle of membership cards from his pocket and put them on the desk by Danvers. 'The membership cards.'

Danvers stared at them, then at Stark. 'Do Special Branch know about them?' he asked.

'No,' said Stark. 'As far as everyone else is concerned, they're still missing.' He removed the rubber band and took out two of the cards, which he handed to Danvers. One was for Dan Harker, the other for Alf Rennick.

'You'll notice that they both have a letter A in the corner.

'A for assassin?' suggested Danvers.

'That's my thought. At a quick glance, there are about fifty others marked the same way.' He tapped the bundle of cards. 'Send out an order for all those with an A on their card to be brought in.'

'Arrest them?'

'No, just bring them in and have them kept overnight. Just in case the King's broadcast didn't persuade them. Tomorrow, we'll talk to them. Get their stories. Sort out the potentially dangerous ones. Some will be like Alf. I want to stop them turning into Harker. And after you've given the orders to bring them in, Sergeant, I suggest you go home.'

*   *   *

Henry and Sarah were in the kitchen with Stephen when he arrived home.

'We heard the broadcast!' Stephen told him excitedly. 'Mr Hickok has a wireless receiver and he brought it into school so we could listen!'

'Great!' smiled Stark, and he sank down on to a chair.

'Tiring day?' asked his father.

Stark nodded.

'The later edition of the papers say there was trouble at the place,' continued Henry. 'Explosions. Shootings. They say people were killed.'

Stark hesitated, then nodded again.

'But you're all right?' Henry asked.

Stark looked at his father, surprised at the note of concern in his voice. Then it struck him that his father had never considered what he did as dangerous; he was a policeman, yes, but one in an office, and offices weren't thought of as dangerous places.

'Yes,' he said. 'I'm all right.'

'Will you be going out tonight?' asked Sarah.

Stark looked at her in surprise. He'd always thought of his mother as one who avoided confrontations or anything controversial. Yet here she was, bringing Amelia into it; there could be no one else she could be referring to.

'Yes,' he said. 'I thought I would. If that's all right with you.'

'Yes,' said Sarah firmly. 'It's all right with us.'

Automatically, Stark looked at Henry, who hesitated, then nodded. 'If your mother says it's all right, it's all right,' he said.

The door was opened by Amelia.

'Servants away?' he asked.

'I've been opening the door to every damned caller since I heard the King's broadcast,' she said. 'Especially after I saw in the papers about the explosion and the shootings.' She looked at him, angry. 'You should have telephoned!'

'You might have told me not to call.'

She reached out and grabbed him by the coat and pulled him in through the door. 'If you try to cut me out again, I'll kill you!' she said. 'Are you staying?'

He pushed the door shut with his foot. 'Yes,' he said.